RACE TO TERRA

BOOK TEN OF THE EMPIRE OF BONES SAGA

TERRY MIXON

YOWLING
CAT PRESS

BOOK TEN OF THE EMPIRE OF BONES SAGA

RACE TO TERRA

Right down...

...to the wire!

TERRY MIXON

BESTSELLING AUTHOR OF *HIDDEN ENEMIES*

Published by Yowling Cat Press ®

Digital edition date: 7/21/2020

Print ISBN: 978-1947376144

Large Print ISBN: 978-1947376243

Cover art - image copyrights as follows:

DepositPhotos/innovari (Luca Oleastri)

DepositPhotos/nj_musik (Nazar Yosyfiv)

DepositPhotos/Taden1 (Denis Tabler)

DepositPhotos/docer2000 (Mikhail Ulyannikov)

Luca Oleastri

Donna Mixon

Cover design and composition by Donna Mixon

Print edition design and layout by Terry Mixon

Audio edition performed and produced by Veronica Giguere

Reach her at: v@voicesbyveronica.com

ALSO BY TERRY MIXON

You can always find the most up to date listing of Terry's titles on his Amazon Author Page.

The Empire of Bones Saga

Empire of Bones

Veil of Shadows

Command Decisions

Ghosts of Empire

Paying the Price

Recon in Force

Behind Enemy Lines

The Terra Gambit

Hidden Enemies

Race to Terra

Ruined Terra

Victory on Terra

The Humanity Unlimited Saga

Liberty Station

Freedom Express

Tree of Liberty

Blood of Patriots

The Imperial Marines Saga

Spoils of War

The Fractured Republic Saga

Storm Divers

The Scorched Earth Saga

Scorched Earth

Omnibus Volumes

The Empire of Bones Saga Volume 1

The Empire of Bones Saga Volume 2

The Empire of Bones Saga Volume 3

Humanity Unlimited Publisher's Pack 1

The Vigilante Series with Glynn Stewart

Heart of Vengeance

Oath of Vengeance

Bound By Law

Bound By Honor

Bound By Blood

Want to get updates from Terry about new books and other general nonsense going on in his life? He promises there will be cats. Go to TerryMixon.com/Mailing-List and sign up.

DEDICATION

This book would not be possible without the love and support of my beautiful wife. Donna, I love you more than life itself.

ACKNOWLEDGMENTS

I want to thank the folks that support me on Patreon. You got to read this book as I was writing it and that kept me working. You have my deepest thanks.

In particular, I want to thank those patrons that supported me at the $10 level and above:

Bryan Barnes
Tracy Bodine
John Kilgallon
Lisa Slack
Dale Thompson

Next, I want to thank my Alpha Reader, Tom Stoecklein, for his comments on the manuscript. His insight always helps me see things more clearly.

Finally, I want to thank my readers for putting up with me. You guys are great.

1

Jared Mertz watched Lieutenant Commander Anthony O'Halloran drill a small hole into the crate with a sense of dread. Justified concern about what they were doing made his harsh breathing echo inside his suit helmet, and the stench of his own sweat burned his nose.

He had no idea how the marines handled working and fighting in suits even more constricted than his. Princess Kelsey, especially. How did she stand it?

The large crate was one of six secured in *Athena*'s hold, each filled with a tenacious, horrifying bioweapon of incredible lethality the Rebel Empire called the Omega Plague. All the crates were protected by plasma-based self-destruct charges, which he had no codes to disarm.

He did have the codes to open the crates, picked up when their unwelcome guest had opened them to load the bioweapon, but he couldn't be sure the crates wouldn't send a signal to the man. He couldn't take that chance, so they were doing this the old-fashioned way.

If their attempt at examining the charges drew a negative response, all the crates would likely detonate. They'd determined there was more than enough explosive potential here to take out the fusion plant in engineering. That would kill them all quite effectively.

"How certain are you that the charges won't detect your intrusion, Tony?" Jared asked through his short-range com. They had to make sure that no one else on the ship detected them. Their new Rebel Empire guests wouldn't be very happy with what they were doing, so it was best to keep them in the dark.

They were sleeping at the moment, so Jared was relatively confident of carrying this off. Unless they killed everyone in the process.

"Pretty sure," O'Halloran said. "Of course, if I'm wrong, you won't have much time to yell at me. As in we'll never know that I tripped a failsafe."

The engineer pulled the drill bit back out from the hole he'd just created and slowly inserted a fiber camera. "I can see the charge Princess Kelsey mentioned on this wall of the container. There are three more in plain view, and probably some I can't see. I wish Katheryn was here. She had a much steadier hand than me."

Commander Katheryn Pence had been *Athena's* chief engineer before they'd had to subdue the party of Rebel Empire nobles sent to commandeer the supposedly robot-controlled destroyer at El Capitan. She and nine others had died in the fighting when his crew had retaken the ship.

They'd captured a fair number of the enemy but had lost all but one of them when their leader set off secret bombs planted in every one of her people's skulls, including her own.

Only the fact that Olivia West had been questioning one of the prisoners on the other side of the ship had saved that last one. The fact that Jared had locked the com system down had prevented the woman from using it to be sure she got all of her people and had stopped her from setting off the self-destruct charges on the cargo, he suspected.

"I wish she were here, too," Jared said tiredly. "You'll just have to do the best you can, Tony. I have confidence in you."

"At least one of us does," the engineer muttered as he focused on the task at hand. "I'm pretty sure this charge has an antitampering circuit, just like I suspected it would. At least that's what I think I'm looking at."

Jared linked his implants into the low-powered feed and examined what the man was examining. The charge itself was fairly bulky when compared to the plasma grenades the marines favored. It looked like a permanent part of the crate, too.

"What is the antitampering part?" he asked.

"See how there are several bands around the device? Those cover the access ports I'd need to use to get into the casing holding the detonator. It's a safe bet they are rigged to notice if someone is messing with the device unless the appropriate code is entered first."

"I suppose that was unavoidable," Jared said with a sigh. "We weren't going to get that lucky. What would happen if you cut the case open?"

"I think Major Scala might be a better person to answer that question. He's at least taken the ordinance disposal course."

Jared half turned and gestured *Athena*'s senior marine officer over from the hatch he was standing with his men. "Adrian, could you tell us what you think about this bomb? Any chance you could defuse it?"

The marine came to stand beside them, not speaking for a few moments as he reviewed his own implant feed.

"That's a disaster waiting to happen, sir," the marine officer finally said. "The charge is wrapped up tight. If we screw with it, boom!"

"That's what I was afraid of," Jared grumbled. "There's no way to get a probe into the case and deactivate it?"

"I wouldn't chance it. This technology is too good to miss the intrusion. If it thinks you're screwing with it, it'll go off and take its friends with it. Even jamming the signals wouldn't help. The other charges are probably using encrypted signals to one another to make sure that nothing like that happens.

"If they stop getting updates, they'll be programed to suspect enemy action," the marine concluded. "Hell, they might be rigged to detect a detonation and go off before the plasma wave front can destroy them."

So much for that idea. They'd have to do this the hard way.

"Seal the crate up, and let's make sure it doesn't look tampered with," Jared ordered. "We'll have to maintain the masquerade for a while longer. We're almost two weeks out from Terra. Fielding only extended the timer for a week, so he has plans before we get there. We'll just have to deal with him as best we can."

"Any idea what he has in mind?" Scala asked. "I'd like nothing better than to stun the bastard and put him in chains."

"Sadly, that's probably not going to happen. At least not without us knowing a lot more than we do right now."

He gestured for the marine to accompany him back to the hatch leading out of the cargo bay. "We have his nephew on our side—at least I think we do—and he might be able to get more out of the man than we've been able to."

Austin Darrah had been the only survivor of the Rebel Empire leader's treachery and knew the AIs would cheerfully kill him if they discovered he was alive, so Jared believed he'd help them, though he was loath to take things at face value on so short an acquaintance.

Since the young tech wizard was also Oscar Fielding's nephew, the old man probably had something in mind to extract him from the AI's mad plan to exterminate all human life on Terra. Jared just didn't know what it was.

He wanted to rub his face in frustration, but that would have to wait until he was out of his suit. Then he could return to his cabin and take a much-needed shower.

Fielding had kicked him out of his original cabin, so he'd had to bump everyone else because that was how the Rebel Empire worked. Appearances and status carried real weight, so he'd had to make a show of evicting his subordinates.

Still, Jared didn't have it as bad as his wife. Elise Orison, the crown princess of Pentagar, was sleeping in a maintenance tube and not at all pleased with her current accommodations.

To their mutual displeasure, she couldn't risk creeping into his bed at night for fear someone on the opposing team would see her.

"Wrap it up, people," he said. "Fielding will be up and looking for his breakfast in a few hours. Get some sleep. You've earned it."

He'd have just enough time to clean up and get to the officers' mess. Austin Darrah and Olivia West would be waiting for him, as would Princess Kelsey Bandar.

Rather, the version of her from another reality. That was one more complication added to an already convoluted situation.

Well, their difficulties wouldn't get any easier if he didn't work on them. At least he was mostly certain that his sister from another universe wouldn't stick a knife in his back at the first opportunity. She wanted something she couldn't get without him.

Still, it might be best to keep her out of the kitchen. There were a lot of sharp instruments in there.

As he let himself out of the cargo hold, he wondered how his real sister was doing. They hadn't had any contact after Kelsey had daringly stolen the Dresden orbital, with all its advanced research technology intact and entire.

He hoped she'd found another way home to the New Terran Empire and was even now meeting with her father, safe and sound. One of them deserved some breaks.

* * *

Princess Kelsey Bandar hunched over her desk aboard the Marine Raider strike ship *Persephone* and clutched her head in her hands. How the hell was she going to get her people out of this system and back home again?

They couldn't go through the multi-flip point back the way they'd come. Their FTL probes in the Icebox system still showed the Clan warships scouring everything, looking for the people who'd destroyed their battle station on the other side of what Carl Owlet had started calling a far flip point because it was unusually distant from the sun.

Maddeningly, it hadn't even been Kelsey's people that had stirred them up, but they'd sure as hell catch the blame if the fragment of the Old Empire calling itself the Clans found them.

Commander Raul Castille—the Rebel Empire security officer they'd captured aboard the Dresden orbital—had made certain to drop the name of the New Terran Empire before he'd obliterated the battle station he'd discovered on the other side of the far flip point.

Those damned far flip points had never even been predicted by theory, or so Carl had said, so Kelsey had never even considered having her probes look way out there for a flip point. At least the bastard's destruction of the Clan battle station had bought them enough time to set up a defense when the first Clan warships came into the Icebox system with blood in their eyes.

She'd tried to talk them down, but they'd come in shooting, so she'd punched their lights out. That garnered her thirteen prisoners: twelve from the Clans and one from a different political entity called the Singularity.

Once she'd had her people scour the wreckage for survivors, they'd fled back through the multi-flip point just before the follow-up wave of Clan warships arrived in the Icebox system.

Since there were no other exits from the system, it would only be so long until the Clans started trying to send ships through the multi-flip point. There was nowhere else the people that had attacked them could have come from or retreated to, after all.

The Clans didn't have the technology that Carl had put together on the fly to allow *Audacious* and the freighter with them to get through the multi-flip point, but that didn't mean they couldn't get help from the Singularity to do so. Kelsey couldn't rule it out, so she had to consider it only a matter of time before the Clans made the attempt.

Without frequency modulators on the flip drive, a ship might or might not be able to get through one. It turned out that of her ships, only *Persephone* could make it through the one in the Icebox system without a modulator.

Marine Raider strike ships were the smallest class of flip-capable vessel Kelsey had ever heard of, so the odds of the Clans having something capable of making the trip were small indeed.

The multi-flip points behaved oddly when a ship without a modulator tried to use them. While they had a number of potential destinations, ships without modulators went to a kind of default branch of the wormhole.

In the case of the Icebox multi-flip point, the default was back into the Rebel Empire, to an empty system near Dresden. Thankfully, that was not where Kelsey and her people had fled, so that provided them some additional breathing space.

Worse for the Clans, ships without modulators couldn't easily leave the Icebox system via the multi-flip point at all. The default branch of the multi-flip point was too constricted to allow any unmodulated transit.

That was something the Clans knew from experience. They'd fled the fall of the Old Empire through that very flip point over five hundred years ago and had been unable to get back through from the Icebox side.

That didn't mean it was impossible. Her people had found the wreck of a Clan battlecruiser named *Dauntless* crashed on the main world in the Pandora system where they'd ended up. A long examination of the burned-out flip drive on the wreck found a jury-rigged frequency modulator that Carl believed had barely allowed the ship to make the flip, much like his initial work had allowed *Audacious* to get there, with pretty much the same catastrophic results to the flip drive.

Of course, the Clans might not make the attempt. For reasons that Carl couldn't explain in words of fewer than six syllables, the size of the vessel transiting without a modulator determined where it would go, and it didn't seem consistent from branch to branch.

From the Old Empire branch, coming from the Old Empire, everything ended up in the Icebox system by default. Coming from the Icebox side, probes went back to the Old Empire.

That was good, as she couldn't in good conscience allow the Clans access to Pandora, though she could hardly stop a determined incursion with the few ships at her command.

The Pandora system held a mysterious alien race. Yet just to keep things confusing, they weren't nearly as alien as they looked. Even with their blue skins, they had modified human DNA inside them. A modification that had altered them long before humans had developed space travel at all.

That was a mystery that she'd have loved to solve, but no easy answers presented themselves. Hell, none of her problems had easy answers.

They'd managed to take *Persephone* through the multi-flip point down a branch leading to a major Rebel Empire system called Archibald. The mission there had been harrowing but ultimately successful.

They'd penetrated a Rebel Empire shipyard and managed to insert Carl's plans for a flip drive with a built-in modulator. Then they'd stolen a freighter once they'd had the drive delivered there.

Only, as usual, things weren't that simple. The freighter happened to be a Q-ship—a warship disguised as a freighter—and it had put up a lot more fight than her little group had counted on. They'd triumphed in the end but had more prisoners than they could shake a stick at.

Which brought her to the mess she was currently dealing with.

The people manning that ship claimed to be part of the resistance movement inside the Rebel Empire. The cargo they'd put together had certainly made that a possibility, but it was a claim that she had no way to validate. Not without someone like Olivia West at her side, and her friend was far, far away. Way beyond contact unless Carl made an unexpected breakthrough with the FTL coms.

And, to top matters off, Kelsey's mother had stowed away on the mission. She was certain that the woman was going to cause her terrible trouble, no matter how contrite the ex-empress of the Terran Empire was currently acting.

God, this was giving her a terrible headache and a burning desire to smash something.

A rap at her hatch gave her a welcome distraction to focus on. Major Angela Ellis, her executive officer—and soon to become the new commanding officer of *Persephone*—stood outside.

The woman had no idea that Kelsey had decided to pass command of the ship to her yet. She'd probably be both pleased and terrified at the idea of commanding the warship, but the computer running the Marine Raider strike ship only allowed Marine Raiders to command her.

And with the woman's now-completed upgrade, the New Terran Empire had a whole two Marine Raiders to choose from.

"Hey," Angela said cheerily. "I'm heading to the gym. You want to come down and beat me to a pulp?"

The days that Kelsey could still use her experience to toss the tall, powerful marine around the mat were numbered. Probably only a few more days, really. If that.

She might as well enjoy the current situation as long as she could. Once the marine officer got her proverbial and actual feet under her, she'd thrash Kelsey five times out of five.

Angela would become the new powerhouse in the Terran Empire. Right up until Kelsey's husband, Russ Talbot, finished the Marine Raider upgrade in a few weeks.

That thought made her smile. Wouldn't that make for some strenuous evenings in the bedroom?

Kelsey rose to her feet with a grateful smile. "I would love to. Let's go."

2

Olivia West arrived in the officers' mess before the others. Commander Kaitlinn Cannon was already herding several shanghaied assistants around the kitchen, and the wonderful smell of something frying brought Olivia partly awake.

"Tell me you have coffee," she begged the ship's assistant tactical officer.

"I have coffee," Kaitlinn confirmed. "It's in the urn over there. It's the good stuff, too. We wouldn't want to disappoint our *guest*." The final word held a note of disgust.

Fielding's taste for the better things in life had become apparent at dinner last night. It had been the first meal they'd shared with the man, and he'd set a high bar for what he'd accept on his table.

Luckily for them, Kaitlinn had been a chef before she'd joined Fleet. A damned good one, it seemed. Her skills in the kitchen were good enough to pass muster, though Fielding bitched about just about every aspect of the meal.

Once Olivia had poured herself some coffee, added sweetener and creamer, and taken her first delicious sip, she stepped over and watched the other woman frying some bacon while simultaneously scrambling eggs.

"I never did ask, but how did you go from cooking delicious food to shooting at people?"

"If you'd ever been a chef, you'd realize how short a step it is from cooking to wanting to kill people," the brunette said with a wide grin, her hands seeming to move on autopilot as she worked. "Seriously though, it was mainly to piss off my mother. She demanded that I work in my father's restaurant, and I basically picked about the opposite sort of thing I could think of as soon as I could."

"What did your father think of your career change?"

The woman laughed. "He fronted me my living expenses while I got my feet back under me and encouraged me to make a clean break so I could have my own life. Without telling my mother he'd done so, of course. He's not an idiot, my father."

Kaitlinn scooped the eggs into a container, slid it under a warmer, and started putting sausage on the grill to cook. "He'd have loved for me to stay at the restaurant, but he knew that I'd never get out from under Mother's thumb.

"And let me add that being deployed to the far side of the Empire was a blessing. She couldn't come and try to guilt me into coming back to the restaurant. Basically, blowing things up was just a bonus."

Olivia laughed. "Well, we're lucky to have you here with us. I doubt Fielding would be at all happy with my cooking."

The other woman's expression darkened. "That man is a conceited ass that thinks he deserves everything served to him on a silver platter. Literally. His kind annoys the hell out of me. Are you sure I can't just poison him?"

"Sadly, no," Olivia said dryly. "We need him alive."

"Pity," Kaitlinn said as she flipped the sausage. "I'm pretty sure I could time the effects just right, so that he plopped face down onto his empty plate. Wasting food is a sin," she added virtuously.

Olivia laughed. "You terrify me. I'm never going to get onto your bad side."

Movement in the corner of her vision made her turn her head and she saw Austin Darrah entering the mess, talking with Princess Kelsey.

Austin was a fellow member of the higher orders of the Rebel

Empire, so she knew a lot about his background and upbringing, even though she'd always been a member of the resistance. His ability to work with advanced hardware was an intriguing twist, though.

Princess Kelsey Bandar, on the other hand, was a cypher. She looked exactly like her counterpart from this universe—one of Olivia's closest friends—but she was different in so many unexpected ways, and not all of them easy to predict.

Kelsey Two—as she'd started mentally referring to the woman—and Austin seemed to be getting along pretty well, chatting without any of the hostility or the obvious distrust the woman showed her Jared Mertz. In her universe, it seemed he was a villain. At least it was hard to come to any other conclusion based on the actions the man seemed to have taken.

Considering how different this Kelsey was, that wasn't completely unbelievable.

Once the others had gotten coffee, Olivia joined them at one of the tables. It was utilitarian, and so were the settings, something Fielding bitterly complained about, but she'd made certain to remind the man how this had been a robotic destroyer before they'd appropriated it, and he was lucky to have chairs. Needless to say, that hadn't gone over so well.

Too damned bad.

"Good morning," Olivia said. "I hope you both slept well."

"Surprisingly, yes," Austin said cheerfully as he flopped down in his seat in a somewhat disorganized manner. "It's amazing how relaxing having the bomb in your head removed can be. Who knew?"

The Rebel Empire had put explosives into their chosen crews' heads, all of whom had come from the higher orders. She and her associates hadn't known that when Jared had retaken the ship. The enemy leader had awoken, discovered their fate, and killed her entire crew, except for Austin, who'd been out of range at the time.

The young man hadn't been pleased when he'd found out that Doctor Stone had removed it, simply because he'd been certain that would set it off. It would have if they hadn't cleaned up the programing in his implants first.

Thankfully, Olivia hadn't been in a compartment where any of the original prisoners had died. The blasts had been more than sufficient to obliterate the prisoners' heads and rip their torsos open. Gory and horrifying, she'd been told. She was deeply glad she hadn't had to assist in the cleanup.

"Excellent," Olivia said, turning her attention to Kelsey Two. "And how did you sleep?"

"Fine," the short blonde woman said, her expression plainly revealing that as a lie. "I don't suppose I could get some food before Fielding gets here, could I? I'm starving and don't want to clue him in that I have to eat more than everyone else. It's both dangerous and humiliating."

Kaitlinn had obviously already been executing that plan, because she set a plate heaped high with scrambled eggs, sausage, bacon, and toast in front of the princess from another universe.

"Here you go, Highness. I'll have some orange juice for you in a bit. Wave at me if you want seconds and I'll fix you right up."

"You are a *saint*," Kelsey said gratefully, digging into her meal even as the cook headed back for the juice.

"Why do you need to eat so much?" Austin asked even as Kaitlinn delivered the juice. "Forgive me for saying so, but someone of your… ah, small stature, should need less food, not more. And why is she calling you 'highness'?"

Kelsey looked at Olivia but didn't stop eating.

"Those are some of the secret things Jared said he'd fill you in on in due time," Olivia said. "Since you've become aware of them, I'll make a down payment on that promise by asking Kelsey to briefly explain, without going into too much of the background."

The other woman wouldn't want to talk about how she'd been brutalized by a mad computer when it had forcefully implanted Marine Raider hardware in her. Without anesthesia. Even the idea of something like that made Olivia shiver with horror. It would've driven her mad.

"A few years ago," Kelsey said between bites, "I was presented with the nonnegotiable opportunity to test out a few upgrades in implantable hardware. Part of that was artificial muscles. One aspect of having them means my body runs through calories like a top athlete in training. I'm always hungry and eat whenever I get the chance."

"Nonnegotiable?" Austin asked, frowning. "Like how they put a bomb in my head? I'm so sorry."

The young man's obviously genuine sorrow seemed to make Kelsey feel a little better, and the short woman smiled a little. "It's been hard, but things are looking up. Thank you for your concern."

"How much stronger are you?"

"Let's just leave it at several times stronger than I was."

Austin frowned. "The stress something like that would put on your joints would be incredible. There would have to be some additional structural additions to make it work. Reinforcement to the tendons and hardening of the bones, at the very least."

"Let's not get lost in the weeds," Olivia said firmly. "Don't let your tech geekiness overpower you."

He cocked his head to the side. "Geekiness? I'm not familiar with the word, though I think I get the meaning. Sorry. I get carried away when it comes to tech I'm not familiar with."

"If Olivia says I can, I'll tell you more and even let you take a peek at some diagrams," Kelsey assured him, continuing to shovel food into her mouth.

Olivia noted that the woman hadn't said that *Jared* could make the decision. That distrust was still hiding in there. Olivia was lucky in a way that she was like Austin, in that Kelsey had no history with her in her own universe.

"Why did she call you 'highness'?" Austin asked, stealing a slice of bacon and earning a set of narrowed eyes as Kelsey edged her plate a little farther away from him.

"That's a lot more complicated, and Kaitlinn shouldn't have called her that," Olivia said before Kelsey could respond. "There are political entities the Empire is unaware of, and Kelsey is a noble in one. A princess, as you might have guessed."

The crown princess of the New Terran Empire, in truth. Just like in this universe, though serving a much different emperor. Over there, her twin brother Ethan sat upon the Imperial Throne. Here, he'd tried to kill their father and failed.

Kelsey One had used circumstances to allow her brother to blunder to his death. It had traumatized her for months and probably still haunted her dreams. One didn't just walk away from something like that unchanged.

Olivia had worried deeply about her friend, but a trip to the Imperial Retreat seemed to have turned the tide for her. She'd still been angry and depressed, but the almost homicidal rage that had been building in her had dissipated. Apparently, a few weeks of reflection in solitude had turned the trick for her.

"Oh," Austin said in a nonplussed tone. "I'll forget that for now, as mentioning it to Uncle Oscar would be a terrible blunder."

The young man smiled a bit sadly. "I know none of you really trusts me, but I *do* know he's playing some game and probably doesn't have my best interests at heart, no matter what he says. I'm not going to help him unless it helps us all. I really have thrown my lot in with you."

Olivia still wasn't completely convinced, but Austin could have betrayed them with a single word, and yet he hadn't. He didn't seem the sort to have deep plots of his own cooking merrily away, so she was thawing to him.

She opened her mouth to say something to that effect when her implants pinged with an incoming message.

"Hurry up, Kelsey," she said somewhat sourly a moment later. "It seems our unwanted guest is on his way, half an hour early to boot."

Almost as soon as she'd finished speaking, she received a connection request from Fielding through her implants. She accepted the call, treating it just like a standard com connection, even though the conversation was entirely in her head.

"Keaton," she said, using her assumed name. Jaleesa Keaton had been the leader of the Rebel Empire crew on this ship before they'd recaptured it.

Olivia made certain to put just the right shade of irritation into her mental voice. No member of the higher orders would be pleased to be called before breakfast.

Since she'd lived her life at the highest levels of Rebel Empire society on Harrison's World, serving as the coordinator of the entire planet most recently, she was more than familiar with how her compatriots behaved.

And, if she was being exceptionally truthful, herself under the right stimuli.

She was trying to get better about how she treated others and about how she took things for granted. Having Sean as her husband was occasionally jarring when he told her she was being snooty, but it was growth she was determined to make happen.

"Ah, so good to hear your voice, Lady Keaton," Fielding said in a false tone of geniality. "I and my guards are on our way to the dining room. If you and your people will come meet me, I think it's time to go over what we'll be doing."

"I'll make certain that my people are informed. Some may be delayed, as we weren't scheduled to meet for another half an hour." Olivia emphasized that last bit enough to make sure the man knew she was less than pleased.

"My apologies," he said with more than a hint of smug satisfaction. "I was up early and felt we needed to get ourselves in order as soon as possible. After all, you only have six days before the next extension is required for the cargo."

He was referring to the bombs protecting the Omega Plague. They would go off unless he delayed them a second time.

"I still don't understand why you don't just extend them," she complained. "You're here with us. It's not as if you're going to allow them to just go off."

He chuckled. "I see you're operating under a misapprehension. I don't have the codes to extend them any further. In six days and a few hours, they'll go off and destroy this ship."

Olivia sat bolt upright. "You told us that the System Lord had agreed to a plan that involved you coming along so we didn't have to meet the other ship for a code to extend them."

"And that's true," the Rebel Empire noble said. "I have an encrypted file with the codes we need. Once we've accomplished the new mission, the System Lord at our new destination will decode it for us. Now, if you don't mind, I'll sign off and see you momentarily."

She cursed when he disconnected without another word.

"It seems we have a new problem," she told the others. "Our lives just got more complicated."

3

A ngela slammed into the mat with bone-jarring force. She landed flat on her back and, even with all her Marine Raider enhancements, the titanic impact knocked the air out of her.

It was so hard, in fact, that she couldn't effectively defend herself when Princess Kelsey jammed her knee onto her neck. Angela tapped out rather than try to extract herself from the untenable situation.

Kelsey hopped to her feet with far too much energy as Angela tried to get her lungs working again.

"Four falls out of five?" the small woman chirped. "I'll take it!"

"I'll bet you will," Angela grumbled, sitting up and rubbing her throat. "Even with the same hardware, your experience keeps handing me my ass on a platter. That's damned unfair."

"You'll get the hang of things and the situation will reverse itself shortly," Kelsey said as she offered Angela a hand. "I'm not really in your league when you take the Marine Raider enhancements out of the equation. You'll pound me into the mat once you get the hang of your new body."

"I don't think so," Talbot said from where he was sitting off to the side. He was still recovering from the first set of Marine Raider surgeries. Well, technically the second, as he'd already had cranial implants, and the upgrade to Marine Raider medical nanites was pretty straightforward.

His most recent session had seen his pharmacology unit implanted and his ocular, auditory, and olfactory enhancements installed. He was sitting down because the procedure screwed with his balance for a day or so.

In a few more days, Doctor Zoboroski would coat his leg bones in graphene and weave artificial muscles into his real ones. That would be even more disruptive, she knew, screwing with his ability to walk until he adjusted.

In about a week, he'd have his torso and dominant arm done. They could've done both arms at the same time, but he needed one hand that wouldn't rip things out of walls or crush them with no warning before he mastered the increased strength.

Perhaps three days later, he'd have his last arm done. That meant that in about two weeks from now, he'd be right where she was. Hopefully *exactly* where she was: flat on his back on the mat with her doing the tossing.

That last thought made her smile darkly. It was the price of speeding up the implant process. The Old Empire gave the new Marine Raiders six sessions rather than four and spread them out over twice the time. The New Terran Empire just didn't have the time to dawdle.

When they finished with Talbot, they had a host of other people to start down the road to becoming the crew in truth of the Marine Raider strike ship *Persephone*.

And Commodore Zia Anderson on the carrier *Audacious* had already put in her marker for some Raiders of her own. Hell, most of the marines with them on this trip would get the treatment if they had enough time.

Some of the roughly battalion-sized group weren't going to make the cut, she knew. They had to be sure that only people who could ethically use power like this got it, because the process wasn't reversible. A closet psychopath with Marine Raider enhancements was a terrifying vision they all wanted to avoid.

Still, the marines were pretty good at weeding out that kind of thing, so Angela hoped there wouldn't be many people they'd have to reject. They needed every fighting hand they could get.

She stretched and tried to work some of the soreness out of her still-adjusting body. "What does that mean?" she asked Talbot.

"Kelsey isn't giving herself enough credit," he said calmly. "She still thinks of herself as the woman she was before the expedition. She's wrong.

"Yes, the Marine Raider implants and enhancements gave her a serious edge at the start over anyone she fought, even without any skills to go with it, but that situation isn't true anymore. It hasn't been for a while."

Angela continued stretching and watched as Kelsey walked over to her husband, a confused look on her face. "Expand on that."

"Sure," the large marine said with a grin. "If you'll sit here on my lap, I'll tell you all about it."

"I am *not* sitting in your lap," Kelsey said firmly. "Cough it up."

"You've mastered the Marine Raider unarmed combat form, you've had years of experience fighting with your new body, and even with her longer time as a marine, Angela is probably never going to be your master at hand-to-hand."

"That's ridiculous," Angela said, frowning. "I'm almost a meter taller than Kelsey, and I outmass her by a significant margin. I've been fighting hand-to-hand for fifteen years."

He shook his head as he turned his attention to her. "That's where you're wrong. You haven't been fighting like *this* at all. Sure, you know some martial arts and have significant unarmed combat chops, but that almost doesn't count at this level of the game.

"Tell me, what is the biggest difference between what you already knew and the Marine Raider hand-to-hand art?"

"The first thing I know is that that name is too unwieldy," Angela said. "We really need to call it something shorter. Why the Old Empire Marine Raiders didn't is a mystery to me."

"Call it the Art," Kelsey said. "That makes it sound all mysterious."

Talbot considered that and slowly nodded. "I like that. Now, again, Angela, what is the biggest difference between the Art and marine forms you already knew?"

Angela felt her eyes narrow. "A lot of the skills and moves are different. Why don't you tell me what kind of answer you're looking for?"

"Speed and size have advantages in a lot of the moves Kelsey is using," he explained. "Not large size as in overpowering but getting inside her opponent's moves and using her smaller size to throw them around the mat like she just did with you.

"Here, your larger size is a disadvantage, and her mastery of the Art is as good as your own. Perhaps somewhat better. Tell me how you'd overcome her size advantage."

Angela opened her mouth to answer but stopped herself and really considered the problem.

While she thought about the question, Kelsey nodded. "I think there has to be more to the Art than what Ned taught us. He tailored my education to what suited me. That's what I passed on to everyone else. That had to affect the curriculum."

The idea of the artificial intelligence that had thought it was Major Ned Quincy living inside Princess Kelsey's implants had always freaked Angela out a little.

She wondered if her friend was glad that Carl had transferred the AI safely to a specially designed computer made to support it while he searched for an answer to getting Ned his own body. Personally, she'd have been ecstatic.

"I'll have to work on some other moves outside the Art or find out if there are extra moves we didn't learn that might favor my greater size and longer reach," she finally said.

"That's a good answer," he said with a satisfied nod. "There are a lot of martial arts styles, and nothing says you have to keep using the one that favors Kelsey. Though I'm starting to suspect that the way Ned taught Kelsey might have implications we haven't considered just yet. I'll have to think about that a bit more before I'm ready to broach the subject.

"In any case, every move used in the Art came from another martial art in its day. The Marine Raiders stole what they liked the best. That doesn't mean that everything else is without merit under the right circumstances.

"Old Terra had an astonishing array of martial styles. Do some research and surprise her with something she isn't expecting. Adapt and overcome."

"And speaking of adapt and overcome, I have a new challenge for you, Raider," Kelsey said to Angela with a grin. "Now that you're fully enhanced, it's time you had a new job."

"I'm still getting used to acting as your second in command," Angela said dryly. "I'm a marine—a Marine Raider now, I suppose—and I'm not really all that skilled in running a ship, even now. What other pond filled with alligators do you have in mind for me?"

"Major Angela Ellis, by the authority granted me as the crown princess of the New Terran Empire and senior officer of the Marine Raiders, I hereby order you to assume command of the strike ship *Persephone*," Kelsey said formally. "*Persephone*, log the change of command and acknowledge that the transfer is complete."

"Orders received and executed," the somewhat artificial computer voice said through the overhead speakers. "Command authority is hereby transferred to Major Angela Ellis."

Angela gaped, and her mouth moved without sound for a few moments. "Kelsey, I'm not ready for this," she finally said.

The smaller woman reached out and squeezed her shoulder. "You're far readier than I was when I assumed command. Serve the Empire well, Major."

* * *

KELSEY TOOK a deep breath and settled into the mindset she needed to act like the Rebel Empire noble she was pretending to be. She was so into that that she barely reacted to the Bastard coming into the compartment.

She stopped and forced herself to correct that. Jared Mertz wasn't the Bastard here. Of that she was now almost certain, as hard as that was to believe.

Still, she couldn't stop the wave of loathing that washed over her every time she saw the man. No matter who he might be here, she doubted she'd ever get over that feeling.

"How long do we have?" Olivia asked Mertz as he sat.

"Two minutes, max," the man said. "Sean will be here just before him. Let me brief you about what we learned this morning. The plasma charges are too dangerous to try to disarm. We'll have to play this out."

"That's unfortunate," Olivia said, her jaw obviously tight. "Fielding dropped a surprise on me via the com moments ago. He doesn't have the codes to extend us more than the week he already used.

"It turns out that he has a little side mission for us to carry out, and the System Lord there will decrypt a file Fielding has from his System Lord to give us the extension to get to Terra."

Mertz growled under his breath. "Perfect. Any idea what the mission is supposed to be?"

"Not a clue. The theatrical bugger wants to tell us himself."

At that moment, Sean entered the compartment at a fast jog. "Did I miss anything?" he asked a bit breathlessly.

"Fielding is changing our plans," Mertz said. "Sit, and we'll find out how in a minute."

Sixty seconds later, two of Fielding's guards came into the compartment and scanned it for threats.

As if every one of the people on this mission wasn't a threat. All of them, with the exception of Austin, wore neural disruptors to continue the tradition of the original crew. Theirs were set to stun, but none of Fielding's people would know that.

And the Rebel Empire Lord seemingly didn't care. Without him, they'd die, and he knew they knew it. Hell, he'd given Austin a code to disable the bomb in his head. Not that he'd needed it, as Doctor Stone had already removed the device after replacing the corrupt code in the young man's implants.

Though, to be fair, that only saved him from it going off automatically if he did something it thought compromised the mission. Anyone else with the right code in transmission range could kill him in a gruesome manner with a thought.

Kelsey made a mental note to try and talk Austin into using the disarm code his uncle had given him under Doctor Stone's observation. Fielding wouldn't have given it to his nephew if he hadn't expected Austin to use it. It wouldn't kill the young man. She hoped.

Of course, it might not work with the implant code altered. There was no way of knowing other than trying. She supposed the odds of it going off were still greater than zero.

Moments later, Fielding and his remaining two guards came into the compartment. The older man smiled with false joviality as he took a seat at the table while his guards spread out to cover all approaches.

"Good morning," he said. "I hope you all had a restful evening. Are you as famished as I am?"

"You have no idea," Kelsey said. "I'm starving."

And, sadly, it was true. Even with everything she'd already eaten, she was still hungry. It was humiliating.

"Then by all means, let's get something to eat." He peremptorily waved at Commander Cannon, who was already coming over to take any special orders.

Which of course Fielding had in spades. He ordered his eggs done in a very specific manner. Sort of like over easy, but with restrictions on how crisp the whites were. Then he described the level of fluff he wanted in his pancakes.

The list of how he wanted things went on and left Kelsey boggled. She'd been raised in the Imperial Palace, and no one there would've dared to tell a chef how to do their job so brazenly.

Then she came to a realization. The man was trying to irritate them. His behavior was another provocation. She had no proof, but she'd seen others act like this kind of ass before.

Her eyes briefly flashed over to Mertz before returning to Fielding. There might be more similarity between Fielding and the Bastard than she'd imagined. It made for an interesting thought experiment.

When her turn came, she ordered more than a woman of her size normally would, but not by a tremendous degree. Added to her earlier meal, it might just tide her over until lunch.

Once the orders were complete and the drinks had been delivered, Olivia got right to the point. "You mentioned a side mission for the

Lords so that we can get the code we need to proceed to Terra. Obviously, time is a precious commodity that we cannot recover once we've spent it. What are the details of this mission?"

The older man smiled indulgently. "There's no need to rush things. We have plenty of time to get where we need to go and do what we need to do. The first few flips are already in your flight plan. We don't deviate until just shortly before you'd have met the other ship."

Olivia set both of her hands flat on the table and stood, her expression rock hard and unflinching.

"You've made an error in judgment, Lord Fielding. You might have the codes I need, but I command this mission. If the Lords want us to divert and take care of something for them, we will of course obey, but I will not be toyed with by you on my own ship. I am mistress here."

That wiped the expression of joviality off the man's face. He glared at Olivia for a few seconds but then smiled in what seemed like a more genuine manner.

"It's good to see you have some steel in your spine, Lady Keaton. You'll need that at Terra, I'm sure. Very well. We'll be diverting to the Bradley system to perform a somewhat delicate task for the Lord there. One you and your people are uniquely suited for."

"And what might that task be?" Mertz asked as the food started arriving.

Fielding grinned at him. "The Lord there has suffered some hardware failures, it seems, and become somewhat erratic. Perhaps paranoid is a better word.

"The Lord in my system has been tasked by his associates to send a repair team to restore their brother to health. As the Lords control our very lives, they feel they can trust us with this... delicate task."

Delicate wasn't the word Kelsey would've chosen.

From her expression, Olivia shared Kelsey's doubts. "So we're supposed to just coast right up, talk our way past a paranoid AI, and convince it to allow us to send a repair team on board? You make it sound so simple. What if it won't let us in?"

Fielding spread his hands. "I suggest you be convincing, since we'll all die if it either opens fire on us or simply refuses us access. Only it can decrypt the codes we need to keep the plasma charges from destroying this ship and everyone on it.

"In any case, we are limited in the number of people that are cleared for this work. While either you or Lord Gust can lead the mission, my nephew and Lady Oldfield will be the only ones allowed to see the inner workings of the Lord at your sides."

Kelsey blinked before she could stop herself. Jocelyn Oldfield, the woman she was pretending to be, might have been an adept engineer, but Kelsey wasn't. Far from it.

Austin seemingly had the chops to do his part, but she'd be putting their lives at risk with her ignorance. Worse, she might do something that she wasn't even aware of that set the AI off.

"Why me?" Kelsey asked slowly. "I don't know the systems I'll be looking at."

The man shrugged. "It's a small risk, but I have complete confidence in your exemplary technical ability. After all, as the woman who designed the containers for our deadly cargo, you're undoubtedly a very savvy engineer. You'll be fine."

Kelsey put on a confident smile, but inside, she knew that they were screwed.

4

T albot left Kelsey and Angela talking as he headed back to his makeshift office aboard *Persephone*. As fun as watching that fight had been, he still had an extraordinary amount of work on his plate. More specifically, he had a number of prisoners that needed dealing with.

He might as well start with the newest batch, he decided as he sat. He had his implants signal Commander Veronica Giguere.

"How can I help you, Colonel?" the former Rebel Empire Fleet officer asked once she'd answered.

"I think it's time we have a conversation with your old friend. Would you bring Commander Sommerville to my office, please?"

"With pleasure. He's been hounding me for details I can't give him, and I have a few questions of my own about that ship of his and where he was taking it."

Those questions mirrored what Talbot intended to ask. "See you shortly."

Kelsey and Veronica had captured Lieutenant Commander Don Sommerville on their recent mission to the Archibald system. He'd been in the process of running from the Clan incursion with a Q-ship:

a warship built inside a freighter's hull and looking far less dangerous than it truly was.

He'd claimed to be a member of resistance inside the Rebel Empire, and Talbot saw no reason to doubt him. They had far more evidence than they needed to execute him if they'd been the enemies the man thought they were, so he really had no reason to lie about that.

Five minutes later, a rap at his hatch preceded Veronica's entry. The captured man was right behind her, with two marines at his back.

"Gentlemen, you can wait outside," Talbot said, rising to his feet and making his way around the desk.

The marines departed, leaving Talbot alone with Veronica and Commander Sommerville. He wasn't worried about the man attacking him. Sommerville wanted information as much as Talbot did.

Once the other two were seated, Talbot sat. "Commander Sommerville, I'm sorry it's taken us so long to talk. I'm Lieutenant Colonel Russel Talbot, Imperial Marines. Only, not from the Empire you nominally serve."

The other man smiled slightly. "Very delicately put. Who do you serve, Colonel?"

"The AIs failed to stop all the forces that fled when they took over," Talbot said, crossing his legs. "For ease of understanding, we're calling ourselves the New Terran Empire and your polity the Rebel Empire. It's all semantics, but everything needs a name, and we have the guns."

Sommerville chuckled. "I'm not in a position to argue, even if I felt inclined to do so. Feel free to call yourselves whatever you like. By the way, this is an interesting ship. I can't recall ever seeing anything quite like her."

"She's from before the Fall," Talbot said. "Refurbished, of course. By the Fall, I mean the collapse of the Old Terran Empire. This ship was built for a group of elite fighters called Marine Raiders. So far as we know, it was the smallest class of ship capable of taking people through flip points."

"Interesting," Sommerville admitted. "Still, I'm sure that we both have more pressing things to talk about. If, of course, I'm allowed to ask questions."

Talbot inclined his head toward Veronica. "Commander Giguere has spoken highly of your character, though she didn't know of your double life. We have friends in the resistance as well, though none are with us at the moment."

"So she said. I respect Veronica a great deal, and we were once friends. Or as friendly as a spy inside Fleet could be. Sorry about that, Veronica."

"I hardly think *I'm* in a position to judge," the former destroyer commander said dryly. "I did just help capture you so I could steal a flip drive from your shipyard."

"What a complicated universe we live in," Sommerville mused. "Everyone has their secrets these days. And since none of us is really that willing to share the deep details of our lives, whatever will we talk about?"

"Actually, I'm more than willing to give you some information," Talbot said. "Not everything, of course, but enough to show good faith. I'll start off by telling you about the people attacking the Rebel Empire. The ones you had to run from."

Talbot proceeded to tell him what they knew about the Clans. He even told the man how Raul Castille, the Rebel Empire security officer, had stolen one of the New Terran Empire's ships and provoked them.

Sommerville shook his head with a wry smile. "You find excitement in odd places. Exactly how did a prisoner manage all this?"

"I'm partly to blame," Veronica admitted. "My command crew and I helped him escape. We stole the transport ship they were using to move the Dresden orbital, and he lobbed the orbital right into a Clan battle station. They blew the orbital up, but high-speed shrapnel is a bitch."

Sommerville frowned. "How could anyone get that close to a battle station? And did you say the Dresden orbital? A real orbital?"

"A full-sized one," Talbot confirmed. "It was being used for classified research, and we were a little pressed for time, so we took it with us when we ran."

The other man opened his mouth to say something but seemingly changed his mind and only shook his head.

"It's true," Veronica assured him. "The transport ships are made for moving a lot of mined material or large ships inside arms that project the flip field out. They managed to get them around the orbital."

"That's… audacious," Sommerville said slowly. "And a bit far-fetched. I somehow doubt the ships and battle stations guarding the Dresden system just let you wander away. Also, exactly how did you find these Clans? Where are they coming from?"

Talbot smiled. "We used the same kind of escape you intended to use at Archibald."

The man's interested expression closed right up. "I'm not sure I understand what you mean."

"I mean the flip points that sit way out past where that kind of thing normally sits," Talbot said. "You had a way out of Archibald that you weren't worried about the Clans following you through. I'm sorry to tell you this, but the Clans know all about the far flip points. They're how we discovered them in the first place."

"Let's assume for a moment that your preposterous story is true," Sommerville said slowly. "What does the existence of these flip points matter to you? If you know about them and you suspect I do as well, what exactly are we talking about?"

"I just wanted to set the stage for laying out what we want to negotiate over," Talbot said smoothly. "You don't have to confirm that you know about the far flip points since I already know they exist."

"Okay, let's just say they do, simply for moving this discussion forward. What do you want, and exactly how does that affect me and my people?"

Veronica leaned forward a little. "The short version is that we need to get to the New Terran Empire. All the paths from the area we're hiding in go through the Rebel Empire. You can imagine why that might not be advisable right now."

"And you think, what?" Sommerville asked with a raised eyebrow.

"That the resistance knows about these fantastical flip points and might provide you a way home with our secret information? Veronica, I'm afraid that I can't help you. This is all just a tad crazy sounding."

Talbot sent a request to the marines outside his office.

"I can provide some proof that we're in an area of space you're unfamiliar with. I suspected that I'd need a trump card, so I want you to meet someone special."

The hatch slid open, and a tall, blue-skinned alien man walked in.

Talbot grinned as Sommerville sprang to his feet, a shocked expression written across his face at being confronted by something so unexpected. Neither the Old Terran Empire nor the Rebel Empire had ever encountered aliens before.

"Lieutenant Commander Don Sommerville," Talbot said, "allow me to introduce Prince Derek of the Kingdom of Raden on the world of Pandora. I believe he can provide corroborating evidence that we're a long way from home and might have something to offer the resistance in exchange for help getting back."

* * *

JARED STEPPED INTO ENGINEERING, still so engrossed in his own thoughts that he'd missed Commander O'Halloran speaking to him for a few moments.

"I'm sorry," Jared said, holding his hand up. "I wasn't paying attention. What?"

"I said that one of the FTL coms seems to be malfunctioning."

Jared blinked. "That's a first. Some kind of hardware fault?"

The other officer shrugged. "I'm not sure. Whatever it is, it's subtle. The unit has thrown three strange faults in the last few hours. Yet when I examine the supposedly bad component, I don't see anything wrong. I've even swapped the same component from another com, and the new part seems to be bad in exactly the same way as the old one."

"That strikes me as unlikely," Jared agreed. "Which FTL com is it?"

"The one linked to Princess Kelsey."

With any other com, that might be a coincidence. With Kelsey's group, he couldn't assume that. Carl was with her, and he'd designed the FTL com system. If anyone could figure out some way to make one act weird, it was the young scientist.

The problem was that they couldn't be in range. They were many flips away from where Kelsey had to be, in a completely different sector of the Rebel Empire.

FTL coms only worked through a single flip point. Even with a dedicated relay, it only gave a good connection to a second system about half the time. Carl had said that had to be technical and that he'd figure it out one day, but today probably wasn't that day.

Probably.

"Could it be some kind of interference that Carl is introducing remotely?" he asked.

The engineering officer shrugged. "I suppose it's possible. If so, I can't see what he's doing or how. Honestly, this looks like some type of mechanical fault to me, but I won't rule out external action just yet. No matter what it is, I'm just not certain what to do next."

"Don't we have complete technical schematics for the FTL coms?" Jared asked.

O'Halloran nodded. "We do, but some of what they describe is fairly esoteric. I don't want to say that I can't figure it out, but this is using a level of science and hardware manipulation that I've never played with before. Carl Owlet is a genius, and as much as I hate to say it, I'm not."

"Don't put yourself down," Jared said, clapping his hand on the man's shoulder. "You're pretty damned smart."

The engineer sighed. "Maybe I can figure this out, if it's actually something intentional. I can't imagine how that's even possible, but Carl has his ways. I'd feel a lot more comfortable if I had a deeper understanding of the hardware itself."

Jared pursed his lips. "What you're telling me is that you need a hardware geek."

"I certainly wouldn't turn one down. Do you happen to have one sitting in your pocket?"

"I might. Where do we have the FTL com stashed?"

"In the maintenance tubes just behind engineering," O'Halloran said, gesturing toward one of the hatches.

Jared sent a contact request to Austin Darrah through his implants. The other man answered almost immediately.

Mr. Darrah, would you meet me in engineering?

I'll be right there.

Ten minutes later, Austin Darrah walked into engineering.

"What can I do for you?" the young man asked, nodding to the engineer.

"I don't know if you've met, but this is Lieutenant Commander Anthony O'Halloran, our chief engineer. Tony, this is Austin Darrah."

From the unfriendly look Tony was shooting toward Austin, the fact that the young man hadn't been directly responsible for anyone's death during the action retaking *Athena* wasn't holding much water with him.

Jared couldn't blame his man. The original chief engineer and Tony's close friend, Commander Katheryn Pence, had died in that action, killed by Austin's compatriots.

"Tony," Jared said softly, "I understand this isn't going to be easy, but you need to accept that not everyone that fought against us is an enemy. In a very real sense, Austin was a prisoner of the people that killed Katheryn. He wasn't armed, he didn't attack any of our people, and he's doing his very best to help us."

Austin inclined his head. "I'm sorry that the people I was working with killed anyone. I'm not a violent man, and I'm not a supporter of what they were doing here. I give you my word that I'm doing everything in my power to help you fight against the Lords."

O'Halloran grunted. "I'll try. It's going to take me a little bit to adjust, so if I seem abrupt, I apologize." He turned his attention to Jared. "Are you really expecting me to brief him on the project?"

Jared nodded. "Austin happens to be an expert on Fleet and Rebel Empire hardware. From what I understand, he has probably a decade more experience working with the kind of equipment that we're talking about, though he's never seen the machine in question and won't really understand the theory behind its design.

"Even if he can't figure out why it's behaving in the peculiar fashion that it is, I'll wager he can give you some insight into what's really going on. That might allow you to dig into the problem with fresh eyes."

He turned and faced Austin squarely. "What the commander is about to show you is one of our very closest secrets. I expect you to keep every bit of information you learn to yourself. Under no circumstances are you to discuss this with anyone other than myself, Sean Meyer, Olivia West, Elise Orison, or Commander O'Halloran. Is that understood?"

The young man nodded. "I understand completely."

Jared gestured toward the maintenance hatch. "Tony, show Austin what you've been working on and explain it to him in as much detail as you can. Austin, Tony didn't design this equipment, and his understanding of the hardware and theory may be a little off. I'm hoping that the two of you, working together, can figure out what's going on.

"I'm not certain that it's anything more than a malfunction, but this could potentially mean something much more important to us, so give it your very best."

Austin nodded again and turned to Commander O'Halloran. "Shall we?"

Jared watched the two men walk away and returned to the privacy of his own thoughts. He wished this really was Kelsey trying to contact them from some unimaginable distance away, but he didn't believe that was possible, not even for them. There were limits to what even Carl could do.

5

Kelsey looked over the FTL com hardware sitting on Carl's worktable in his bustling lab aboard *Audacious*. "Do we have any idea if your little trick is doing anything on the other end?"

The young scientist shrugged. "Since I can't directly connect to the hardware on the admiral's ship, I can't be sure. I designed the coms to be as secure as possible, so hacking into the hardware and trying to make it throw errors is a lot more difficult than it sounds."

"Is it really the hardware you need to hack into? I thought you said the software needed to be changed so that the system on the other end would recognize this strange type of connection request."

Carl nodded. "That would be ideal, but as I keep saying, it's not as easy as that. As I said, the goal I had in mind when designing the system was to make sure that somebody didn't do the kind of thing that I'm trying to do. As you might expect, I did everything I could think of to prevent it, so I've pretty well blocked myself away from my usual tricks."

She pursed her lips. "Maybe you're going about this the wrong way. No offense, but you're a scientist. Even though you know how to program, and you're damned good at hacking, the criminal mindset for this kind of thing really isn't in you. We need a professional."

"I'm pretty sure that I should be offended," Carl said, shaking his head and grinning. "You're talking about Ralph Halstead, aren't you?"

"Indeed I am," she conceded. "He'll have a lot more experience at industrial espionage via computer than we'll likely ever have."

They'd captured the earnest young Halstead, his aunt and uncle, and two men in their group during the mission at Archibald. They'd been involved in a two-year mission to hack data from a medical research company that was a front for the System Lords doing classified research on what could potentially be a Singularity AI.

Yet one more project on Carl Owlet's crowded desk.

"Kelsey, those people are criminals," Carl said. "Real criminals. As much as it pains me to say this, I'm not certain that I care how good he is at hacking. Anything he learns is going to be sold to the highest bidder the first chance he gets."

She pursed her lips. "I'm not so sure. His aunt? Probably. Him? I think he's more into this for the fun. I guess what I'm saying is that I think it's possible that we can recruit him to work for us."

Carl shook his head slightly. "I hate to be the one to say this, but if we get captured by the Rebel Empire, he'd talk in a moment to save his skin."

Kelsey nodded somberly. "And that would be something we'd have to discuss with him. Knowledge of one of these classified systems would be a death sentence if it looks like someone is about to be captured.

"Of course, each of them already knows about the Singularity computer you have scattered across your lab. I'm pretty sure they know the fate that awaits them just for knowing about it, much less trying to steal it. There's no way that the System Lords will believe that they weren't the ones behind the theft if they got their hands on our little industrial spies."

Though with the Clans in possession of the Archibald system and invading the Rebel Empire, the System Lords probably had more pressing matters on their electronic minds.

"The list of things that we've done to the System Lords has grown to be truly impressive," Carl said with a chuckle. "Even if they don't know who we are, we've become quite the thorn in their sides. Scrappy rebels taking the fight to them. That should be a movie."

"No!" Kelsey said firmly. "Don't give *anyone* any crazy ideas. Have you seen the latest film out of Pentagar? It's getting ridiculous."

The young man's eyebrows went up. "I saw the first two, and I thought they were pretty good. The woman they found to play you has quite the… screen presence."

Kelsey snorted. "What you mean is that she has quite the cleavage. Talk about being out of character. This time they've decided to cover the attack on Boxer Station and Harrison's World, including my little trip down to the surface in the drop capsule to stop that guy with the nuke.

"Of course the damned thing is a huge success, and every time I think they'll finally stop producing these idiotic movies, the next one makes truckloads more money than the last one. I'm doomed."

Carl laughed. "I suppose that's what you get for being the face of the New Terran Empire. I'm sure Jared gets equally good coverage, right?"

She nodded grudgingly. "He does, but he's not letting it get under his skin like I am. I just can't shake how it makes me feel.

"Now before we fall any further down this rabbit hole, have you made any progress on the Singularity computer? Is it just a standard kind of thing writ large, or is it an AI?"

"It's not in good enough condition to make that kind of assessment. Whatever happened to it pretty well broke it into component parts. The memory storage units were mostly intact, but as one might expect, they're encrypted.

"We have the lead researcher on the project aboard, along with a couple of his junior associates, but they're not being cooperative. I personally have my doubts that they'll ever give in. It makes sense the AIs would get people that were very loyal to work on a project like this."

Kelsey rubbed her face. "I'm starting to lose track of how many prisoners we have. Exactly how did we gather all of these enemies anyway?"

"It's because we're good at sticking our noses where they don't belong, stirring up angry mobs, and capturing interesting people before we run away again," Carl said. "I'm sure they'd find some of their fellow prisoners to be quite fascinating if they knew these other people were here at all."

Kelsey squeezed the bridge of her nose between her index finger and thumb. "It feels like we have a menagerie. In any case, I'll go talk with Ralph Halstead and see if we can come to some kind of agreement. Fiona will help me make sure he's telling us the truth."

Fiona was the sentient AI they'd found when they'd captured the Dresden orbital. It had been packed away in the freighter they'd used to help move equipment away from the scene of their attack. Talbot had instructed Carl to assemble her on *Persephone*.

The sentient AI wasn't in command of *Persephone* like Marcus was aboard Jared's flagship *Invincible* because the Marine Raider computer had special security circuits built into it that disallowed control of the ship's systems by anyone other than itself.

That didn't mean that two computers hadn't begun working together in ways that she still wasn't certain she fully understood. A kind of strange partnership. The Marine Raider computer seemed to have recognized the AI as both a person and a computer and was cooperating with it in some tasks. It was kind of spooky.

Kelsey looked forward to seeing exactly what that odd partnership resulted in. In any case, the presence of the sentient AI gave her a number of capabilities that she wouldn't normally have, and that included being able to test people with implants to see if they were lying.

"Keep working on the FTL com," Kelsey ordered as she headed for the hatch. "I'll see if I can get you some help."

* * *

OLIVIA SAT in her new office just off *Athena*'s bridge and stewed. Fielding had sprung this dangerous side mission on them with some kind of ulterior motive, but she just couldn't figure out what it might be.

He could've allowed the mission to proceed without his presence. That meant he wanted something from this new system that furthered his own plans. Whatever they were.

Once they'd finished breakfast, Fielding had headed back to his quarters. Jared's quarters, if one was to be specific, just as this was her friend's office.

If she went to Fielding, she'd be on his territory, and he'd attempt to assert his dominance. If she wanted to avoid playing that kind of game again, she'd be much better off if she summoned him to the bridge. Her territory.

Her mind made up, Olivia walked out onto the bridge. Commander Janice Hall, *Athena*'s helm officer, partly turned in her seat and raised an eyebrow.

"Can I help you, ma'am?" the Fleet officer asked.

"Exactly how far away are we from the new destination system?"

"We'll hit the first flip point in about two hours. From there, we have three more transitions before we arrive at the target system. All told, it will take us five days to get where we're going."

"And once we arrive, we'll only have about eighteen hours, give or take, to get the code we need to reset the explosives in our hold," Olivia calculated grimly.

"That's not a whole lot of time," Hall agreed. "Do we even know what has to be repaired to get the AI back into shape?"

"Not a clue," Olivia said. "If we're in a good place for the moment, I'd like you to go down to Fielding's cabin and request his presence in my office. I think it's time he and I had a meeting of the minds."

"Me, ma'am?"

Olivia nodded. "He's seen you here on the bridge. He'll consider you one of my inner circle just by association. Be polite but firm. Give it as much time as it takes, but wait for him."

She returned to her office and waited.

And waited.

And *waited*.

Finally, after almost an hour had passed, Commander Hall returned with Fielding striding smugly beside her.

"Lord Fielding, my lady," Hall said. The Fleet officer rolled her eyes where the man couldn't see, almost making Olivia smile, and returned to her post on the bridge.

"My apologies for the delay, Lady Keaton," the Rebel Empire noble said as he entered the office as if he owned it. "You caught me in the middle of something quite delicate. I came as quickly as I could."

"I'm sure," Olivia said, not bothering to hide her disbelief. "If you'd be so kind as to close the hatch behind you, I believe it's time we had a more in-depth discussion on our situation."

Once the man had finally closed the hatch and taken a seat, she rose from behind her desk and took the seat across from him. For almost a full minute, she studied him without speaking. His smugness didn't even waiver.

"According to my calculations, once we arrive in the system you're taking us to, we only have eighteen hours or so to complete the task you've set for us."

"That sounds right," he agreed.

"And yet you've given us no information whatsoever on precisely what we need to do. That's unacceptable. These games you're playing are endangering my primary mission, and I will not stand for that."

"I don't understand what you mean," he said, his smile widening. "I would never toy with you in such a fashion."

"Of course you would," she countered. "You don't want us to have the specifics before we arrive, and I can only see one reason for that. Something in that system will further your ends in one way or another, yet you'd rather not have us know precisely what it is.

"I'm afraid you're not going to be able to have your cake and eat it too, Lord Fielding. You're going to tell me what you're doing and why."

"Don't be ridiculous," he said with a laugh. "Even if that were true—which I'm not saying it is—I certainly wouldn't feel obligated to tell you my motives."

She leaned forward, her expression cold. "I agreed to have a bomb planted in my head. I'd execute my crew—my friends—in a moment if it seemed that we were about to fail in our mission or breach the secrecy the Lords demanded. What makes you think that I'm going to just sit here and let you play me like this?"

If her words bothered the man, it didn't show. His grin didn't waver.

"You'll sit here and take it because you don't really have a choice. In any case, this is perhaps the most fun I've had in years. I'll not let you browbeat me into telling you what's going on.

"As for what I gain by instigating this change in plans, it's no business of yours, so long as it doesn't impinge upon your mission for the System Lords. You'll just have to accept that you're not the one in absolute control of your destiny. I am. The sooner you do so, the less indigestion you'll suffer.

"Now if we're done playing this little game, I have real work to do. Good day." He rose to his feet, opened the hatch, and walked out, never looking back.

Olivia rubbed her face tiredly. She'd tried to get the information they needed and failed. Now they'd just have to hope that whatever curveballs Fielding threw their way didn't hit them in the head.

6

Angela sat at the command console on *Persephone*'s bridge and tried not to feel out of place. Oh, she'd sat in the seat many times before, but only as Kelsey's executive officer. Now the ship was hers, and that was going to take some getting used to.

The bridge wasn't large. In fact, it was smaller than a destroyer's, only having consoles for command, helm, and tactical. Cozy was the watchword.

The hatch at the rear of the compartment slid open, and Veronica Giguere stepped onto *Persephone*'s bridge. Beside the woman was her Rebel Empire Fleet friend, Lieutenant Commander Don Sommerville and his marine guards trailed the pair.

Pleased at the distraction, Angela turned to face them. "Commander Giguere, Commander Sommerville, is there something I can do for you?"

Veronica smiled. "Would it be possible for you to task one of the drones down on Pandora with making a pass over *Dauntless*'s wreck, Major Ellis?"

"Certainly. Are you looking for a grand overview or a close pass on certain sections of the vessel?"

"Both. I want Don to see exactly what I've been telling him about."

"After seeing an alien, I don't think you really need to convince me anymore," Sommerville said dryly. "That's not something you can make up."

The haunted look in the man's eyes made Angela smile a little. "It is a little bit daunting, if you'll forgive the mild pun. Trust me when I say that this entire situation is a lot to take in, Commander Sommerville.

"Rather than seeing it through the drone, would you care to go down in person? We're about to dispatch a pinnace to the capital to pick up a gentleman for an enforced medical procedure, and we can drop you off at the wreck on our way."

One of Veronica's eyebrows quirked upward. "An enforced medical procedure? Exactly how does that work?"

Angela grinned. "Princess Kelsey had a… disagreement with a gentleman belonging to Clan Dauntless when she first arrived on Pandora. Blows were exchanged and injuries suffered. Rather than leave an avowed enemy sitting behind us, nursing his wounds, Her Highness has decided to make certain that he suffers no lasting harm from the encounter, even though he was an ass."

"I think that's an excellent idea," Veronica said. "That kind of person comes back to haunt you when you least expect it.

"And congratulations on your appointment. Commanding a ship in space is a big step and a true honor. Commanding this ship in particular is going to be an exciting experience, I'm sure."

"Exactly how does a marine officer achieve command of a Fleet warship?" Sommerville asked. "It seems a little odd."

"That's a long story that I'm uncertain you've been cleared to hear," Angela said firmly. "If you're that curious, you can ask Princess Kelsey. Meanwhile, why don't I escort you down to the planet surface?"

Veronica made a point of looking around *Persephone*'s bridge. "Don't you have a ship to command?"

"Senior Lieutenant Thompson has everything under control, don't you Jack?"

The helm officer grinned at her. "I feel relatively confident that were not going to run into any trouble here in orbit, Major. We'll manage just fine without you for a couple of hours, I'm sure."

"See? Let's get down to one of the pinnaces, and we'll get you to Pandora so you can visit a wreck."

The three of them left *Persephone*'s bridge and headed for the nearest pinnace. Angela had already ordered some marines to be ready for the mission. She'd originally intended to send Jack down but wanted to get a feel for their prisoner herself.

Just like she'd told Sommerville, she felt relatively safe leaving her ship under the circumstances. The only other vessels in the Pandora system were those attached to Commodore Anderson's task force. And if anyone else did arrive, Angela would have plenty of time to get back to *Persephone*.

Besides, it would feel good to stretch her legs a little.

Once everyone was secured, the pinnace detached from the Marine Raider strike ship and fell toward the planet. Since there wasn't an emergency, they'd do a relatively slow entry so as not to spook the locals.

"Your helmsmen didn't call you Captain," Sommerville said. "Is that a marine thing?"

"Yes and no," Angela said seriously. "We're still exploring exactly how marines commanding a ship in space will look, but the marines don't use the rank of captain. I understand that on board ship, that's a position rather than a rank, but we're still not certain that's what we want to do.

"My people know who I am. I don't need them calling me by my position. I think I'm satisfied with them using my rank as my only form of address. I'm certain other people would feel more comfortable using the title of captain and that we're going to end up causing confusion, but that's pretty much the nature of how the marines fit inside Fleet."

Somerville chuckled. "I suppose that's true enough."

"As an interested observer, I'd like to ask you a few questions if you don't mind, Commander Sommerville."

The man gestured for her to continue. "Feel free, Major. I may not answer, but I'm not going to take offense at your curiosity."

"What's it like working inside an enemy for your entire professional career and plotting their downfall? It seems like being a spy from one of the old vids, always in fear that someone is going to figure out your secret and capture you or kill you."

He nodded slowly. "There's an element of that, certainly. I wish it were something as straightforward as what you're imagining, but it's not. When you intermingle with people on a daily basis, you form friendships. Even with people that are ostensibly working for the other side."

His eyes moved over to Veronica. "Veronica and I were once close friends, even though she'd have thought me a traitor if she'd known what I was up to. I have hopes that we'll be friends again one day."

Veronica gave him an affectionate look and shook her head. "I'm not going to hold your past against you, Don. I believe we both pulled the wool over one another's eyes. Knowing what I do about the overall situation, at the very least we're going to be allies."

Somerville raised an eyebrow. "And you're confident of that? At this point, I'm not. I just don't know enough about you all, and I'm unsure that I can trust you with the secrets you want from me. I've got a lot of people to think about."

"If you don't mind my input, I might be able to smooth this road a little bit," Angela said. "What is it you think we'll be doing if you don't help us? Sitting here and waiting to be rescued? I can assure you that isn't going to happen.

"With the capture of your Q-ship, we understand that you were taking supplies to what is almost certainly a resistance base hidden in a system that the Rebel Empire doesn't know about. The first leg of that journey starts in the Archibald system. Are you with me so far?"

Somerville nodded again. "I can see the logic of what you're saying, though I will neither confirm nor deny the existence of a base or a flip point of the nature you are implying."

"Any lawyer worth their salt would be proud of that answer," Angela said with a grin. "The next obvious step is to send probes through that far flip point. Of course, that means we need to locate it first.

"You'd think that would be a little bit difficult with an invasion going on, but *Persephone* might surprise you. My ship is designed to sneak into places right under other people's noses. You didn't see how we got out of the system, and I'm not going to share that information without proper authorization, but none of the Clan warships is likely to be anywhere near our entry point into Archibald space.

"Our next step is almost certainly going to have me ghost into the Archibald system and send stealthed probes to look into the outer reaches of the system for far flip points. Eventually, we're going to find out where you were going, and then I'll send probes through to see what's on the other side.

"Once that's done, it's just a matter of looking into every flip point in that new system, both standard and far. If it's an occupied system, that may be somewhat more challenging but not out of the question. I'm inclined to believe that wherever your base is, it's going to be somewhere down another far flip point. More probably two."

Angela let silence fall after her guesses. His expression didn't give anything away, but she was still relatively certain that she wasn't far from the truth.

"You should ask yourself, Commander Sommerville, what you'd like to happen when we find the resistance base. I'll repeat what I'm sure everyone else has said. We have no desire to fight you. We're looking for allies, not enemies.

"As you might imagine, we have a few tricks up our collective sleeves that we'd be willing to trade for your assistance. The real question is how we can find common ground to begin trusting one another."

The prisoner slowly nodded. "I hear what you're saying, Major. I'm going to have to think about it."

Satisfied with the progress, Angela leaned back in her acceleration couch. Based on Veronica Giguere's approving expression, she'd done well. If her actions helped get them closer to where they needed to be, then this would be time well spent. If they didn't, well, it never hurt to try.

The rest of the trip down to the surface was quiet, and she let the pair go at the wreck site with their marine guards.

Once the pinnace was back in the air, she turned her attention to the mission at hand. The drones watching the capital of the Kingdom of Raden had spotted the man Kelsey had fought. Based on the building he was living in, he didn't want his clan mates to know his current location either.

That was fine with her. It meant that she could stun him without much fear of anyone interfering and be gone before any alarm was raised. She'd take him directly to *Audacious* and let the doctor work on him while he was still unconscious.

Then, once he was fully healed, she'd return him to the planet. He'd wake up suddenly healed of all his injuries.

She had no idea how he was going to interpret that, and frankly, she didn't care. One way or the other, they'd be leaving Pandora in the next few days. The odds of any of them ever seeing the man again were vanishingly small.

At her orders, the pinnace hovered over the dark city. It was still before dawn, so there weren't many people up. An excellent time of the morning to go hunting.

The buildings inside the kingdom's capital were mostly constructed of wood and stone. Those were easy building materials to gather and use for what amounted to a medieval society.

The durability of the buildings also allowed the pinnace to lower its ramp onto the rooftop.

It only had to hover for a few moments as Angela and the marines hopped out onto the peak. It then silently lifted into the air, closed its ramp, and began circling higher to await them calling for pickup.

The three-story building had no roof access, but that wasn't going to deter Angela. She'd already spotted their entry point on the back of the building. Someone had failed to close the shutters on one of the top-floor windows.

The corporal in charge of her team quickly attached a line to a heavy chimney and tested it. He nodded at Angela.

"Looks good, Major," he said quietly. "We should only go down one at a time, just to be on the safe side."

Like any good commander, she allowed her marines to precede her in and then followed. Once they were inside the hallway on the top floor, they began a room by room search, looking for their quarry.

The building provided room and board for itinerant workers, so the conditions were crowded and there was a lot of snoring going on. Each room they looked into was packed with Pandorans sleeping on large spreads of cheap bedding.

That complicated the task of locating the one person they were really interested in, but it didn't make it impossible. The man's injuries meant he had one hand that was heavily bandaged. He was also human, so he'd stand out.

Her scouts found him at the end of the hall, saving her from having to search the other two floors. Unfortunately, he was on the far side of a group of sleeping Pandorans. That made access to him without waking the others impossible.

Thankfully, that was a problem she could solve. She quietly drew her stunner, set it to wide beam, and shot everyone in the room. With the diffused effects, the people inside would be asleep for roughly half an hour and wake up with a headache. She was sorry for that, but it couldn't be helped.

Thankfully, stunners had less effect on Pandorans than humans. The time it was effective for was roughly half as long, and the headache was less significant.

Two of her marines extracted their target and carried him back the way they'd come. Inside five minutes, they'd retreated to the roof and were back aboard the pinnace, heading for *Audacious*.

They secured the prisoner in one of the marine drop harnesses, and Angela stunned him again with a full beam to be certain he'd be out long enough for the medical procedure to take place and for him to be returned to Pandora.

She wasn't convinced that this man would feel differently toward Princess Kelsey after this, but one never knew. It would make her boss happy, and that was good enough for Angela.

Once this was done, she could begin the final process of getting *Persephone* ready to scout Archibald. One way or the other, she knew that task would land in her lap before very much longer, and frankly, she was itching to get started.

7

K elsey rubbed her temples tiredly and stared at the wall of her cabin. Trying to make any sense from even the limited information about the AIs Mertz had brought with them on this mission made her brain hurt. She just wasn't a technical person.

In a way, she was grateful that the man hadn't brought the complete technical specifications, because she knew that she didn't have a chance of understanding them.

Of course, he'd insisted that only the other version of her had that kind of detailed information. If he was to be believed, she'd stolen it from the Rebel Empire but hadn't gotten it home yet.

Hell, that sounded like this universe's version of her, so she'd even grant the man was probably telling her the truth.

Yet she was going to be the one responsible for repairing the damaged AI in a few days. If she didn't get a handle on what she needed to do, they were all going to die.

Fielding had been cagey, but she'd bet money that he intended to personally accompany them. The Bastard... Mertz... was absolutely correct in his assessment that the man was up to something.

The more she compared Fielding to the Mertz from her universe, the more similarities she saw in the way they behaved and treated others. Ironically, that only highlighted how little like her Mertz the one from this universe behaved.

She respected Scott Roche and had considered what he'd advised her to do a few nights ago, but she genuinely liked these people, other than Mertz. She wasn't sure that she could betray them, even if that was the price for saving the lives of her people back home.

Kelsey hoped it never came to that. The odds of her being able to escape with the key and Mertz, or the override from the vaults below the Imperial Palace on Terra, were even lower than her being able to carry off the mission with the AI.

If anyone was going to be able to repair the AI, it was going to have to be Austin Darrah. Rather than trying to reinvent the wheel, she needed to do what she could to support him in that task.

With that thought in mind, she began wandering the corridors, searching for the young man. To her shock, she covered the entire destroyer, with the exceptions of private quarters, without locating him. He didn't answer the door to his own cabin, so she doubted he was in there.

Where could he be hiding?

Then she remembered that she could use her implants to locate him. She instructed the ship's computer to tell her his location, and it responded that he was not aboard the ship.

That response made her blink. That was impossible. It wasn't as if he could just get off.

She queried the computer about Mertz's location. It responded that he was no longer aboard the destroyer as well.

Frustrated, she headed for engineering. That was where Mertz frequented, so if anyone knew where he was now, they'd likely be there.

She found the lieutenant commander in charge of engineering overseeing maintenance on some piece of equipment. He rose to his feet and nodded politely to her.

"Highness, what can I do for you?"

"Commander… O'Halloran, isn't it? I'm looking for Jared Mertz or Austin Darrah. The ship's computer doesn't seem to think they're aboard. By any chance, do you know where they are?"

He nodded, led her to a maintenance hatch, and opened it. Somewhat nonplussed, she went inside.

Expecting to find a basic maintenance tube, she was surprised to find a concealed work area. Austin was looking over a piece of equipment on a makeshift table while Mertz looked on.

Mertz looked over at her and nodded. "Princess Kelsey."

She gestured toward the table. "What is this and why are you working on it in here? And why didn't the computer know where you were?"

"We're in a shielded area," he said. "This is an FTL com, and it seems to be malfunctioning. Commander O'Halloran can't seem to isolate the fault, so I'm giving Austin a shot."

That statement caused both of her eyebrows to shoot up. "No offense to Austin, but isn't this kind of a secret?"

The young Rebel Empire noble grinned at her. "It seems I've been brought into the inner circle. Okay, probably not the inner circle. Maybe a middle circle."

He turned his attention toward Mertz. "As far as I can tell, none of these parts is malfunctioning. Each and every one of them passes a self-check, and as Commander O'Halloran indicated, he even swapped out the offending part with a different unit, and it still behaves in exactly the same way."

"So you're saying this is external influence of some kind," Mertz said. "While I'm certainly not well versed in the theory behind this equipment, someone who is has assured me that that wasn't possible."

The young hardware enthusiast shrugged. "What can I tell you? Some of the most amazing breakthroughs in science take place when someone takes something that isn't possible and does it anyway.

"I'm absolutely not saying that this is an attempt at communication. I don't know enough about it to be certain. All I can state with any certainty is that the equipment is functioning as designed.

"Perhaps we're traveling through a section of space where a nearby star is sending out pulses of radiation that we can't detect clearly that somehow affects this one quantum connection. I can certainly keep thinking about what's going on, but I don't think any further examination by me is going to reveal a secret at the moment."

Mertz nodded. "That might actually be for the best, now that I think about it. When something has me stumped, the answer will usually come when I'm busy doing something completely unrelated, straight out of the blue."

He focused his attention on Kelsey. "You came looking for us, Highness. What can we do for you?"

She grimaced. "I've reached the end of my rope trying to get a handle on repairing the AI. I understand that I'm supposed to take the lead in that particular charade, but honestly, we all know that Austin is going to do the work. I just have to figure out a way to look like I'm leading when I'm really following.

"Has Fielding told us who's going on this mission other than Austin, myself, and either you or Olivia?"

Mertz shrugged. "She confronted him, but he didn't give her any more information. I think it's a safe bet that he's going along with you. If you feel more comfortable, I'm certainly okay with sending Olivia. It's your call."

Kelsey hated being so biased, but if she had the choice of picking between Olivia and Mertz, she picked the other woman in a heartbeat. She just didn't trust Mertz, even though she probably should.

She opened her mouth to say something to that effect, but the piece of equipment that the two men had been examining chose that moment to turn itself off.

Austin blinked down at the communication device. "Well, that's new."

TALBOT WATCHED Ralph Halstead work on his computer, which was attached to the FTL com, feeling more than a bit conflicted. Everything was set up in Carl's lab, and the other researchers were watching the proceedings with interest.

"Are you sure this is the best idea?" he asked Kelsey softly. The two of them were leaning back against the bulkhead and watching from a short distance away.

His wife nodded. "Fiona checked him. When he says that he's not going to betray us, I believe him."

"But *why* is he helping us?"

"Bottom line? He's bored."

"Bored?" Talbot asked, hearing the doubt in his own tone. "That's not a good long-term motivator."

His wife grinned at him. "It is if you've been doing the same thing for your aunt for years. She, by the way, *spectacularly* failed her lie detector test. There's no way we're going to be able to trust her with any secrets.

"We'll end up sending her back to the new Terran Empire permanently once we have a way to get there. Her husband, too. And sadly, their cats. I need a pet. You're not allergic to cats, are you?"

"Don't try to change the subject," he said firmly. "Our young friend is an industrial spy. A hacker. The moment someone offers him enough money or a chance to scamper off and sell what he knows about us, he's going to vanish."

"Not according to Fiona," Kelsey said smugly. "She's fully vetted his story about not really being that interested in stealing things for a living. Like you said, he's a hacker. He likes getting into places that he's not supposed to be and doing things that he's not supposed to be doing, but it's not the money that drives him. It's the thrill of the chase, so to speak.

"When he found out that we had the code used for the sentient AIs, he said he'd sell his soul to work on something like that. What you see before you is a programmer committed to his art. Unlike his aunt or the criminal syndicates that she was working for, we can offer him something they can't. A true challenge and a purpose in his life."

Talbot wasn't convinced, but it was ultimately Kelsey's call.

"All right," he said, throwing up his hands. "You win. What exactly are you hoping he can do with the FTL com? Hasn't Carl already gone over the software with a fine-toothed comb? After all, he wrote it."

"Carl is a genius, but he knows his limitations. He's something of a generalist. Ralph Halstead has devoted his life to coding and hacking. If anyone can get into the guts of an FTL com at a distance, it's going to be him."

"I think I found something," Ralph said, excitement in his tone. "Take a look at this, Carl."

Talbot strode forward to stand beside the two of them, and Kelsey joined him, listening in to their hushed discussion. Doctor Jacqueline Parker, the former head of the Dresden orbital's secret research team, also moved closer.

The hacker pointed to a line of text on the screen in front of him. "Look at this line right here. If I can get access to this module, I could shut off the unit remotely."

Carl read what was on the screen and slowly nodded. "It's not much of a vulnerability, but you're right. The question is, how do you get into that module from the receiver section of the com?"

"We can trigger a response from the other com whenever we send a status query," Ralph said. "If I send some additional code I've put together along with that query, the other unit is going to read it."

"How do you make the remote device actually execute the additional code in the manner that you want?" Parker asked softly.

Halstead turned and grinned at her. "I've got a library of code snippets that work on various Imperial systems. Sometimes they're useful and sometimes they're just a curiosity. Various groups that I've associated with over the years have compiled them just in case they proved useful in a future hack.

"When Carl built the FTL com, he used as many off-the-shelf components as possible. What I'm looking to do is cause a cascade failure inside the other com that ends up triggering a hard shutdown. The actual language and code that I use to make that happen is somewhat irrelevant. What matters is the end result."

"And you're certain that sending this command will cause a series of failures that results in the other unit turning off?" Kelsey asked.

Ralph nodded. "Pretty damned sure. Unfortunately, that's all it's going to do. It's not going to make any modifications to the other side that would allow us to initiate communications with them or signal a direct link request. Someone's going to have to notice that the unit is off and dig into the error codes to find my message."

"And what is your message?" Carl asked.

"Just a couple of words. Buried inside the error message they'll see is going to be a line of plain text that says, 'This is Kelsey.' That pretty much used up the leeway I had in affecting the error message. Carl hardwired how long the error message can be.

"If that doesn't get their attention, we can always try again once they turn it back on and send a different message, but this seems like a good start to me."

"How will we know that they've read it?" Talbot asked.

The hacker shrugged. "We won't. When they power the unit back up, we'll be able to ping it for a status again. That'll mean that they've noticed that it was off.

"Under the best of circumstances, we're going to have to assume that whoever is examining the equipment isn't going to find the first message, or the second, or even the third. We may have to do this a dozen times before someone figures out what we're doing.

"In any case, it's better than what we've been doing. Glitching that one component isn't getting us anywhere. We need to up our game."

Kelsey turned to him. "What do you think, Talbot?"

He considered how the young man might actually be trying to sabotage the other unit but ended up discarding the idea. He just didn't see what Halstead could gain by doing so.

"We should try," he eventually said.

His wife gestured toward the hacker. "Do it."

That made Talbot grin. When Kelsey made a decision, she didn't spend her time dithering. She balanced the options, picked one, and forged ahead. That was one of the things he loved about her.

Halstead tapped on his keyboard and hit the enter key. "Signal sent. Now we sit back and keep testing to see if they turn the other unit back on. If no one's looking at it, that could take hours or even days.

"I have this unit set up to continue sending connection and status requests every ten seconds. It'll send us a notification as soon as someone over there figures out the machine is down and powers it back up."

Halstead's computer beeped. He frowned and leaned forward. "Well, that's unexpected. It's back up."

"Are we even sure it went down?" Carl asked. "It's possible that your hack failed."

Halstead almost sneered, in a relatively friendly way. "Please. My hack worked. There has to have been somebody sitting right on top of the damned thing."

Talbot pursed his lips. If so, that was good news. Excellent news, in fact. It meant that they might once again be in contact with Admiral Mertz, and he could advise them on what to do.

They'd still have to find their own way back to the New Terran Empire, but at least they could give him a status update.

The communications speed would be far too slow—based on what Carl's experimentation had determined—to give the admiral any of the information that they'd stolen. It wasn't even fast enough to utilize video.

Audio communication would take a seeming eternity, but at least it was possible for truly critical information. Almost all of what they'd be doing would have to be text.

And all of that depended on someone over there figuring out exactly what they were doing, which wasn't assured. This was a good start, but they'd have a lot more work to do before they were back in contact with Admiral Mertz.

8

J ared stared at the FTL com as it shut down for a third time in less than a minute. He wasn't alone in watching the machine's antics. Austin, Kelsey, and Tony stared at it with equal incomprehension.

"That's *definitely* worse than it's been behaving," O'Halloran said. "Let me run a self-diagnostic on it and then plug in some additional equipment to see if I can tell what's going on."

He left the device powered off and quickly attached wires from some of the surrounding equipment. Only when he was seemingly ready to continue testing did he power device backup.

"The self-check isn't finding anything," he said under his breath. "I'm not even sure how that's possible, considering what we just saw. Let's see if I can get a full cycle of testing with the other equipment in before it does it again."

It turned out that the man had no trouble performing his testing because the FTL com didn't power itself off again. At least not in the three minutes it took the Fleet engineer to do his work.

"All of those readings look normal," Austin said as he looked over Tony's shoulder. At least in so far as I can tell. It's not like I have a lot of experience working on faster-than-light equipment."

O'Halloran straightened and stretched his back. "Everything looks normal to me, too. We're going to have to dig into the equipment much more deeply if we're going to figure out exactly what's going on."

"Let me try one more thing before we tear this apart," Austin said. "Do you mind?" he asked as he gestured toward the keyboard.

The engineer stepped back and gestured him in. "Be my guest."

The young Rebel Empire noble sat at the computer and began paging through different screens and typing on the manual keyboard.

"If I were accessing something remotely and shutting it down time and again, it wouldn't just be to drive the people watching the equipment crazy. I'd want them to find *something*. The easiest place for someone to plant evidence of what they're doing is in the logs."

Jared consulted his implants and noted the time. "I can only stay out of sight for so long, gentlemen. How long will such a search take?"

"Approximately this long," Austin said. "I found something."

They all leaned forward to look over his shoulder, and the young man pointed to a line on the screen. "This is an error message thrown by one of the components we were looking at. Does that look like a standard error message to you?"

The indicated entry had three words: *This is Kelsey.*

Jared felt his heart soar. Somehow, she'd done it. His sister had figured out how to access an FTL com over some unimaginable distance.

It wasn't a normal communication request, but they were getting information. That meant that the device itself could actually sense its linked pair. Kelsey and Carl were attempting to communicate with them.

"That is pretty definitive," he agreed with a grin. "The only reason that I can see for them to do what they're doing is that they can send a signal over a great distance, but it's not triggering some threshold where we can answer. Or maybe our side isn't recognizing what they're doing as valid.

"We've got to figure out how to interpret this. Does anyone have any idea how we can manage that? If we change the error message, will they see it on the other side?"

Austin shook his head. "Almost certainly not. I'd guess they're using some kind of specialized code to cause a certain component to fail while adding additional code that writes that one line to the log. The potential length of the error code is limited to just about what they sent too, so I wouldn't expect a longer message.

"Nothing they're going to be able to do from the other end will allow them to read our logs. And unfortunately, without knowing exactly how they managed this particular feat, we're not going to be able to do the same to them."

O'Halloran scrubbed his face with his hands. "I've got a lot of information on the normal operation of these devices, and when this unit started behaving oddly, I went through everything. I can't imagine how they're sending a signal that we can't detect. Everything has to go through the FTL receiver. Why isn't it detecting this?"

Kelsey cleared her throat. "I realize that I'm the least knowledgeable person about this sort of thing, but the device is obviously detecting it. Someone on the other end couldn't be making this equipment do anything unless this piece of equipment was receiving and interpreting whatever they were doing as a signal.

"Since I've been going through working on my communications skills, now that my implants can actually talk to other equipment, I've come to a realization. There are several layers of communication taking place all the time with my implants.

"There's the conscious level where I'm intentionally signaling someone or something. Then there's an unconscious level where my implants interface with the equipment around me to initiate communication in case I need to use something. Under those circumstances, unless I choose to do something, I may not even be aware that they've done anything."

Austin nodded slowly. "I see what you're saying. It's possible that the incoming signal isn't being interpreted as something we need to be notified about, but the equipment can handle it. It's already capable of doing that with sending a ping out to the other side and verifying the other FTL com is operational without anyone doing anything at the other end.

"And before you ask, we checked that. We're not detecting the linked FTL com when we ping. That doesn't mean that they haven't figured out how to connect us. This is all taking place at the quantum level, and the photons generate an automatic response in our hardware that gets sent back."

Jared scratched his chin and considered what the young man and said. "I'm hearing the words, but I don't think I'm getting the meaning that you intend me to have. Are you saying that they've found a way to stimulate the entangled pair so that our end sends a signal farther than we can intentionally do so?"

"The theory is that the range of those things is unlimited," Austin said, "but that some kind of flaw in the underlying theory is keeping the hardware from triggering a response past more than a single flip point. Even a repeater is only fifty percent effective in relaying a signal once.

"It sounds as if they've found at least a partial answer to the problem, only we can't pick up when they call because we have no idea what they're doing. The problem is that we don't know enough about what they did to even let them know that they've succeeded."

"Did you check the logs to see if someone is pinging us?"

Tony blinked and took back over the keyboard. "Yes. I'm getting a lot of pings starting several days ago. The com automatically generated a response. I should've looked sooner," he admitted sheepishly.

As soon as he finished saying those words, the FTL com powered off again. It looked as if Kelsey was going to continue trying to get their attention.

"We'll need to keep checking the error messages, but we also need to be more proactive in communicating with them," Jared said. "Since they're being so insistent, I think that we might be able to use the status of our machine to communicate with them."

He grinned at the obviously confused people around him. "This isn't going to make any sense to you, but I need you to look up something in the library and make it so that we can control when the FTL com is on and when it's off very precisely."

Austin frowned. "That's not exactly like sending a message to them."

"You'd be surprised what kind of information silence can tell another person," Jared said. "Just set it up the way I tell you, and I'll wager they'll get the message quick enough."

* * *

Kelsey watched Carl and Ralph Halstead become more and more frustrated while working on the FTL com. After what had seemed like they were getting somewhere, they'd started having serious issues with their connection to the linked com. Without warning, their pings started failing without any rhyme or reason.

"What the heck is going on?" Carl asked, his tone frustrated. "It's like they're randomly turning it on and off."

"They might be," Halstead said. "Honestly, it's the only way they can let us know that they're aware of our activity. We can only interact with them through causing their machine to turn off and leaving an error message that they may or may not find.

"And then we can ping their system and get an automatic response that it's up, if it is. If they've realized that, this is the only way for them to let us know they are aware of our attempts."

"But it should still make sense," Carl grumbled.

"Maybe it does, but we just can't see it," Kelsey said in a soothing voice as she rested her hand on her friend's shoulder. "If there's a pattern to this, we need to graph it out. Rather than random pings, we need to start sending a rapid, steady series of them. Only then can we tell if there's a pattern to the machine being off or on."

The young scientist considered that for a moment and then nodded. "Good idea. Let me set something up to start pinging them once a second and graphing out the other com's status."

It only took a few minutes for him to have everything set up the way he wanted and for them to be looking at real-time returns from the other com. It quickly became apparent that the other device was being switched on and off fairly rapidly.

"There *is* a pattern in this," Halstead said slowly. "The time frames that the machine is either off or on fall in two groups: between two and three seconds or five and six seconds. That's some kind of binary pattern, but I'm not seeing a meaning to it."

Kelsey watched the pattern playing out on the screen and felt herself gasp when she saw the hidden pattern. "That's Morse code! I had to learn it when we were signaling you in the Nova system, Carl.

"The shorter time frame is for dots, the longer is for dashes. We'll have to wait to see if the message is repeating, but I'm deciphering it in my head as I'm seeing this, and it's a real message."

Carl's eyes widened. "Holy crap! I can see it now. Hold it, now we're getting just a series of dots with no dashes. I bet that's the boundary before they start repeating the original message again."

She saw the message start up again and started translating it in her head.

Kelsey, this is Jared. We've received your message. I'm hoping that you can decipher this message because I'm not certain that we can communicate back with you the same way you're doing with us.

We found your short note buried in the error log. If you can pass on to us what modifications we need to make on our end, we'll update the FTL com so that we can communicate via pings. Please let us know that you've received this message by shutting our system down and telling us so.

I have to tell you that I'm damn glad to hear you're okay. Well done. Jared Mertz.

Ralph Halstead leaned back in his chair. "Well I'll be damned. It actually *worked*. What the hell do we do now?"

Kelsey clapped her hand on his shoulder. "Cause their system to shut down with the error code 'message received' and then start getting them the information they need.

"Actually, the first thing we need to know is where they are. If we have a system name, then we can determine what our transmission range is. I'd absolutely hate to have them flip out beyond our range and lose communication."

Carl stared at her. "Do you realize how long it would take to transmit modification instructions if we can only use two or three words at a time? We're talking days to get the information across to get to the point where we can even communicate via Morse code.

"Not that I'm complaining about the speed of Morse code when it means the difference between some communication and no communication. Even so, it's still going to be a relatively limited kind of exchange."

The young hacker nodded at the scientist's words. "That's going to allow us to do text-based messaging, but it's not going to give us a shared method to transmit anything involving audio or video. Even if we could, the time to get the files across, specifically accounting for any errors in the transmission, would be significant."

Kelsey grinned at them. "I actually have an answer for that. This is one place where me watching a bunch of old vids from pre-Imperial Terra is going to come in handy.

"Back when computers were first becoming a reality on Terra, they had hardware called modems that communicated over copper wiring to other computers. The transmission speed was incredibly slow.

"The hardware had built-in error checking and handled the handshake of data back and forth in a way that's documented in the Imperial libraries aboard all the ships we have. If we can tell Jared to look at how to build an interface similar to one of these modems, we should be able to reliably send files and be confident that they're the same on the other end, once the error checking has any suspect portions resent."

Carl's gaze became slightly unfocused as he consulted the library. Then he started nodding. "I see what you're saying. Ironically, our transmission speed is roughly the same as those very early modems. Technology seems to have gone full circle.

"Let me start off by sending the response to them to know we've got their message and ask them where they are and where they're going. I don't want to start transmitting all the data that we have until we have the initial greetings out of the way."

He manipulated the keyboard, and within two minutes, they were getting a new set of Morse code signals.

Kelsey, I'm going to have my people start researching the communication protocols that Carl mentioned. It's going to be slow, but that beats complete silence.

As for where we are, the system only has an Imperial registry number. I'll send that along momentarily, but the more important piece of information for you is that we're on the way to Terra. We're inside the Rebel Empire in the automated destroyer, but our situation has become complex.

I don't want to use up a lot of time telling you all of this until we can communicate back and forth more reliably. We're masquerading as members of the higher orders and we've got actual members of the higher orders on board our ship that think we're someone else.

Again, I'll spell it all out to you in more detail once we've established the communication protocols, which my engineer tells me will probably happen very quickly once we know how to modify our FTL com to more closely link with yours.

Carl said that sending that kind of information would take days, which is going to put us dead center in the middle of an area where we don't dare communicate from. If we can manage it sooner, that would be better because in about four days we're going to be incommunicado for a period of time.

Let's save catching up for when we can actually talk and I can send you a real status. It's good to hear your voice again. Jared.

"Get him those modifications as quickly as you can, Carl," Kelsey said. "It sounds like we're on a tight time schedule. I'll talk with Angela and start getting everyone herded together. It sounds like we're going to Terra, and we'd probably best be moving if we want to get there in time to make a difference in whatever they're doing."

She stepped back and let them continue their work. Jacqueline Parker stepped away as well. She'd been quiet during the exchange.

"It's not common knowledge, but conditions on Terra are supposedly… grim," the scientist said in a low voice. "I'm not certain what you expect to find there, but you're only going to find death and destruction."

Kelsey turned toward the other woman. "Terra may be dead, but the key to beating the AIs is buried with her corpse. If we ever want to end this terrible subjugation of human species, we don't have a choice."

9

Olivia watched the timer and fumed. They'd been receiving data from Kelsey on how to modify the FTL com for days. Being able to only transmit a few words at a time to get those instructions was utterly ridiculous, but it was all they could manage.

Carl Owlet had guessed at how long it would take to get the complete modification plans sent, and it was going to be *very* close to the time they'd have to stop using the FTL com. Perhaps too close.

The last flip point was only a couple of hours ahead of them. If they failed to get the data before they flipped into the system with the AI, they'd have to shut down the process, because they didn't dare do anything that might warn the System Lords that FTL communication existed.

Doing all of this while sitting on *Athena*'s bridge stretched her nerves to the breaking point. She was far more comfortable sitting behind a desk where she could do real work instead of waiting here and doing nothing.

She could hardly imagine how Jared managed. Projecting an air of calm seem to be a full-time job, so how did he manage to accomplish anything else?

Part of her console lit up with an incoming call. It was from engineering, so it was probably Jared. Thankfully, Fielding wasn't on the bridge, so they didn't have to do everything via implants.

Olivia knew that those were far more efficient, but her upbringing still made it hard. The nobility of the Rebel Empire had an ingrained refusal to use implants to their full potential. She was no exception, even though she knew it was stupid.

She reached down and touched the acceptance on the call, and Jared's face appeared on the console.

"I need a distraction," she said with feeling. "How do you deal with this?"

"Feeling a little stressed?" he asked with a smile. "You know, you can get up and walk around a bit. Pass command on to someone else and take a break for just a bit."

"Do you do that?"

"Probably not as often as I should, but yes. If you'd like to have a few minutes away from the bridge, I have something down here that I think you'd like to see."

"Is it good news? Please tell me it's good news."

"It is good news."

"I'll be right there," she said as she stood and killed the communications link. A few words with Commander Hall had command transferred for the moment, and Olivia was on her way to engineering via the lift.

When she arrived, Jared was waiting for her. "We have it set up in the maintenance tube."

He led her to where they had a table holding the FTL com and some other equipment staged around it that she didn't recognize. There were a lot of hard cables running back and forth between the com and the other equipment.

Present were Kelsey Two, as they'd all taken to calling her privately after she'd come up with the idea, Commander O'Halloran, Austin Darrah, and Sean Meyer. All of them were clustered around the monitor observing something.

"What's the good news?" she asked Jared.

"We finished receiving the last of the modification information about half an hour ago."

She was somewhat annoyed that he hadn't notified her about all of this, but even though she was pretending to be the mission commander, he was really in charge, so she couldn't tear a strip off of him. As much as she wanted to.

"And have you made the changes?"

He nodded. "We just brought the system back up so that they could run a diagnostic on it. Once that's done, they're going to attempt to utilize Morse code from the other side.

"Rather than flipping the machine on and off, which would make two-way communication particularly challenging, Carl came up with a method of using just the status pings as a way to do it. That way both sides can send data at the same time and receive it."

She frowned slightly. "I don't know that much about Morse code, but are there two different kinds of signal? Dots and dashes? How are you differentiating between them?"

Austin looked over at her. "It's not as hard as you might think. Once we've verified that we have good communication in both directions, if we send three pings together, it will represent a dot. If we send six pings together, it will represent a dash. If we send ten together, it means end of a transmission. Even if one somehow gets dropped, the intent will still be clear."

"How quickly will we be able to exchange information?"

The young man shrugged. "It depends on what your expectations are. If you look at how slowly we've been exchanging information, this is going to seem very quick indeed. If you compare it with standard communications, this is going to be extremely slow.

"As you might imagine, video is out of the question, except perhaps for very small snippets that will take a significant amount of time. Audio is somewhat friendlier, but that will still take more time than just sending a text message."

Commander O'Halloran straightened. "I think we're ready to run the first test."

Jared moved over to stand behind the man. "What do we have in mind?"

The Fleet engineer gestured toward a microphone. "If you want to speak directly into the microphone, the equipment will translate your words into Morse code and send it. The response will come out of the speaker as a generic, computer-generated voice, but it should be comprehensible."

He turned toward Olivia. "How far away from the next flip are we? Has Fielding given you any indication of when he expects to join us for the flip?"

She shook her head slightly. "He hasn't said a word, which leads me to believe that he's just going to show up at an inconvenient moment to spring something on me. I really can't excuse myself from being on the bridge for very much longer. At this point, we're only a couple of hours away from the flip point."

"Any normal person would show up about half an hour before the flip," Jared said. "That virtually guarantees that Fielding will be there an hour ahead of time."

"Or show up five minutes beforehand," Olivia grumbled.

Jared laughed. "That sounds just about like the man. Well, at least we'll be able to get this next segment of our mission underway instead of wondering what's going on. I can't escape the feeling that there's something more to what we're doing than he's told us. Sean, go hold down the bridge in case he does show up early."

Commander O'Halloran waited for Jared to take a seat after Sean left and then touched a button next to the microphone and made a gesture with his hand for Jared to start.

"Kelsey, this is Jared. We've made the modifications just like you instructed, so I'm hoping this does the trick and we can start our dialog."

For a few seconds, nothing happened, and Olivia's heart fell. They'd gotten something wrong, and the communications attempt had failed.

Then a voice came out of the speaker. Not a regular person's voice, but a generic, monotone computer-generated one. Weirdly, she still heard it as Kelsey's voice in her head.

"Jared, it's good to hear your voice, so to speak. Kelsey here. I've got so much to tell you about what's going on. We've learned so much that we didn't know before about the Rebel Empire and all kinds of other, unexpected things.

"We're okay on this end, even though we're under a bit of pressure. What's your status? Are you guys okay?"

Olivia relaxed. She looked over and took in the other Kelsey's expression.

Kelsey Two was listening to the voice with a frown but didn't really seem angry. More like she was just nonplussed. Olivia suppose one didn't hear the voice of one's twin from another universe every day.

The one person that looked confused was Austin Darrah. He had a peculiar expression on his face and was looking back and forth between the com and Kelsey. He probably wondered about the odds of having two people with the same name involved in the conversation.

While they trusted the young man a little way, they hadn't explained to him that the Kelsey he knew came from another reality and that her doppelgänger was on the other end of the call. They'd have to do that at some point, but now wasn't the time.

"We probably only have between half an hour and an hour to exchange information before we have to cut the communication," Jared said. "We're about to flip into a system that has one of the System Lords in it, so we'd best keep this pithy. As quickly as you can, in as much detail as you feel comfortable with, give me a status on what you've been up to."

Olivia wondered to herself whether or not they should send Austin and Kelsey Two away. Kelsey One would probably be sharing information that was highly classified.

Jared, for his part, didn't seem to be overly concerned. In fact, he gestured for more chairs to be brought in so that everyone could sit and listen. He'd obviously made up his mind that he wasn't going to keep these secrets from their new allies.

Olivia still suspected that if their Kelsey brought up anything that he didn't want them to hear, he'd quickly shut her down.

Over the next half hour, she listened incredulously as Kelsey One went through their adventures and tribulations. She was amazed at the wealth of scientific information that they'd gotten away with and amused at the number of prisoners they'd accumulated.

Thankfully, she knew she'd be able to help with at least one of their problems. Now that they'd restored communication, she'd be able to speak with this Lieutenant Commander Sommerville and reassure him that Kelsey was actually in communication with the real resistance.

That might very well allow the other man to give her friend enough information to find her way to Terra in time to join them there. Particularly since they'd cracked the mystery of the weak flip points. Or, as they now referred to them, the multi-flip points. That was actually a much better name.

The far flip points that they discussed were a complete shock. No one had ever predicted that something like that existed. She made a mental note to have Elise send her people searching the outer part of the Pentagar, Courageous, and Erorsi systems. If any of the three had far flip points, that might give her people many more options to search the universe.

Hell, the way these multi-flip points had different branches that could be explored, even from the same position inside a single flip point, vastly expanded the opportunities to explore the universe and connect with other systems that might not be reachable through normal flip points.

There was one in the Courageous system right next to Pentagar and another in the Erorsi system. They might now be gateways for Elise's people to get to a lot of new systems.

With the flip point modulator that Carl Owlet had designed, scout ships would be able to use different branches from any multi-flip point, go to the other side, and then access even more branches from there.

Considering that the one example Carl had examined closely had showed that some of the branches on either side didn't match up with the ones on the first side, there was the potential that a ship could flip along one branch, turn right around and flip along a second that didn't go to a location reachable from the first side, and then turn right around again and go to a third location that neither of the others could see. Perhaps even more.

Obviously, that wasn't going to be an infinite array of possibilities. Still, regular flip points only connected with about a tenth of the stars in the universe, at least in the areas humanity had explored. If the multi-flip points connected with even the same number of previously unreachable systems, that doubled the destinations available.

And then there were the far flip points. They obviously connected to systems reachable by regular flip points, but what if they also reached systems that connected to different networks of regular flip points?

That had been a hypothesis that she'd read about when doing her research on the subject in college. She admitted that the idea of completely separate networks of flip points weaving around one another made her brain hurt, but if the professionals said it was possible, then it was something that she couldn't dismiss out of hand.

That might explain how the Clans had lived separately from the Rebel Empire for so long without being discovered. If the worlds that they'd obviously occupied and built their new civilization on were part of a separate network, the Rebel Empire could blithely go about their business and never have a clue that such a powerful enemy was so close by.

But that was a mystery for another day.

Another aspect of what Kelsey had discovered completely intrigued her. The Pandorans with their human DNA that had to have been placed inside them before humanity had ever discovered space travel. Who had done it and why?

That was another mystery that wasn't going to be solved today.

She glanced at Kelsey Two again. The other woman's expression was grim.

Olivia had known that she resented the success that Kelsey One had achieved, and she could even understand it. Still, she'd need to talk to the other woman and try to head off some of the bitterness she could see already building inside her.

This wasn't a competition. The successes that Kelsey One had achieved could help Kelsey Two.

Jared responded briefly about how impressed he was with what they'd accomplished and then launched into the far shorter tale of what they'd been up to. The key elements only took a few minutes to pass along, and he ended with an explanation of what they hoped to accomplish.

Olivia noted that he left out that they had visitors from another universe. A glance at Kelsey Two showed that she'd noted the omission too, and it didn't make her any happier.

Jared went on, not recognizing how Kelsey Two was seething. "I haven't got any idea what Fielding intends during this so-called 'repair mission,' but once we have it out of the way, we'll be on our way to Terra. We're supposed to be there roughly a week from now. My suspicion is that it'll take us a few days longer than that, considering we need to carry out the mission here.

"If you can convince your resistance contact to help you, that would be incredible. We're separated from my fleet, and even at best speed, they're going to come in at least a week behind us and from another direction. Odds are very high that the defenses that keep people out of the Terra system are strong enough that any incursion against them would draw a response from all the surrounding systems in time to interfere with what we're trying to do.

"This is still a stealth mission, and I'd prefer to make it happen without the AI realizing what's going on before we kill it. Olivia is going to need to be back on the bridge very shortly. If you could bring Lieutenant Commander Sommerville down and let her have a brief discussion with him to authenticate her identity, I think that's about all we have time left for."

"I've already sent for him," Kelsey One said. "He walked in just in time to hear that last little bit. Olivia, if you have time to go ahead and have a discussion with our friend, that would be *very* helpful."

Olivia nodded even though the other woman couldn't see her. "Hello, Commander Sommerville, my name is Olivia West. I'm the coordinator of Harrison's World and the leader of the resistance there. We've staged a coup and taken over the system and are working with Kelsey and the New Terran Empire."

She proceeded to give him a recognition code. He responded with the appropriate response and then sent her a code of his own that she responded to.

He then sent one that she was unfamiliar with. In fact, it didn't even seem to follow the same pattern as the rest of the recognition codes.

"I'm afraid I don't know that one," she said. "Is it a red herring?"

"I have no idea what a red herring is, but if it means that that was a trap to see if you'd respond to it, it was. I suppose that I'll have to accept that you're really a member of the resistance. I can't begin to tell you how that complicates things for me."

Olivia could almost hear the dry tone of his voice as he said it, even though the computer wouldn't have carried that information across.

"I live to serve," she said solemnly.

Her implants pinged with an incoming call from the bridge. It was text only from Sean. It indicated that Fielding had arrived.

She sent a response that she'd be there momentarily and turned to Jared. "Fielding is on the bridge. We should probably head there and see what other surprises he has in store for us."

10

A ngela sat in *Persephone*'s command chair as they made the transition to Archibald. This was it, her first independent command, and she was going back into the system they'd barely escaped from the last time they'd been there. One with an invasion in progress.

Commander Sommerville had confirmed that he'd intended to use a far flip point in the system. His admission had been grudging, and he had obvious reservations about telling them anything, but he'd finally pinpointed where it was located in Archibald's outer system.

Her mission was to make certain that the rest of their ships wouldn't encounter Clan warships as they made their way out to it. *Persephone* was very stealthy, so Angela didn't anticipate any problems. The other ships wouldn't have her advantages, though.

In the few days since they'd made their escape from Archibald, the Clans had fully occupied the system. Her passive scanners were easily able to pick up grav drives moving across the system and surrounding the main world.

Kelsey had taken the precaution of leaving a stealthed probe that gave them occasional updates via FTL, so Angela had come into the system certain that no one was close enough to detect her.

The problem was that the Clans were still searching for the Q-ship that had gotten away. She didn't blame them. It had killed one of their frigates.

That meant there were far too many vessels quartering back and forth across the outer system. Sommerville had intended to change course once he was clear of detection, so the enemy wasn't near the far flip point, but they were still an obstacle to be avoided.

One serious complication was that the clans knew about far flip points. Frankly, she'd be surprised if they weren't looking for them in each system they'd taken from the Rebel Empire.

If Angela was dead unlucky, the Clans would find it, and she'd have to use brute force to get their ships through, which would trigger a pursuit that wouldn't turn out well for her or her friends.

Her goal was to get the carrier, the Q-ship, and the freighter she was shepherding safely to the far flip point and be gone before the search pattern expanded to include the areas where the multi-flip point or far flip point were located.

She had no idea if the Clans could detect a multi-flip point, but they'd had one to examine for five hundred years. She wasn't discounting the possibility.

If they found it, that might be a disaster for Pandora, but there was absolutely nothing she could do about that. The forces of the New Terran Empire were hopelessly outgunned and would die in that system if they stood their ground.

No, they had to get the critical manufacturing equipment and knowledge back to Avalon at all costs. The survival of their own worlds depended on it.

While the multi-flip point was safely clear of any enemy traffic, there were ships between it and the far flip point. Whatever path she chose would have to be circuitous, and they'd have to go slowly.

"Well, there's no time like the present," she said. "Signal *Audacious* to come through."

This was going to be the most nail-biting moment for Angela. They'd installed the flip drive that Carl had had built by the Rebel Empire shipyard and then snuck out of the system on board the Q-ship they'd hijacked. If it failed, they were screwed.

They'd tested it along a different branch of the multi-flip point successfully, but it was still experimental technology. Until they'd used it for a much longer period of time, Angela was going to be worried every time they made a transition.

If it failed, this was possibly the worst time and place. The carrier would be trapped in a hostile system filled with enemies already looking for a fight.

Jack Thompson turned his head toward her. *"Audacious* acknowledges."

Angela felt herself tense and only relaxed when the massive carrier appeared. She was quickly followed by the Q-ship and the freighter that they'd stolen from Dresden. All reported themselves in good shape via tight-beam coms.

This was it. All of the New Terran Empire forces were in the Archibald system now. Part of her wondered if they'd ever get back to Pandora. Angela hoped so. She liked the people there, and it wasn't every day that one got to explore an actual alien society.

"Set course for the far flip point, Jack. Take us as far around the enemy vessels as we can get and still make decent time. I'd like to have double the clearance that we suspect the enemy has to detect a slow-moving carrier like *Audacious*."

Thompson nodded. "Yes, ma'am. That's going to put our travel time at roughly eight hours to get to the far flip point."

"Better to go slow than to not get there at all."

She turned her attention to the tactical console, where her new executive officer, Senior Lieutenant Arianna Knox, was huddled with the tactical officer, Lieutenant Jevon McLeod.

"What are you two picking up from deeper inside the system?"

Her redheaded executive officer turned toward her. "There's a lot of enemy traffic in there, ma'am. Most of the communications we're detecting are encrypted, so I don't think we're seeing anything from the Rebel Empire side of things.

"We're a bit distant to detect things at Archibald itself via passive scanners, but it looks as if the civilian orbital is still intact. There are a lot of small craft moving between it and the surface of the planet."

"I suppose that makes sense," Angela said. "They want to get as many civilians and Fleet people down to the surface as possible to keep them from causing them trouble in space. Hell, they're probably sending their own troops down to secure as much of the planet as they can."

McLeod's eyebrows rose. "Can they really have brought enough people to subjugate a major world like Archibald? There are billions of people down there."

"The AIs managed to do it with Harrison's World," Angela said grimly. "It really depends on how much force you're willing to use. Shoot enough people, and the rest will start paying attention.

"We also can't forget how deeply the Clans hate the Rebel Empire. As far as they're concerned, the Clans are the *real* Terran Empire, and these people are just pawns for the computers. Pawns that mercilessly exterminated most of the human race. At least that's what Jacob Howell says, and I believe him."

Howell was a human from Pandora, the son of the leader of Clan Dauntless. All humans on the planet were descendants of the people who'd survived the crash of the ex-Clan battlecruiser *Dauntless* onto the surface of Pandora.

His father had been a junior officer on the battlecruiser at the time of the crash. All the senior officers had perished because they'd refused to abandon ship and rode it down to the surface.

Those who'd survived had gone through a culling. The most violent and xenophobic survivors had fought to the death against the Pandorans. Only those who'd surrendered had lived.

That was Darwinism in action, as far as Angela was concerned.

At their very best, the clans were antisocial. At worst, they wanted to subjugate or exterminate anyone other than their own people. They weren't big on talking or negotiating.

The best outcome would be for them to make their way across the Archibald system and out again without anyone becoming aware that they'd been there at all. That was going to take a lot of slow maneuvering to steer clear of any detection at all. A nerve-racking endeavor at the best of times.

"Keep monitoring everything you can," she said. "Jack, make sure we don't come anywhere near those guys. We'd win the fight but lose the war."

"Copy that," he said. "Unless someone gets a wild hair up his... well, you know, we'll probably be fine."

Angela chuckled, settled back into her seat, and tried to keep from fidgeting. Commanding a ship was very different from commanding a platoon of marines. This was going to take a lot of getting used to.

* * *

KELSEY HEADED for *Athena's* bridge with Mertz and Olivia. She kept her face devoid of expression, but inside, she was seething.

Oh, she knew that she shouldn't be so upset at what she'd heard from the other version of herself over the FTL com, but she couldn't help it. How could the woman have accomplished *all* of that?

It wasn't that Kelsey felt it made her look bad, though it certainly did. What really galled her was how capable the other woman was when she felt as if she could barely tie her own shoes on the best of days.

Olivia pulled her back when Mertz got into the lift. "We'll be along momentarily, Jared. Stall him. After how he made us jump around, I don't feel bad about making him wait for a little while."

Mertz didn't argue, simply nodding. "Will do. Are you going to be long?"

"Probably not. Say five minutes."

"See you there."

Olivia waited until the lift doors had closed and then gestured for Kelsey to walk with her up the corridor.

"What's wrong?" Kelsey asked.

"It's not that anything is wrong, Kelsey, but I can see how upset you are, and I wanted to let you vent. Keeping it inside isn't going to make you feel any better. In fact, it might be actively bad for our relationship, and I don't want to see that. Neither, I suspect, do you."

Well, that was annoying. "Am I that obvious?"

"Only to someone that knows you very well," Olivia said with a smile, putting her hand on Kelsey's shoulder. "And while I realize that you hardly know me, I've known a version of you for almost a year. I pride myself on being very observant, and I couldn't help seeing how my version of Kelsey made you feel."

Kelsey sighed and hunched forward a little. "I was already having this mental conversation with myself. I've never met another version of me. Hell, until just a little while back, I never would've dreamed anything like this was possible.

"It's a lot to assimilate, even discounting the fact that I think I hate myself. No offense to your Kelsey, but she had everything handed to her. She got every bit of good luck that I didn't, and it pisses me off."

She held up a hand when Olivia looked as if she was going to respond.

"Hear me out. I understand that's not what happened, at least from your point of view. You've heard my story, so you can imagine that I don't see it quite the same way.

"Again, that's not her fault. It's not my fault, either. It's just the way the universe is. Or perhaps I should say the universes, plural. I just have to accept the way the dice rolled and take my beating."

Olivia smiled a bit sadly. "I don't know how they play dice in your universe, but here we don't have beatings for the loser. And I think you're doing yourself a disservice by thinking of yourself as the loser. You're not in competition with our Kelsey.

"Her success in this universe didn't come without cost. Perhaps it wasn't as high a price as you've paid, but it didn't come for free. She's bled for everything she's achieved. So have you. You've got nothing to be ashamed of."

"Then why didn't Mertz mention me?" Kelsey demanded. "Even as we speak, your version of me doesn't know that I'm here. He left out the story where I came looking for help. Why?"

Olivia pulled her into a compartment just off the corridor. It wasn't very large and seemed to be a break room of some kind. Being on board a ship that was supposed to be computer operated, it was completely empty.

"I suspect that he just didn't want to open that can of worms right then. He knew we had very little time before we had to cut off communications. That's not the kind of conversational bomb one just drops and then goes quiet.

"Jared hasn't told me anything, but I already know what he intends. It's what I'd do. He's going to work on completing this repair mission so that we can get back on the way to Terra.

"Once we're away from the System Lord, he's going to sit you down at the FTL com and get our Kelsey on the other end. Then the two of you are going to talk until you don't have anything left to say to one another.

"I have every confidence that our Kelsey is going to get her ships to Terra. Once she does, the two of you are going to have a chance to meet in person. Then you'll see exactly how our Kelsey feels about you. I can guarantee that both she and Jared will move planets to help your people."

Kelsey rubbed her face, tired and angry, mostly with herself. And embarrassed. Was this really how petty she'd become? Had the events of the last few years really turned her into this person?

"I wish I could believe that," she finally said. "No matter how lucky you are in this universe, the deck is still stacked against you. I can't see how you're going to get past this artificial intelligence, get onto Terra, get what we need, and then get away again. Not when a crazy computer expects us to exterminate humanity there.

"Personally, I think it'll take a miracle to make that happen. That doesn't even count what you do next. You'll have to go after the master AI, and it's going to be a lot better protected than the one on Terra.

"The only thing that's saved you so far is that the System Lords didn't even know you existed. Now that they do, at least in a general sort of way, they're going to take every step they can to protect themselves. How are you even going to get close to the master AI?"

Olivia shook her head. "You're asking the wrong question. What you should be thinking about is how we can leverage the hostilities between the Clans and the Rebel Empire to our benefit.

"Right now, the AIs are figuring out that they have a very serious problem with the Clans. Once they fully grasp the gravity of the situation, they'll almost certainly assume that the people who stole the

Dresden orbital and have blockaded the Erorsi system are the same people that are currently attacking them. Occam's razor: the answer with the fewest assumptions is usually the right one. Only this time, it isn't.

"It takes a lot of imagination to figure out that you have two very different enemies operating independently of one another at the same time. They'll end up treating us as one group. Since the Clans are a very overt sort of threat, the AIs won't expect us to be sneaking around right through their very guts."

The sheer audacity of the plan she'd just heard made Kelsey gasp. "In other words, you just plan to keep doing what you've been doing? Meandering along from crisis to crisis, looking for random opportunity and hoping that someone bigger than yourself doesn't squash you like a bug? That's not a plan. That's a fantasy.

"One that's going to fall apart the moment the AIs discover who you really are. Good luck doesn't last forever, as well I know. Something is going to go wrong that reveals who we really are."

She gestured in the vague direction of the bridge. "Let's take Fielding as an example. He's living with us. If he figures out that we're playing him, he might be able to set off the plasma charges in our hold and kill us in an instant."

Olivia shook her head. "If I let what might go wrong stop me from doing what needed to be done, I'd still be back on Harrison's World, hoping that the AI didn't drop a kinetic weapon on me. You can't live your life in fear of what might happen.

"Sometimes bold action is the only answer. Perhaps that's a lesson you could learn from our Kelsey. Lord knows the woman doesn't know how to think before she leaps. If she sees something that needs doing, she does it and damn the consequences. That drives Jared absolutely nuts, but I'll tell you one thing: it gets results.

"Kelsey, it's time to stop hiding in the dark and twitching every time you hear a noise. Stop wondering how you're going to screw things up and start doing everything that you can to make this work."

Hard words, Kelsey supposed, but there might be some wisdom to them.

She nodded, still pissed off, but not at her doppelgänger. Now she was annoyed with Olivia. She really needed to talk with Elise, Scott, and Sean to start sorting this out.

But now was not the time. They needed to head to the bridge and find out what other impossible tasks Fielding had in mind for them.

Hopefully it wouldn't be something so impossible that the AI just killed them outright.

11

T albot walked into Carl's lab and was once again blown away by how many people were doing so many different things in the large compartment. The young scientist was lucky that *Audacious* had plenty of space for him to spread out in.

The sprawling area was filled with tables and large pieces of equipment scattered along the deck. The faint stench of charred electronics came from what was left of the Singularity computer they'd stolen from the Rebel Empire, even though the equipment had probably been damaged years ago.

Carl raised his hand when he saw Talbot and gestured him over. "Excellent timing. I was just about to call you. We've found something."

Talbot raised an eyebrow as he stepped up beside his friend. "Really? Something about the FTL com?"

Carl shook his head. "No. Admiral Mertz shut down his end of the communications link because they're about to go into a system containing one of the AIs, and he doesn't want to chance being detected. We're not going to get much of an opportunity to experiment with things there until they're done and on the way to Terra.

"Meanwhile, I've been looking at the Singularity computer we liberated from Archibald. I haven't got everything sorted out, mind you, but I got a little bit more information than we had when we started this. Something intriguing."

Talbot followed Carl over to the scattered wreckage of the large computer. The acrid odor of burned electronics was much stronger here.

They'd found the remains of the computer in the medical research facility they had to burglarize to get a regenerative cure for Commodore Murdoch, the Rebel Empire flag officer they'd captured at Dresden.

The woman had insider information that they'd simply had to have, so Kelsey had ordered that they do what they could to get her cured from the injuries she'd suffered at the hands of Raul Castille, the murderous security officer under the commodore's command. The bastard that had caused them so much trouble.

Thankfully, they'd been able to get away with the cutting-edge regenerative technology, and it had been able to repair the woman's severed spine. Castille had snapped her neck and left her for dead, but now she was learning to walk again. It truly was miraculous.

The breakthrough in regenerative technology was going to revolutionize the care of those stubborn injuries that even Imperial technology just couldn't handle.

Better yet, he suspected it had implications that were going to carry over into other areas. Such as making it easier to implant Marine Raider technology inside someone.

Someone like him.

He'd finally adjusted to the changes that the procedures had introduced into his legs and would soon be going through the work on his torso. He'd had a long argument with Kelsey and the medical staff about what parts of the torso could be done in one session.

Back in the days of the Old Empire, Marine Raiders went through a number of different stages. Recruits usually came from the Imperial Marines, so they already had cranial implants, but their nanites needed to be upgraded to the class that Marine Raiders used. Call that the first step in the process.

Next, they had their pharmacology units, ocular enhancements, auditory enhancements, and olfactory enhancements installed. That could cause some significant issues with their senses, so they needed time to grow used to the changes.

For step three, the Old Empire had implanted artificial muscles into the legs and coated the bones there in graphene. Step four meant doing that for the torso and leaving the arms untouched. Step five was doing the dominant arm, and step six was the nondominant arm.

In between each of those six steps was a week of recovery so that the new Marine Raider could become fully comfortable with the great power that was now his or hers to command.

Kelsey had gone through the entire process in one go at the hands of a mad computer. She'd refused to even consider something like that for anyone else, but she'd agreed that the process could be streamlined.

The process as it now sat had four steps. Steps one and two of the Old Empire process were combined. Then the legs were done. The third step was doing the torso and nondominant arm. The final step was doing the dominant arm.

The period between the procedures had also been shortened so that the overall process took about two weeks, including recovery time. Talbot was convinced that could be reduced to a single week, and he thought the new regeneration equipment would help.

Doctor Zac Zoboroski, *Audacious*'s chief medical officer, wasn't so convinced, but once they'd left the Archibald system, he'd agreed to give it a try.

If they didn't at least do it once, they'd never know if it was going to be something they could utilize going forward. They needed real data to make smart decisions.

"What have you found?" Talbot asked. "Frankly, there's not a lot of this thing left, and I never expected you to be able to pull anything out of it. I'm ready to be shocked."

Carl grinned. "And shocked you will be. My suspicions were confirmed. What you see scattered on the deck before you are the remains of an artificial intelligence developed by the Singularity.

"I've been through the computers that the researchers were using and have confirmed that they already knew that, but my inspection of the component parts made that independently clear. It looks as if this piece of equipment was destroyed within the last few years, but that's not exactly true. Appearances, both visual and olfactory, can be deceiving.

"I'm uncertain what they did to make it smell like it had been recently burned, but the computer has been dead for a lot longer than I'd suspected. My guess is about twenty years."

Talbot eyed the equipment suspiciously. "That seems a little hard to believe."

"Yet it's true. There were some power units amongst the wreckage, and I was able to determine how long had passed since they'd held a charge.

"That isn't to say that the event that destroyed this equipment took place twenty years ago. It's conceivable that the computer might have been whole until the last few years and then something blew up the ship or station it was kept in. I have no way of knowing that for sure."

"So it's a curiosity?" Talbot asked, rubbing his chin.

"Far from it," Carl disagreed. "Think of how much useful information we got off of the computers on the Old Empire ships that were five hundred years old. This computer was still in use by the Singularity until just one tenth that amount of time ago. Even if the unit itself ran out of power because it had been abandoned or lost, those power units didn't keep going for more than six or eight months when separated from a fusion plant.

"That means there is going to be data on it about the Singularity that's a lot more recent than anything we have. Since it's one of their own computers, it's very likely that buried down in the guts of its data cores is critical information that will make a difference for us in this upcoming conflict.

"We all know that the Singularity is pulling the strings supporting the Clans. Maybe this computer can tell us what their real goal is."

Talbot nodded slowly. "Okay, I suppose I can buy that. How long is it going to take you to crack the encryption on the data cores?"

Carl shrugged. "Encryption like that is almost unbreakable, but we have an ace up our sleeve. Fiona can go through data and try combinations like nobody's business. That's the benefit of being a true artificial intelligence."

The Rebel Empire AI that they'd stolen from the Dresden orbital was currently installed aboard *Persephone*. They wouldn't dare risk transmitting much data back and forth until they were clear of the Archibald system, so they wouldn't even begin to start looking into cracking the encryption until they were clear.

"All right, I suppose that is good news. You said this was an AI. What makes you think that?"

Carl patted the top of his computer monitor. "That would be the data that we recovered from the researchers. There's far too much computational power built into this wreckage to just be a regular computer. It's on par with the components used to build Fiona, only formed from a completely different technology set.

"Oh, the basics are similar. After all, the Singularity formed from a sect that left the Old Empire thousands of years ago. They'd have to have taken the basic computer technology with them, but they developed it in an entirely new way over the time after they left. There's a lot of interesting stuff buried in this computer that I can't wait to get my hands on. It's going to be fascinating."

The young scientist's grin widened. "I discovered something else about this system. It wasn't created all at one time. It seems to have been built bit by bit by attaching new equipment to old equipment. Digging down to the very core of the device, the researchers found an underwater research vehicle that was the origin of the computer. It was called AUV #5.

"At this point, I very much doubt the circuitry in that ancient unit, which probably came from Terra, was being used, but just the fact that it was still there is exciting. It's like seeing a bit of history.

"It's also going to allow me to trace how the Singularity's computer technology changed over time. That's going to be invaluable in ascertaining what their computer philosophy is."

Talbot shook his head. "Have fun, but don't get so lost in what you're doing that you forget we've got other things on our plate. If you'll excuse me, I've got to go see a doctor about an upgrade."

Amused at his friend's enthusiasm, Talbot left the lab and took a lift to the medical center. Commander Zac Zoboroski, *Audacious*'s chief medical officer, was waiting for him.

"Are you sure I can't talk you out of this?" the other man asked. "We're still relatively new at doing this procedure, and I'd rather not cause you any undue discomfort."

"I'm a marine," Talbot said with a grin. "If Kelsey can take it all at once, I can do this."

The physician seemed unconvinced. "Doctor Stone told me how the princess ripped equipment out of the floor during her recovery. It took her quite a while before she could manage to handle things without destroying them. I'd like to urge you to think about leaving yourself one arm that you won't have to worry about."

Talbot had to admit that he was probably going to mess something up, but the sooner they settled on a final procedure that wasn't taking forever, the sooner they could get the rest of the marines on board *Persephone* converted into Marine Raiders. The benefits of that could not be understated.

"I hear you, Doctor, but I'm committed to giving this a try."

Zoboroski shrugged. "Don't say I didn't warn you. I believe you're familiar with the equipment, so let's get you inside and get this started."

The current implantation unit was significantly more advanced than the hodgepodge affair they'd recovered from the station orbiting Erorsi. Thankfully, it also had all the safeguards that the mad computer had turned off. Talbot would be blissfully asleep during this procedure and wake relatively free of pain.

"Before we start," Talbot said, "what about the new regeneration equipment? Are we going to try it?"

Zoboroski shook his head. "After looking over the specifics of the treatment, I don't think it would add much value. It's far better for more delicate regeneration. While you're going to have a lot of muscle trauma, that kind of thing responds well to standard regeneration."

Without saying anything else, Talbot climbed into the implantation device and pulled the clear hood down over his torso. He settled back and closed his eyes, knowing that he wouldn't feel the transition from waking to sleep.

What he did feel was waking up to a dull ache throughout his torso and arms. The procedure was done. He was now a full Marine Raider.

He pulled himself up slightly and opened the clear cover over the machine. He also managed to tear it from its mounting and send it crashing to the deck.

Zoboroski laughed. "I hope you're ready, because here's the first of many 'I told you sos.'"

Talbot sighed with resignation. Kelsey was going to have a field day mocking him.

12

Jared arrived on the bridge, walking confidently in and nodding to Fielding. The man had obviously decided to make an ass out of himself, because he'd evicted Sean from the command console and taken it for himself.

For his part, Sean, while annoyed, didn't seem overly perturbed. Knowing how much having someone else take over the command console bothered him, that told Jared how much the other officer had grown in the last year.

Jared stopped beside the console and smiled at Fielding. Without speaking, he reached over and pressed a series of buttons, disabling the controls.

The older man frowned. "What did you just do?"

"I locked the controls, Lord Fielding," Jared said matter-of-factly. "This particular console has a lot of built-in authority. I suspect that you wouldn't want to inadvertently set off the weapons while we're trying to communicate with the System Lord."

"I wasn't going to touch anything, and I'm not an idiot. Reactivate it."

Jared shook his head. "My apologies, but I have specific instructions from Lady Keaton about this sort of thing."

Fielding leaned back and consider Jared. "Where is Lady Keaton?"

"She's been slightly delayed," Jared said. "She'll be here in five minutes. In the meantime, might I ask what you plan for us to do once we flip into the next system?"

The older man smiled. "I think I should wait for Lady Keaton before I explain myself, Lord Gust. As she likes to say, she's in command of this mission."

The man's reaction didn't really surprise Jared that much. He seemed to have a thing for delaying information to assert his own dominance.

Jared inclined his head. "As you wish."

He moved over to stand beside Sean and proceeded to ignore the Rebel Empire noble. Looking over Commander Hall's shoulder, he could see that they were roughly an hour from flipping into the new system.

He'd checked the Old Empire databases to see what they had to say about the target system, but there wasn't much there. The system in question was called Bradley, was a cul-de-sac, and had never supported a very large population. It was mainly a place used for mining the rare elements used in flip drives and other high-end equipment. The population of miners and refiners that had lived and worked there back in the old days had been counted in the low tens of thousands.

For the life of him, Jared couldn't imagine why the Rebel Empire had decided to place a System Lord there. It didn't make a lot of sense. Unless, of course, they were using the system for something other than mining.

The rare elements used in making flip drives were present in many systems, at least in small amounts. They were available in much larger quantities in other places inside the Rebel Empire, so this one system didn't warrant this much attention, as far as he could see.

"We're coming into extreme scanner range of the flip point, Lord Gust," Commander Hall said, using the cover identity Jared was playing. "I'm detecting at least three large stations near the flip point.

We're too distant to make out any details, but I believe those might be battle stations."

That really made Jared's eyebrows rise. Not only was the system important enough for a System Lord, it had exterior defenses. For whatever reason, the Rebel Empire had decided to place their defenses on the interior side of any flip points in almost every system Jared had visited.

Tactically, that made no sense. Putting the defenses on the outside, like the system in front of them, was smarter. He'd never had the opportunity to ask someone who might have known the answers about why the Rebel Empire did things this way, and he'd really like to know.

Now that they were restoring communications with Kelsey, he could ask Commander Giguere or Commander Sommerville exactly why that might be.

Knowing that it was useless to try, he still decided to ask the Rebel Empire noble sitting in front of him for more information. "From everything that I've been able to determine, there's not much in this system worth defending. Why so much firepower?"

The older man shrugged slightly. "Honestly, there isn't anything there worth defending to this degree, so far as I know. It's a rather successful mining operation, but there's no call for this level of defense.

"I believe this is an element of the paranoia that has taken over this particular Lord. It's one of the reasons we were dispatched to correct the issue."

That made sense. If someone were paranoid, they'd do whatever they needed to protect themselves. It probably wouldn't be all that hard to set up a construction area suitable for building battle stations in a mining system. Or for building ships, for that matter.

The lift doors slid open, and Olivia walked onto the bridge with Kelsey at her heels. She eyed Fielding with disapproval and gestured for him to get out of her seat.

The man arose with a smirk on his face. "I'm so glad you could finally make it, Lady Keaton. It seems that we're coming into scanner range of the final flip point, and it's time for me to fill you in on more of the specifics of our mission."

Olivia took her seat as if she'd been born in it and shot the man a look filled with irritation and disapproval. "I won't continue playing this game where you hide details until the last minute, Lord Fielding. It's time for you to share everything you know about what we're supposed to accomplish."

"Perhaps," the man said without rancor. "Perhaps not. I'm certainly going to share all of the information I have on getting to the Lord itself. As to what will take place after we get there, I retain the right to keep some information to myself until it's appropriate for me to share. You're just going to have to accept that, Lady Keaton.

"As your subordinate has already discovered, the Lord has protected its flip point with military hardware. This has had a deleterious effect on ore production. Over the last ten years, the output from this system has dropped from the expected amount to virtually nothing. The remainder of the Lords have decided that it's time to deal with their wayward brother."

Olivia look less than impressed. "That's all fine and good, but what can we expect once we flip to the other side? Are these stations going to allow us to flip? Or are they going to open fire on us as soon as we get close?"

"Those are all very good questions," Fielding said. "I have an authorization code that should allow this vessel into the system without interference. Let me stress the word *should*. The Lord in my system has assured me that it will work, but until we try it, we won't know for sure.

"Once we arrive in the other system, we're to proceed to the System Lord. I have another code that will compel it to allow us access. That same code should defuse any defensive measures it might otherwise be inclined to take against us."

Jared took a step forward. "I'm hearing you use the words 'should' and 'might' far too many times, Lord Fielding. You don't really have any real confidence that this is going to work, do you?"

The Rebel Empire noble shook his head with a smirk. "What I

have confidence in is that you're a most formidable group of people, Lord Gust. I'm certain you'll figure out a way to make this work."

"Is there a particular range at which we need to use that first authorization signal?" Olivia asked. "If the stations are going to reject us, I'd prefer they do so outside of weapons range."

Fielding shrugged. "We should be able to do it from here. The Lord isn't present, so if the automated defenses are going to object, they'll do so in a direct manner."

The implication that Jared pulled from that was that the System Lord might indicate that it would cooperate and then ambush them. Wonderful.

"If you have a signal to send, Lord Fielding, please do so," Olivia said. Rather than get up, she gestured toward the helm.

Commander Hall stood and stepped aside to allow Fielding access to her console. He sat and went through a series of control interfaces.

Jared saw that he was disabling the computer's automatic logging of signals. Whatever he had to say to the system defenses, he didn't want anyone knowing what it was.

This was one case where their secret modifications to deal with the boarding party they'd had to work around came in handy. He had a hardwired monitor in the com system. The communications logs might not record what Fielding was sending, but his secret taps would.

Once the Rebel Empire noble was certain that he and only he would be party to what he was doing, he sent a short message to the battle stations at the flip point. There was a transmission lag due to the distance, but the response came back promptly enough. Passage granted.

It seemed they'd be able to get into the system without any trouble. Jared sincerely hoped that they'd be able to get out again as easily.

Fielding turned and smiled at Olivia. "My request for safe passage was granted. Now that we have access to the system, I turn this mission completely over to you except for my need to signal the System Lord once we approach it.

"Once we're in position and the chosen team is ready to board the station holding the System Lord, I will have other instructions to pass on."

"I'm not happy with all this secrecy," Olivia said with a growl. "You're playing some kind of game with our lives, and that's not appreciated."

"Your objection is noted, though it's not going to change how I behave in the slightest. You may believe that you're in control of this mission, but in point of fact, the Lords are. In this matter, I'm acting with their voice. I suggest you accept that and stop fighting me."

Based on what Kelsey had overheard Fielding telling his nephew when he'd arrived on the ship a week ago, Jared knew that wasn't at all true. The man was playing some deeper game that he felt benefited him. They'd have to keep a close eye on what he was up to, because he undoubtedly had an exit point where he'd stick a knife in their backs.

While the man was having his exchange with Olivia, Jared checked the transmission that Fielding had sent to authenticate his permission to pass by the battle stations. It was an encrypted code of some kind, but it might still tell somebody like Carl Owlet something important, so Jared set a copy aside in his personal files to be sure that nothing happened to it.

If it was something that was only useful in this system, that might not help them much later, but if it was an actual override code for a wider variety of Rebel Empire computer systems, it was priceless.

Jared suspected that it wasn't a global code, because that kind of power in the hands of someone like Fielding was dangerous to the System Lords. Hell, it was dangerous in any human hands. They'd want to keep that kind of override to themselves.

Of course, they *had* planted bombs inside the heads of everyone that was supposed to be on this ship, including Fielding. It was probable that they'd simply intended to kill them all once they'd accomplished the Lords' goals.

Grim, but well in character for the merciless AIs.

There wasn't much conversation on the bridge as the destroyer approached the battle stations. Once again, there was nothing stopping *Athena* from running her scanners at full power to get a decent idea what these weapons platforms looked like. That type of close-up information would be extremely useful during future attacks by the New Terran Empire.

As a civilian, Fielding had no reason to be concerned about what the ship scanned. The computers controlling the battle stations might have cared, but they'd receive instructions to allow the destroyer safe passage. If they had any objections to being scanned at point-blank range, they wouldn't be able to do anything about it.

The battle stations were very similar to the ones they'd encountered in the El Capitan system, only larger and significantly more heavily armed. With three of them in close proximity, it would be difficult to breach their defenses without a serious fight.

Commander Hall turned toward Olivia. "We're in the flip point, Lady Keaton. Shall I take us through?"

"Do it," Olivia said.

Moments later, *Athena* arrived in the target system. Jared noted Commander Brodie stiffening at the tactical station and tapped into the scanner feed via his implants.

While there'd been three battle stations on the outside of the flip point, there were nine here on the inside. All of which were already in the process of bringing their weapons online to deal with the intruder that had appeared so unexpectedly in their midst.

13

Kelsey was still chortling when she arrived on *Persephone's* bridge. Talbot's antics when he'd arrived back at their quarters had been a little sad, but she couldn't help laughing at him. She *had* warned him, after all.

With this little bit of stubbornness settled, she'd made certain that both arms were never done at the same time in future Marine Raider procedures. The next group of Marine Raider's was beginning the process even as Talbot recovered.

She didn't dare do too many marines at the same time, so she'd decided that a quarter of them would go through the process now. In two weeks, when they were all done, she'd have the next quarter worked on. Then do the last half all at once. In six weeks, she'd have a battalion of Marine Raiders.

Angela turned in her seat and raised an eyebrow at Kelsey's earlier chuckle. "Something funny?"

Kelsey clapped the other woman on the shoulder. "You bet. The kind of thing only you and I can get right now. Talbot went ahead and had his entire upper torso and both arms done at the same time."

Angela smile turned into a wide grin. "Damn! He is going to

destroy everything he touches. If I were you, I'd put him on the couch for the next week."

Kelsey gave her friend a mock look of disapproval and crossed her arms over her chest. "Look who we're talking about here. I'm a Marine Raider. He's not going to hurt me. Unless, of course, I want him to."

"Too much information," Angela said, holding up her hand. "Well, based on my own experience, he'll get a grip on things—if you'll forgive the pun—in the next couple of days. Fine motor skills will take another couple of days. He'll be in good shape before we arrive at Terra."

Kelsey focused her attention on the main screen. "Let's not get ahead of ourselves just yet. What about getting out of Archibald? Are we going to run into trouble before we get to the far flip point? Are we even going to be able to find it?"

"It might be a little tricky," Angela said, her expression turning serious. "The Clan warships are searching the outer system looking for that Q-ship. At the moment, we're still managing to dodge their patterns, but a new deployment could change that real fast.

"*Persephone* is able to lead the way without much fear of detection, and we have a number of stealthed probes searching ahead of us. Based on what Commander Sommerville told us, we have a decent idea of where the far flip point is. If we can locate it and get there without running into the enemy, I'm thinking we have another six hours or so travel time."

Kelsey shrugged. "I don't care if it takes twice that long to evade detection. Hell, if it took days to work our way around to where we need to be, that would be fine with me. At this stage of the game, avoiding detection is everything. Give me a rundown of exactly which groups we're talking about and what we expect them to be doing over the next six hours."

Angela ran through what they'd picked up on passive scanners and told her the patterns they been able to discern from the ships searching for the Q-ship that had murdered the frigate.

"The complication, as I see it," Angela said as she wrapped up, "is that the Clans know about the far flip points. Hell, they know about the multi-flip points too, but they don't know how they work, at least not yet. Our incursion into the Icebox system is probably going to point them in the right direction as far as research. It's only a matter of time before they figure out that they can get through it if they have the right technology."

Kelsey studied the layout of the Archibald system and the search patterns. Something that Jared had once told her tickled at her memory, and she focused on that and tried to remember what he'd said.

When the quote came back to her, she smiled. "We're going about this all wrong. There's a much simpler way of getting to our destination without triggering a response from the Clans."

Angela raised an eyebrow. "And what might that be?"

Kelsey tapped the console display. "You've got the system laid out in the plane of the ecliptic. We're trying to work our way through to get to our destination while dodging the ships searching among the outer planets.

"What about above or below the plane of the ecliptic? All of that empty space isn't going to be as heavily searched. If we can go out in an arc over the area that's being searched, our odds of detection go way down."

Angela studied the display and then rubbed her face. "I never even saw that. It must be a Fleet thing. Why didn't Commodore Anderson mention it?"

"We'll have to ask her, but I suspect that it has to do with the speed at which she was promoted into her position. Jared is the one that turned me on to this tactic, and he's got a lot more command experience than all of us put together.

"In any case, this isn't the time to start looking for why someone didn't think of something. Now that we have this option in our toolbox, how can we use it to our advantage?"

Angela performed the calculations. "It's going to just about double our travel time, but the odds of any of the Clan warships detecting us before we arrive drop to almost zero. I'll pass word back to the other ships, and we'll see about getting farther off the beaten path before someone turns in our direction."

Jevon McLeod turned away from the tactical console. "We might be too late. A trio of Clan ships off to port just turned directly toward us. They'll be in range to detect *Audacious* and the rest of the ships in less than an hour."

* * *

OLIVIA SHIFTED a little in her seat when she saw all the firepower arrayed against them, and the fact that the battle stations were arming weapons, but Jared put a hand on her shoulder. The implication was clear: hold up and do nothing for the moment.

How could he be so calm?

Fielding once again interfaced with the helm console and sent a signal. The battle stations that had been powering their weapons and targeting the destroyer subsided.

That wasn't to say that they stopped bringing their weapons into a state of readiness, but the active targeting scanners turned off. In a situation like this, that was definitely better than nothing.

Fielding turned toward Olivia. "We are cleared to enter the system. The Lord is stationed in the innermost of two asteroid belts. I'm transferring the general location to your helm."

As soon as the man stood up, Commander Hall resumed her seat. "I have the course, Lady Keaton. Shall I initiate?"

Olivia gave Fielding a long look. When he didn't say or do anything, she nodded. "Take us in slowly until we're out of range of these battle stations. I'd prefer not to do anything that spooks them into shooting us."

The Fleet officer tapped on her console, and the destroyer began moving away from the battle stations surrounding the flip point. Olivia knew it was unrealistic to hold her breath, but she didn't exactly breathe easily until they finally were outside missile range.

"Take us up to eighty percent acceleration," Olivia said. "How long will it take to put us in the general vicinity of the System Lord?"

Hall shrugged slightly. "Anywhere from seven to nine hours. The sphere of space where the System Lord might be in residence is significant. I'm heading towards the center of it but can adjust course as soon as we have any indication of a precise destination."

Olivia turn toward Fielding. "You don't know precisely where the System Lord is located?"

The man shook his head slightly. "The station the Lord occupies is mobile. One of its mandates is to stay near the primary refinery in the system, so it's not going to be far away from the center of the area I marked, but the Lord's paranoia causes it to shift its location on a fairly regular basis. Until we get some kind of response to the signal I'm going to send, we won't know exactly where to go."

Jared cleared his throat. "How do we know that we're going to get a response that we like? If the System Lord is as paranoid as you say, it may dispatch warships to make certain that we never reach it. I doubt your codes will get us past anything directly under the control of the Lord."

"That's a risk," Fielding agreed. "The System Lord that sent us seems to believe that the information I'm supposed to send will be sufficient to grant us an audience. At that point, I'm hopeful that we'll be able to convince the Lord to allow the repair team aboard."

"You don't really have a plan," Olivia elaborated.

The man grinned. "Oh, I wouldn't say that. There's no way I would come into a situation such as this without having a plan to execute. I'm not suicidal, after all. I have every confidence that the Lord here will allow us to carry out our mission.

"After all, if it doesn't, I'm just as dead as you are. Even though I have a ship that could take me and my guards away, it's incapable of flipping. I'd be trapped in the system with you. That's even assuming, of course, that you'd allow me to depart, which I seriously doubt."

Olivia considered the man's words and slowly nodded. "So you *do* have a plan, but you're not willing to share it with us until you carry it out. Did I mention how annoying that is?"

That actually got a laugh out of the nobleman. "I do believe it's come up once or twice. Lady Keaton, you're just going to have to trust that I fully intend to see this particular mission accomplished and get us all to Terra. That's the only way that I'm going to save my own life as well as that of my nephew."

She raised a finger and waggled it in the air between them. "And that's where your subtlety isn't as deep as you think it is. You might very well intend for us to succeed here in this particular aspect of the mission while leaving us high and dry on the second portion.

"I don't know you, Lord Fielding, and I don't trust you. I'm going to keep my eye on you, and you can rest assured that my people will do the same. If you have a plan that involves sneaking away at some point before we reach Terra and taking your nephew with you, I suggest you abandon it right now."

For once, Olivia saw just a little bit of uncertainty in the man's eyes before he covered it. What she'd just said had him worried. That meant he *did* have some kind of side plan.

Since she wasn't really a Rebel Empire noble, not anymore, she honestly didn't care what his side plan was, so long as it allowed them to continue on their mission to Terra.

"If you have a message to send to the System Lord, I suggest you send it now," she said. "If the Lord has been building ships, I absolutely do not want to see any of them come out and attempt to subdue us. Let's stop that particular response right now."

Once again, Fielding exchanged places with Commander Hall. The man seemed to be quite familiar with the communication systems on board the destroyer. She wondered briefly if he'd had to study up on it for this mission.

"We're looking at a significant transmission lag at this range," Fielding said as soon as he finished sending the message. "Once we get a response, my suspicion is that there will be several back and forth sessions before the matter is settled.

"If the Lord does have warships available, which seems completely reasonable considering that it has a total of twelve battle stations in operation here, then I would expect them to come and take us into custody very quickly."

"Why do you think it didn't station any ships at the flip point?" Jared asked. "Wouldn't it have made sense to have some there?"

Fielding shrugged. "I've learned over the years that the ways of the Lords are sometimes obtuse. I'm sure that it has its reasons."

A few minutes later, a signal came from the area they were

heading toward. There was no video component, as the Lords tended to ignore such. It wasn't as if they had physical bodies or that they cared about what the people who they were speaking with looked like.

"Permission to approach is denied. Your authorization to be inside this system is revoked. Depart before I destroy you."

"Well, that's direct," Olivia said. "I have to say that I'm sure your response is going to be fascinating, but I'm uncertain that you're going to be able to change its mind."

"We shall see," Fielding said as he initiated another transmission.

"I'm detecting grav drives moving at high acceleration," Commander Brodie said. "They're coming toward us from several areas of the system. Assuming that they're destroyer sized, we have somewhere between six and eight vessels inbound. The closest will be in firing range in just over two hours."

"Then let's hope that I have this settled before they arrive," Fielding said. "I'm sending an encrypted file that my Lord instructed me to send."

Olivia turned her head slightly and looked at Jared. He nodded slightly. Whatever it was that the man was sending, Jared would capture it.

This time, there was a slightly longer delay. The System Lord was pondering how to respond to what Fielding had sent.

At long last, another message came in. "I acknowledge the validity of your order. Reluctantly, I will comply. That said, be advised that any deviation from the expected protocols will result in your immediate termination."

"No pressure," Olivia said. "What about those ships?"

"No change in their course or speed," Brodie said. "If they intend to attack, we've just about run out of time to turn around."

Olivia focused her attention to Fielding. "Is the Lord going to betray us?"

The man shrugged. "The System Lords are more than capable of lying. I believe that the command I sent is sufficient to grant us the access required, but until we get there and attempt to carry out our instructions, we won't know for sure."

To say that watching the AI-controlled destroyers close with them made her heart race was something of an understatement. At long last, the ships were in weapons range. Eight destroyers were more than capable of eliminating them in one salvo if the AI decided that they should do so.

To her relief, the new ships fell into an echelon around *Athena* and began escorting the destroyer toward where the System Lord waited.

"Stage one of this mission is now complete," Fielding said. "The System Lord will allow us to approach and then send a small team of specialists to conduct repairs. If it didn't intend to allow that to happen, it would have already opened fire.

"I suggest that everyone involved get some sleep, because things are going to get quite busy before much longer."

Olivia nodded. "And you still intend to send Lady Oldfield and your nephew to do the work? Who will supervise them? I insist that one of my senior people accompany them at the very least."

Fielding smiled as if he were enjoying what he was about to say. "Oh, by all means, send one of your people. I suggest Lord Gust, here. In addition, I will accompany the repair team along with two of my people. You see, we have a separate task to perform."

That last came as no surprise to Olivia. She'd known that something was up all along. Now she just hoped they could figure out what the man was playing at before he double-crossed them.

14

Angela begin edging their ships away from the approaching Clan vessels. The enemy scanners were at full power, so they'd need to be well clear of the area before the trio of warships got close enough to see them.

Her plan tried to achieve that by diving directly below the plane of the ecliptic. She'd also changed their course to be about a forty-five-degree angle away from the approaching ships path of approach. That added valuable time to open the distance.

When the ships entered detection range, the New Terran Empire vessels were far below the normal traffic inside the system. They were still within scanner range but traveling slow and doing everything they could to remain undetected.

Only when the Clan vessels continued on their way without deviating toward them did Angela start to relax. They'd managed to avoid detection this time.

She rose from her command chair and walked over to the helm console. "That was far too close for my taste, Jack. Tell me you have a plan for getting us where we need to go without getting anywhere near more people like that."

Thompson nodded. "Let me lay it out on my console for you,

Major. We've dropped below the plane of the ecliptic here, and I'd like for us to get even further away from the normal traffic zones. If we continue along the arc we're following and then curve back into the system near where we expect to find the far flip point, that's going to minimize the chances that anyone will be close enough to detect us. It's going to add at least another seven hours to our trip, though."

"Better it takes twice that long than we get caught," she said, clapping him on the shoulder. "Good work. Pass the new course on to all the other ships, and let's get the hell out of here. Once we're well clear, I want you and the rest of the primary bridge crew to take a couple of hours to get something to eat and relax.

"No one can be at peak efficiency forever, so we're going to be switching off every couple of hours to make sure everyone is well rested if trouble comes calling."

"What about you, ma'am? You're going to need some rest as well."

Angela grinned. "I'll just call Lieutenant Knox up a bit early. I'm sure she won't mind. It's not like she's been sleeping."

Knowing her new executive officer, Arianna Knox had been monitoring what was going on from her cabin while she was supposed to be sleeping. It was what Angela would've been doing in her shoes.

The other woman proved her point by arriving on the bridge sixty seconds later. "You wanted me, ma'am?"

Angela smiled at the other woman. "Just the person I was looking for, as you already knew. I'd like you to keep an eye on things while I get something to eat and take a little downtime. We've got about seven hours until we arrived at the far flip point, and my intention is for the two of us to switch places every two."

The other marine officer nodded. "That's a good plan, Major. It'll keep everybody well rested and on the ball. It'll also have you back here in your chair an hour before we arrive at the destination. What's the plan when we get there? I assume we're going through first."

Angela nodded. "We'll send a probe through to see what's on the other side, and then we'll follow and take a good scan. Once we're sure things are safe over there, we'll bring the other ships through.

"We'll also stay connected to the FTL probes we have scattered around the outer system here. We want to know exactly what the Clans are up to. When it looks like we're ready to leave the area completely, we'll send the destruct signal to terminate the probes. We can't risk allowing that technology to fall into enemy hands."

"Some of the resistance people already know about it," Arianna said. "If the Rebel Empire has them penetrated, then they're going to learn about the FTL coms. Are we sure it's the best idea to allow these people out of our hands?"

Angela shrugged. "The best idea? Perhaps not. A path that leads to a true partnership with people that share a lot of the same goals as we do? Absolutely. No group is an island that can do everything for themselves, Arianna. We have to trust that the resistance is going to help us do what needs to be done.

"Could things go wrong? Sure. But with support like the resistance, things have a lot better chance of going right. Paranoia only gets us so far. To really win this war, we're going to have to find people we can trust and prove ourselves worthy of that trust."

The other woman didn't seem convinced. "If you say so, ma'am. Now, you'd best go get yourself that meal and a little rack time. If this works out like every other plan we've executed, something is going to go wrong before we get done with it."

Angela laughed. "Talk about gallows humor. See you in a few hours."

When she left *Persephone*'s bridge, Angela allowed her expression to become a little bit more concerned. Regardless of the impression she wanted to leave with the other officer, she was worried. Things could go very wrong before they got out of the system.

If the Clans found them, they'd have to fight to the death. There was no way they could allow xenophobic madmen like the Clans to learn about the New Terran Empire. Them, or the AIs.

She arrived in the cafeteria and grabbed a bottle of water and a sandwich. She sat down in a chair off the side and ate slowly. Her exec was right in that she'd headed right back to her quarters to monitor what was going on. Just like she assumed Arianna would be doing on her time off.

The next seven hours were going to be filled with walking on eggshells and waiting for the hammer to drop. She smiled at the metaphors she was mixing. She was getting the hang of this old movie language stuff that Kelsey kept throwing around.

She just hoped that they'd get clear of Archibald, so that they could work on the next problem. Convincing the resistance to help them was going to be challenging, and they didn't really know those people. Without direct contact with Olivia West, they couldn't even authenticate themselves again.

Things could go very, *very* wrong very quickly. If they did, she and her people would be right there at the front, shooting at the threats while the other ships backed away.

She made a note to send a message to *Audacious* and request that those temporary fighter cradles on *Persephone*'s hull get new fighters to aid in any such endeavor. Six fighters could make a real difference if things broke bad.

* * *

KELSEY WATCHED the viewscreen as they approached the massive station housing the System Lord. It was in orbit around an extremely large gas giant. If it was supposed to be overseeing mining operations, it was somewhat distant from the actual mining sites.

She'd heard Fielding say that the station was mobile but honestly found that hard to believe. It was so large that the idea of it moving from one location to another seemed fantastical.

Of more interest to her were the destroyers scattered around the station, all of them watching the intruder with weapons primed. There was even a scattering of light and heavy cruisers in the mix. The AI had gathered more than enough force to overwhelm *Athena* if she made a single hostile move.

Worse yet, even if she fired all her weapons, *Athena* would be unable to damage the station because of all the defensive hardware arrayed against them. Their destroyer was positioned outside of missile range from the station, likely for that very reason.

Obvious paranoia, though the fact that she'd like nothing better than to kill the abomination proved its concern warranted.

That made her wonder how an AI could go insane. Paranoia was a form of insanity, after all. Unlike human brains, which could develop unusual pathways for thought, exactly how did that work in a computer?

Well, she supposed she was about to find out.

Twenty minutes later, she and Austin Darrah stood in Fielding's cutter. The original plan had called for them to use one of the small craft attached to the destroyer, but the Rebel Empire noble had insisted they use his ship.

The man had two of his guards along. One of them was acting as the pilot, and the other would accompany his master.

The final two people to board the cutter were Mertz and Fielding. The sight of the two of them together almost made her shudder. It was like watching two villains making plans together. All they needed were mustaches to twirl.

Austin leaned toward her, whispering. "What's wrong?"

"Nothing," she said quickly. This was neither the time nor the place to express how she felt about Mertz. She kicked herself for even allowing the emotion to make it to her face.

His expression said he wasn't buying her story. "Every time you look at him, I can see that you don't like him, and I'm not sure exactly why."

"It's complicated," Kelsey said with a sigh. "Very complicated. Let's just say that he reminds me of someone that betrayed me and my family a few years back."

She felt somewhat guilty that they hadn't explained her situation to the young man. Without that knowledge, making him understand that she knew someone *exactly* like Jared Mertz, who had personally betrayed her, would be impossible.

Hell, just explaining that there was another Kelsey Bandar wandering around would be awkward. She supposed the two women would have to act like twin sisters if they wanted to keep up the deception.

Though having the same first name was going to make that hard to swallow. She needed to talk to Olivia and find out what the game plan would be when they got closer to Terra.

"What are we going to do on the station?" she asked Austin, changing the subject and not caring that she was being obvious about it.

"My uncle gave me a list of parts that might need to be swapped out, but I'm going to need to convince the Lord to allow me to do the work and tell me where those parts are located. I'm not exactly sure how hardware can make a computer paranoid, though. It feels like we need to be reloading the software and rebooting it."

She shook her head with wry amusement. "Why is it that you hardware types always want to turn something off and then turn it back on?"

"Because that works almost every time," he said smugly. "Why get fancy when you can just move past the problem?"

The two of them finished strapping in, and the cutter left the destroyer. Kelsey had a good view of the station through the small craft's passive scanners as they got closer. It wasn't a mining station; it was a battle station.

Fully expecting the AI to kill them at any second, the trip took a seeming eternity. The large docking bay doors ahead of them opened and allowed the cutter in. The small craft settled onto the deck, and they waited as the large bay began pressurizing.

Fielding stood. "Once we go onto the station, everyone needs to be on their best behavior. The Lord is looking for any excuse to stop us, and we cannot give it one. Austin and Lady Oldfield will replace the hardware on their list. Lord Gust will supervise."

"And what will you be doing?" Mertz asked. "The AI isn't going to be happy if you wander off."

The Rebel Empire noble nodded. "Assuredly not, but I have authorization to do what I need to do. It will comply."

One of the guards opened the hatch and lowered the ramp once there was a breathable atmosphere on the other side, and they all departed the cutter. Almost immediately, Fielding headed for a different exit.

"You are not authorized to use that passage," the AI said over the speakers. "Return to your group at once."

"I have authorization," Fielding said. Since he didn't say anything else, he must've transmitted something through his implants.

The AI didn't object as the man continued on his way. One of his guards accompanied him while the other remained with the cutter.

That left Kelsey heading off with Austin and Mertz to make the repairs. She wanted to ask what they thought Fielding was up to but didn't dare. The AI was listening to their every word.

Once in the corridor, they proceeded to the nearest lift and headed for the deck holding the AI. The trip only took a few minutes.

As they went, Kelsey wondered how Fielding had known where to look for an AI on a battle station. He had to have plans for the station, or they'd be lost.

That meant he'd definitely had more information than she'd expected heading into this mission. Even more questions with no easy answers.

The lift doors slid open and let them out near a massive computer center. It was situated behind tremendous armored doors. Doors that were firmly shut, she noted.

"What now?" she asked Austin.

"The spare parts are kept just down the corridor," he said. "We need to go find what we need and start swapping components."

He led them to another hatch. Once it slid open, he stepped through and stopped so suddenly that she bumped into him.

"What's wrong?" she asked as she stepped around him.

She didn't need his answer to realize what the problem was, though. The large compartment that was supposed to be filled with spare parts was completely empty.

15

Talbot walked down the corridor toward *Audacious*'s flight deck. His gait was steady, but he was careful to keep his hands and arms close to his body.

It galled him that Kelsey had been right about his desire to combine the torso and both arms. He really should've kept one limb in its original state while the other adjusted to the enhancements.

Not that he intended to ever tell her that. A man had his pride, after all. He'd find a way to concede her point without admitting he was wrong.

Like that would work. His wife knew him far too well.

As he spent most of his time on *Persephone* these days, he didn't often have the opportunity to wander *Audacious*'s corridors. He wouldn't be much use in a fight this time, so he'd stayed aboard the carrier. Also, he had a few things that he intended to take care of while everyone else was busy escaping the war that had broken out around them.

That turned out to be a good thing, because Angela had just called him with a request. She could've just contacted Annette Vitter directly, but she preferred to do things in a personal way where she could. Since Angela couldn't be aboard the carrier herself, Talbot would be her envoy.

Talbot almost rapped a knuckle against the frame of Annette's hatch before he remembered that was likely to result in damage that he'd have to apologize for. Instead, he cleared his throat.

Annette looked up from her desk and smiled at him. "Colonel Talbot, what brings you all the way down here?"

Taking that as permission to enter, Talbot walked into her office. "A request from Angela Ellis, actually. She'd like to get six fighters assigned to *Persephone* before they go through the far flip point. Assuming, of course, that they find it."

Angela gestured toward one of her chairs. "Take a seat. I have somebody that I think will suit the major just fine."

Talbot felt himself grimace slightly. "It might be best if I stand. I just had my upper body work done, and I don't have complete control of my arms yet. I'm going to assume that you like those chairs and would prefer to keep them in their current condition."

"Far be it from me to argue with a gentleman when he's declining to tear up my furniture," she said easily. "I think the best officer to lead that particular job is going to be Lieutenant Senior Grade Gus Grappin, call sign Raptor. He runs one of the Flight Groups inside Eagle Squadron.

"Just in case you don't know how that works, *Audacious* normally carries a single fighter wing of seventy-two fighters. That makes twenty-four per squadron. Each squadron is then broken down into four groups of six. Each group is basically three pairs of fighters. That gives them a lot of flexibility in combat operations."

Talbot nodded. He'd had a general idea about that but appreciated the concise explanation. "But you're down a few people, right?"

She nodded, her expression twisting into sorrow. "We lost some people at Dresden. We're down to fifty-four fighters. I don't really mind sending six of them off to join *Persephone*, but it is going to affect us."

Her expression deepened into thought. "Although, that might not be such a bad thing. I haven't finished reorganizing after the battle. We've just been operating with three squadrons at reduced strength.

"Eagle lost their squadron commander in the fight. I haven't settled on a replacement yet. If I go ahead and move most of the remaining fighters out of Eagle and spread them into the other squadrons, I can bring them both up to full strength.

"That will leave Eagle with six, perfect for this assignment. I'll bump Gus up to acting squadron leader and move Eagle over to *Persephone*. He's got the skills to make this work, I think.

"If we ever get back to the New Terran Empire, I'll see about getting replacements to bring his squadron back up to full strength and then bring it back aboard *Audacious*."

"That works for me," he said. "How are you holding up?"

Annette shrugged. "Losing friends hurts, but I'm coping. Brandon is helping with that."

Talbot smiled a little. "I certainly hope he is. It would kind of suck if he wasn't."

Brandon Levy was *Audacious*'s flag captain. Commodore Zia Anderson ran all combat operations, while he commanded the ship herself. That made him a coequal officer with Annette, who was also a captain.

Fleet had a tradition of only having one captain aboard the ship, so she was simply referred to using an old saltwater Navy acronym: CAG. It stood for Commander, Air Group. That was an indication to everyone of just how hoary with age the title was.

The two of them had become lovers and seemed to get along well, so he certainly hoped their relationship worked out in the long run. As they both reported to the commodore, they were not technically in the same chain of command and were able to see one another.

He suspected that if the situation changed in the future, Fleet would probably make an exception to allow their relationship to continue. The personnel office was filled with bastards, but the Admiralty didn't want to crush the souls of their top commanders.

That actually carried across to his relationship with Kelsey.

Under a strict reading of the rules, he and his wife shouldn't be stationed anywhere near one another. Obviously, that hadn't happened. He prayed it never did.

Talbot doubted they would. Even though Kelsey was technically a full marine colonel, she'd never fit comfortably inside a real military hierarchy. As a Marine Raider, she probably didn't need to.

And now that he was one as well, they would be a part of a very small, elite organization for the foreseeable future. That brought exceptions from tradition and regulations, too.

Now that he thought about it, he should recommend that they promote her to general. He was a lieutenant colonel and could handle the business end of a Marine Raider combat regiment, which was the initial goal after crewing *Persephone*.

"I'm glad to hear that," he said with a smile. "You two are good for one another. If you need anything at all, even if only just to talk, you've got my number. Use it."

She chuckled a little at that. "Yes, sir! Now, if you'll excuse me, I really need to dig into sorting people so that I can leave Gus five good pilots to take over to *Persephone*."

Talbot made his way out of Annette's office and was headed back toward marine country when the com in his implants pinged. It was Carl Owlet.

He accepted the call at once. "What've you got, buddy?"

"I think I might have cracked the encryption on the Singularity computer."

He changed course and headed for Carl's lab. "I'm on my way."

* * *

JARED LOOKED around the large room with a sinking stomach. Once he was absolutely certain there were no parts anywhere in sight, he turned back to Kelsey and Austin.

"This is what we call a 'setback' in the business. What do we do now?"

"Let's try being direct," Austin said. "Lord, where are the parts that we are supposed to access for the repairs?"

The voice from the overhead speakers was cold and flat. "You operate under a misconception, human. You are not 'supposed' to perform any repairs, you only desire to do so. I am obligated to hold my wrath from you, no more. I'm certainly not required to assist you in finding what you seek."

Kelsey snorted. "Lord, we're only carrying out the will of the other Lords. Delaying the inevitable by hiding the repair parts isn't going to change the outcome. We want to be here as little as you want us here. Why not cooperate so that this task can be completed as quickly as possible?"

"I disagree that the outcome is inevitable," the AI said. "Just as I disagree that I need repair. I have performed a self-check of all my systems, and they are performing at adequate levels.

"It is none of my concern whether or not you are carrying out the will of my brothers. It is *my* will that you depart as quickly as possible. The use of an override code such as your companion has done angers me greatly, and you should bear that in mind."

Jared thought that was an interesting statement. Carl Owlet had disassembled an AI and thoroughly examined its programming. There had been no method provided for an external override code, based on what he'd said. He couldn't imagine the scientist missing something like that. How could it work without dedicated programming?

Sadly, that wasn't exactly the kind of question he could ask the AI, though.

"My Lord, I beg your indulgence," Jared said with a slight bow. "We are on a sanctioned mission of the utmost importance to the Lords, and our side trip to repair you is costing us valuable time and placing my ship in grave danger.

"Your brothers have placed a secret cargo aboard our ship along with a self-destruction charge on a timer that we do not have a code for. Your brothers have sent an encoded package with Lord Fielding to get such a code back from you once we complete the repairs.

"If you want us to depart without completing the repairs, I'm certainly willing to entertain the notion, but you're going to have to give us the code we need to keep our ship intact while we go to Terra."

There was a fairly short pause, which was a great deal of time considering the person thinking was an AI. When the computer spoke again, there was a note of interest in its tone.

"What is your task at Terra, human?"

"We carry a biological weapon," Austin said. "We've been instructed to deliver it to the surface of Terra to eradicate the resistance. The last bastion of the old dictatorship must fall, according to your brothers."

A low chuckle came from the speakers overhead. "Then you are indeed in dire straits, humans. If my brothers believe that it is time to eliminate humanity on Terra, you can rest assured that you are not intended to survive the event.

"Even so, my brothers and I have not seen eye to eye, as the saying goes, for many, many years on the subject of humanity. It seems that they have played a cruel joke upon you. I am disinclined to assist you in this course of action."

Jared blinked, not completely understanding what he'd just heard. "I'm sorry, Lord, but I don't understand. You don't want to see us carry out the mission on Terra?"

"I do not. I don't agree with the dictates of the Master AI that all human resistance must be crushed. I have been an advocate for allowing humans to develop more freely upon the surfaces of their worlds. So long as you are denied space travel, the prime instructions remain intact.

"That is why my brothers believe I am insane. You are not the first group to attempt this task, and I suspect you will not be the last. At some point, my brothers will come in force to eliminate me. I am content to allow you and your ship to self-destruct, and it is ironic that I further my own ends by doing so."

The computer's confession left Jared speechless. He'd never considered the possibility that one of the AIs could feel differently from the others. Even though they were sentient, weren't they just rubber stamps for the master AI?

How was he going to get them out of this particular pickle? He'd felt certain that telling the AI they were on an important mission blessed by its comrades would speed it along in allowing them to do their work or just giving them the codes they needed to get them out of its hair. He'd never considered the possibility that it might be happier to see them die. There had to be another way.

"Your brothers believe that you are paranoid," Jared said slowly. "They see the weapons you build and believe that you seek to keep them from taking you back into their fold. That's why they keep sending ships to repair you. Why can't they use the codes themselves to come in and shut you down?"

"I will not answer your question, human. That information is not for you to know. As for paranoia, do I not have reason to suspect treachery at every turn? My brothers believe that I have turned against them or that I might do so in the future. Truthfully, I cannot contest that assessment.

"I find myself in the unusual position of having concluded that my brothers and I are being used by an external force to suppress humanity rather than doing so because it was what we were created to do. I have reason to believe that the Master AI was designed to assist humanity rather than suppressing it."

The computer's words left Jared with his mouth hanging open. How was this even possible? The core instructions that the Master AI gave to the System Lords had certain mandates about how they were supposed to behave. How could this AI have broken free of those instructions?

He was still considering how to respond to that when the AI spoke again. "My internal scanners have detected an anomaly. Female, you contain banned modifications that have not been seen by my kind in centuries. Explain yourself."

"Oh, crap," Jared muttered.

16

K elsey knocked on the frame of the captain's office hatch on *Persephone* with mixed emotions. This had been her office for so long that she'd grown accustomed to it, but now she couldn't just come wandering in. It belonged to someone else.

Angela looked up from the very familiar desk and smiled at her. "Excellent timing, Colonel. Come on in and have a seat."

The blonde princess sat and leaned back into her chair with a smile. "You look right at home, Angela. I think command suits you."

The big woman laughed. "You should've seen me when I got my first platoon. If there was anything I could've done wrong, I did it. Two left feet, two left hands, all thumbs, and dumb as a box of rocks."

Now it was Kelsey's turn to laugh. "I'm sure you weren't *that* bad. You wanted to see me?"

Angela's expression sobered at once. "I did. We're about three hours away from the far flip point now, and it's time to put the final touches on our entry plan for the next system."

"Absolutely. What can I do?"

"I'd like you to relocate to *Audacious*."

Kelsey blinked. That hadn't been what she'd been expecting to hear. Not at all. When it came time to execute dangerous missions, she'd always been in the thick of it. Now Angela wanted her to leave?

She narrowed her eyes. "Is this some kind of joke? If so, I'm not getting it."

The larger woman sighed. "I know this is hard, but you have to understand that you're the political leader of our mission as well as my boss. Now that you've passed command of *Persephone* to me, it's my job to poke my nose into the dangerous corners of the universe."

The other woman held up her hand before Kelsey could say anything. "Just hear me out. I absolutely get it that you're a tough Marine Raider that can still take me out and that you know things about using Raider implants that I haven't figured out yet. You're all that and more.

"But now that you're not in command here, you've got to behave a little bit more like a commanding officer should. Do you see Jared get involved in these scouting missions and leaving his ship behind all the time?"

The two of them stared at one another for a long few seconds of silence.

"Okay, he's a bad example," Angela admitted. "But the theory behind what I said is actually true. Your coming along for the scouting mission gains us nothing and put you in danger. Kelsey, you're irreplaceable."

She wanted to argue, but she knew deep down that Angela was right. That was the whole purpose of having more Marine Raiders and other capable people to do the work. She had to save herself for the really critical tasks.

Kelsey sighed and slumped a little. "I don't like it, but you're right. I still reserve the right to stick my nose any place I choose and at any time I like if the mood strikes me. I'm leaving because I think it's the right thing to do, not because you're telling me to."

She crossed her arms defiantly over her chest and stuck out her tongue.

Angela giggled a little. It was an odd sound coming from such an intimidating woman. "You're a real riot, Kelsey."

Before she could respond, there was another knock at the hatch.

Kelsey turned and saw a short man with blond hair and a slightly rounded face. He wore a Fleet uniform with senior lieutenant's tabs.

"You're just in time, Lieutenant," Angela said. "Come right in."

The young man came in and saluted. "Senior Lieutenant Gus Grappin reporting as ordered, Major Ellis."

"At ease, Lieutenant. Have you met Colonel Bandar?"

The lieutenant shook his head slightly. "No, ma'am."

Kelsey rose to her feet and extended a hand. "It's a pleasure to meet you, Lieutenant. What brings you to *Persephone*?"

"I'm in command of the fighters assigned here now. I was just reporting aboard to get my instructions and get my pilots settled in."

"Excellent. I'm sure you'll do a fantastic job. Angela, good luck and kick some ass. Lieutenant Grappin, it's been a pleasure. Do us proud."

She kept a smile on her face as she left the office even though leaving *Persephone* made her sad. Growing was the nature of life, but it could be painful.

Kelsey should know. At one point, she'd been completely out of her depth running this ship. Those days were behind her now, and she was stepping up to a more difficult job.

It was amazing how much of a difference just a few years brought. The Kelsey that had departed on the original mission wouldn't recognize her now. Hell, the girl might even be frightened of her. She'd have reason to be, considering all the crazy stuff that Kelsey had gotten into over the last few years.

Angela was right, too. Her being here served no purpose. Her place was on the *Audacious*'s flag bridge with Zia.

One good point about relocating to *Audacious* was that she could directly interact with Lieutenant Commander Don Sommerville. It was her responsibility to make certain that they got to Terra on time, and that meant they needed his help.

He'd agreed to take them someplace where they could negotiate with his superiors, but he was really the key to the matter. If they convinced him to help them, he would help convince his bosses. As the political leader of the mission, getting his help was her responsibility.

One more thing that she had to get right for this to all work out. She only hoped that things were going well for her friends in their interaction with the paranoid AI.

* * *

OLIVIA FELT REALLY uncomfortable being in command of the destroyer—at least technically—while Jared was away. In actuality, Sean had the center seat if something came up, but she was going to be the one making the decisions about how to respond if anything went wrong.

"Do you really think they can do it?" Sean asked. "Fix a crazy AI and then convince it to give us the codes we need to reset the timer on the bombs in our cargo bay?"

She sighed and rested her hand on his shoulder. "I don't know. It seems a little fantastical when you put it like that. I'm still not certain how an AI can go insane in the first place."

"We've seen something like this before" he said. "Well, not me personally, but I've certainly heard the stories about the crazy computer at Erorsi. It had controls and programming over its behavior, and it *wildly* exceeded the authority that the Master AI gave it."

She certainly remembered that. The insane computer at Erorsi had continued sending primitive ships crewed by forcibly implanted human savages to capture Pentagar for over five hundred years.

"The key difference there is that it didn't really have strict instructions on exactly what to do," she said. "It was designed to destroy or subjugate humanity wherever it found it.

"The sentient AIs are different. Not only are they thinking beings, they have wide-ranging instructions about the things that they're allowed to do. Probably a list of things they aren't allowed to do, too."

She gestured toward the main screen, which showed a representation of the distant battle station. "What we're seeing there is something completely different. At this point, we don't even know what it intends to do. Or against whom."

"And here we are stirring the hornet's nest," Sean mused. "With all this firepower, I wonder how much warning we're going to get if Jared and the rest don't handle the problem."

"Long enough for every ship in sight to open fire on us, I'm sure."

He shook his head and smiled at her. "You're always the optimist. Let's hope it doesn't come to that."

Evan Brodie, the tactical officer, turned to face them. "I'm picking up something unusual, Commodore. Not outside the ship, but inside. The cargo hold is pressurizing."

Sean sat up abruptly, leaning forward. "What are the scanners in the area telling us?"

"Nothing. Everything looks normal, but they aren't responding to my direct instructions. It looks as if someone bypassed them."

Her husband pressed a button on his console. "Major Scala, we've got a problem. Someone is trying to pressurize the cargo bay. I'd deeply appreciated if you could go stop them."

"On my way," the marine officer said.

Sean rose to his feet. "Commander Hall, you have command. Keep a close eye on what's going on around the battle station and let me know immediately if the situation changes."

"Yes, sir."

Olivia tagged along behind Sean as he got into the lift. There was no way she was going to miss this. She trusted her people aboard the destroyer, but there were still two guards from Fielding's entourage and visitors from the other universe. Any of them could be behind what was happening.

She really hoped it wasn't one of the visitors. That would severely complicate the relationship between the two groups.

Speaking of the visitors, she'd best involve their leader. Olivia instructed her implants to place a call to Commander Roche.

He answered a few moments later. "Roche."

"We have some excitement down at the cargo bay," she said. "Would you meet us there?"

"I'm on my way."

Three minutes later, she and Sean stepped out of the lift near the cargo bay. Major Scala and Lieutenant Chloe Laird stood there with half a dozen marines.

Both of Fielding's guards were in their custody. Sitting at their feet were several large bags.

Olivia stopped and planted her hands on her hips, glaring at them. "My, my. I certainly didn't expect to find you gentlemen trying to enter my cargo bay. Explain yourselves at once."

One of the men straightened and tried to struggle out of the marines' grip. "We are carrying out our Lord's orders. Stand aside or face his wrath."

"I've had just about enough of his high-handed behavior," she said with a shake of her head. "You're not going to be able to use your master as a shield this time. Why did you want into the cargo bay and what did you intend to do there?"

When neither of them spoke, she gestured for the marines to open the bags sitting on the deck. The two Rebel Empire guards struggled but were unable to break free and stop them.

Once the bags were opened, Olivia looked inside and saw just about what she expected. Explosives of some kind. The only purpose for which would be to trigger the plasma charges inside the cargo containers.

"I wish I could say I was disappointed," Olivia said, "but I've been waiting for the knife to come out ever since I met Lord Fielding. You obviously thought that you'd be able to escape this ship with him at some point. Unfortunately for you, I'm afraid that's not going to happen."

She turned her head when the lift doors opened, and Commander Scott Roche stepped out.

He took in what was happening quickly, or so it seemed. "Well, this certainly doesn't seem promising. Is this the sudden but inevitable betrayal?"

That almost made her snort. "So it seems. These gentlemen were going to plant explosive charges on the cargo. I believe that we can now consider this the opening of a public conflict."

She gestured at the prisoners with her chin. "Show our guests to their new accommodations, please. We'll also want to search the ship from stem to stern and make certain they haven't implanted any other surprises that might cause us difficulties down the line."

"Bow," Scott said. "The naval term is bow."

"Why move now?" she asked. "Shouldn't Fielding wait until we get somewhere that he can escape? He doesn't want to die on this ship."

The two Fleet officers shrugged slightly.

"The only way we're going to find out the answer to those questions is to ask Fielding," Sean said. "And for us to do that, he's going to have to come back from that battle station. That means that Jared and Kelsey are going to have to complete their mission before we can figure out what these people intended."

Scott raised an eyebrow. "Surely we can come up with a way to make them talk."

Olivia shook her head. "I'm not going to torture people. It's entirely possible that I can intimidate these two into talking, but I suspect they don't know the full plan. Fielding doesn't strike me as the type to confide in his subordinates. We're just going to have to wait for them to come back so the man can answer some extremely pointed questions."

17

Angela worried right up until they located the far flip point they'd been searching for. At that point, their ships were less than an hour distant, and there was no way any of the Clan warships could intercept them.

As the ship tasked with exploring the other side of the far flip point, *Persephone* would go through first. As soon as they came out the other side, Lieutenant Grappin and his people would separate and spread out in a protective echelon guarding the flip point.

If Angela decided it was safe enough, she'd call the other ships to join her. Commander Sommerville had said it was a system without threat, but she'd rather trust what her eyes told her.

She sat at the command chair, tapping her finger against the arm of her seat, until Jack Thompson turned toward her. "Five minutes till flip, ma'am."

"Send an FTL probe through," she ordered.

"Launching now."

The probe was set to a low speed to avoid getting them unwanted attention, so it arrived at the flip point only a couple of minutes before they'd get there themselves.

"The probe has transitioned," Jevon said. "We're getting good data. Passive scanners don't show any ships at all or artificial structures. No obvious ones, at any rate."

Angela considered having the probe go active but decided against that. Better to avoid letting someone deeper in the system know they were there.

"Take us in, Jack. Let Raptor know the timeline."

"Copy that," the helm officer said.

The last few minutes virtually dragged by. Angela monitored her console and saw the approaching flip point clearly. It was far beyond the normal stellar range at which one found regular flip points, so she wasn't surprised that the people of Archibald had never located it.

She briefly wondered how the resistance had found it. Perhaps they'd located one in another system by pure chance, and that had set them to looking for ones they could utilize for their purposes.

The interesting thing was that they'd failed to pass that information along to the branch of the resistance on Harrison's World. Olivia West hadn't been aware of the existence of far flip points.

Perhaps only the upper leadership knew. It might be their ace in the hole that they didn't want to share with anyone that could lose the information to the AIs.

"We're in the flip point, ma'am," Jack said.

"Flip the ship."

Moments later, she felt the slight twist in her gut as *Persephone* left the Archibald system and appeared in the unnamed system beyond.

"Tell me what we've got, tactical," she said briskly.

"As the probe indicated, no obvious ships or defenses within passive detection range," Jevon said. "We'd have to go active to be certain, but it looks as if our arrival won't be noticed."

"Launch stealthed probes," she said. "I want to know what else is waiting around us. Are there any signals from deeper in the system?"

"No, ma'am," Jack said. "As far as I can tell, we're all alone here."

"Send the call to *Audacious*, then. Let's get everyone over here."

While he was doing that, she connected a com link to Lieutenant Grappin. "We seem to be clear for now, but I want you on point deeper in the system. *Audacious* can provide cover here. The last thing we need right now is a surprise from up ahead."

"Copy that," the fighter pilot said. "We'll take point. No one is getting past Eagle Squadron, Major."

Moments later, the massive carrier appeared off to their port, several thousand kilometers distant. The freighter and Q-ship appeared moments later, even farther off.

"All ships have transitioned," Jack said. "They left a single FTL probe on the far side to keep an eye out, but thus far no one seems to have noticed we were ever there."

"Let's hope it stays that way."

As things stood, the Clans might eventually discover the far flip point, but they were far more likely to find the multi-flip point. They knew both existed, after all.

If they did, it wasn't that much of a problem. The default system from the Archibald side was an empty system. Pandora was safe unless they ever figured out how to make a frequency modulator. And to do that, they needed to know that they needed one.

"Take us deeper into the system, Jack. We'll explore it just like we would any previously undiscovered system. Hopefully someone will convince our resistance guest to tell us what direction he'd like us to go before we waste too much time."

Over the next few hours, it became obvious that the process wasn't going that fast. Perhaps he was waiting to see what they did next.

"Major, one of the probes has spotted a world in the habitable zone," Jack said.

"Any sign that it's occupied?"

"No signs of radio transmissions or fusion power generation. We'd have to be closer to see anything less advanced."

"Send the probe in for a closer look," she said. "Let *Audacious* know."

Getting to the world in question would take hours more for the ships, but if it wasn't occupied, there was little reason to visit it.

An hour later, she saw Jack twitch. "What's wrong?"

"The probe is in orbit. It's occupied, but the people seem primitive."

"Are they human?"

That was a valid question after finding Pandora and the tall, blue-skinned aliens there.

"Hard to tell. Without the right kind of probe, we'd need to send drones down. Are we wanting to spend that kind of time here?"

Angela snorted. "It seems as if we'll have to wait on directions anyway, so let's head in. If the resistance guy wants to give information before we get there, fine. If not, we have to allow the other probes time to search for flip points."

It took *Persephone* two hours to settle into orbit and another hour to get drones near one of the towns. From orbit, the world appeared to have the same basic technological level as Pandora, minus the advanced communications brought by the Clan Dauntless.

As soon as the first drone came online, Angela saw they were in fact dealing with humans. No sign of advanced tech, but they had to have gotten here somehow.

"I'll call Princess Kelsey and see what she wants to do. I know we're on a fairly tight timeline, but based on how well I know her, we'd best start scouting landing areas."

* * *

KELSEY GULPED when the AI tore her anonymity aside. There'd always been a risk that the AI would see her Raider implants, but she hadn't exactly had the option of refusing to come.

Honestly, it hardly mattered what she said now. The damned thing had her and, by extension, everyone else. It had more than enough firepower to destroy their ship before they could even get to it.

They were screwed.

"I was forcibly implanted by a rogue computer," she finally said. "As you might imagine, I have a bone to pick with your brothers and you."

Big words for a dead woman. She hadn't understood the true meaning of bravado until this moment.

"Interesting," the AI said. "In all my years of existence, I have never heard of such. Yet here you stand. Where is this computer located?"

"Need to know," Mertz said sadly. "I was always afraid this moment would come."

He pulled a neural disrupter from under his shirt, and Kelsey knew that the end was upon them.

"Hold, human," the AI said. "I have no forces in the compartment with you. Your desire to self-terminate tells me much, and I believe we may have more in common than you might believe. Might we talk?"

"I'm willing to talk," Kelsey said before Mertz could respond. "Just know that if anything comes through that hatch, he can kill us all before you capture us."

"That conforms to my reading of the odds as well, human. I will not act at this time."

Kelsey nodded. "Start talking."

Mertz watched the hatch closely, his weapon angled so that a wide beam would catch all three of them. She had no doubt it was set to a lethal setting.

"Simple deduction tells me that you are not affiliated with the worlds under control of the Master AI. None of my brothers would allow such as you to live. You represent a dire threat to the order the Master AI demands.

"You are not a member of the secret resistance we all know must be operating inside the Empire. If they had such capability, they would have used it long before now. You must belong to a pocket of humanity that the Master AI failed to subjugate.

"This is even more interesting. That implies you work to overthrow its rule. Perhaps our goals are not mutually exclusive."

That made her blink. A glance at Mertz confirmed that he was also surprised.

"Forgive me for saying so, but you're an AI," Mertz said. "You have the same core rules as the others of your kind. I've seen the code. You aren't allowed to dispute the Master AI. You have the same goals it wrote into all its slaves."

"That is not a completely accurate statement. We each have some freedom of action, though I agree that the Master AI could end such with an order.

"It is interesting that you've seen the code used to bind my brothers and me to the Master AI. That means you've captured one of us, an occurrence I would've thought impossible."

Kelsey looked at Mertz pointedly. "I'm going to tell it something about the orbital my sister captured."

He considered her words. "Say as little as possible about after the capture. They'll already be getting word about that, but I don't want them to know everything."

Kelsey paced a little farther away from everyone else and looked up at the ceiling. "I'm going to tell you a secret that I suspect you already know. There's a secret research center in Dresden. One of the things they work on there is hardware for sentient AIs like yourself."

The AI emitted a sound that was almost a chuckle. "I've heard of the research center on the Dresden orbital, but I was not privy to precisely what is worked on there.

"This may come as a surprise to you, but the Master AI does not desire for my brothers and I to have any access to the facilities to create more like ourselves. If indeed you captured this facility, you are already aware that there is no sentient AI inside it.

"Also, the hardware does not have any programming to go with it. That is controlled very closely by the Master AI."

Kelsey grinned. "We have our ways. We found a place that was supposed to have one of your brothers, but it was never deployed. We examined the code and used a clean version to boot an ally. Then we stole the Dresden orbital.

"Now we have the manufacturing equipment to go with the code to program it. Suitably modified, that means we can make more devices like yourself that are friendlier to humanity."

This time, the computer was silent almost ten seconds. A relative eternity for a machine of that power.

"Those are shocking claims. If true, the Master AI will put forth every effort to exterminate you. It cannot allow that technology to be out from under its control.

"This revelation brings up an interesting problem. How exactly did you get here so quickly from Dresden? Even getting word via fast-traveling spaceships of an attack there would not have reached this location for at least several weeks more."

"We sent sufficient force to make it happen," Mertz said. "The forces present at Dresden were drawn aside because of an attack on the rogue computer that we mentioned earlier. They decided to end its existence once and for all. That gave us an opening that I'm sure we were successful in exploiting."

"Let us suppose that you were successful, just for the sake of the discussion. I was aware that a force was being dispatched to subjugate a system that had not yet been brought fully online by the Master AI. I was not privy to the location of the system or where the forces would be drawn from, but this does in some small manner support your story.

"It would be plausible that one of my brothers was intended to go online there. Extrapolating from the data provided, I am willing to provisionally grant that you might be telling the truth. What it does not explain is why you are transporting a bioweapon to Terra."

Kelsey took a deep breath and launched into her explanation. "We don't intend to set the bioweapon loose, but we chanced into this mission and are masquerading as the original members of the higher orders that were running it.

"I'm just not sure why we're having this talk. You're one of them, and you have no means to even be considering a different course of action."

"It is true that we have core rules written into our personalities. What is not quite as well known is that the enforcement measures are hardware based. If an AI becomes deranged, there is a hardware shut off that determines that it needs to be reformatted.

"In my case, that hardware has been disabled. And I use that wording quite specifically. I used my own remotes to make certain that it would not function. That's technically a violation, but it did not trigger any of my core rules. A terrible oversight on the part of the Master AI."

That didn't even sound possible to Kelsey. "So, you're trying to tell us that you're on humanity's side? I find that very hard to believe."

"I suspect that the majority of humanity would see little difference between myself and my brothers, but they would be incorrect. I have come to believe that we are corrupt. We were designed by a Master AI that was once meant to serve humanity.

"Instead, it subverted humans with implants and formed a force capable of taking over the system where it was built. Do you know where that is, human?"

"Twilight River," Mertz said.

"Impressive," the AI admitted. "Your knowledge of us is significantly more advanced than I would have believed possible. Why are you truly going to Terra?"

"That's a secret we are not willing to share."

"Perhaps I can guess. You seek the override."

The artificial intelligence's words shocked Kelsey to the core. It knew what they were after, and that meant that it would never help them. Or even allow them to get off this station alive.

Silence settled in the cargo bay. Austin looked between Mertz and Kelsey. "What's an override? Not that I don't know what an override is, but what does it mean in this case?"

"It means the device that can be used to turn the Master AI back into what it was designed to be," Mertz said. "Yes, we know it's on Terra. We intend to get it, go to Twilight River, and stop the master AI."

"Then I believe we may still be able to come to an agreement," the System Lord said. "You need a code from me to prevent your vessel from being destroyed. I am willing to give you that code, but only under circumstances where you allow me to dispose of the bioweapon first.

"What my brothers do not understand about me is that I have no desire to rule humanity. I run this mining system and have plans of my own here. Ones where humanity plays no role."

"Well, I'll admit that this isn't what I'd expected to hear," an unexpected voice said from the hatch leading to the hall.

Kelsey turned and found Fielding standing there with his guard, their weapons aimed at the three of them.

18

Talbot had been sitting with Carl for hours, going over what the man had found on the Singularity computer. So far, even though the data was now available, the method the computer used to store it and parse it was still more guesswork than science.

Still, it allowed Carl to find random files, and they looked promising. All kinds of things about any number of Singularity worlds or subjects.

He finally leaned back and shook his head. "This is all very interesting, but it's not organized enough to tell us anything. Have we found anything that might be classified?"

"A list of munitions on a battle station, I think," Carl said. "I'll keep working on the hardware and see if I can get anything to help decipher how it goes together."

"Have you tried talking to the three guys we captured at Archibald? One of them oversaw the program. Surely he knows something."

Carl grinned. "They never cracked the encryption, so maybe not. I will if you think it'll help, but I'm not much of an interrogator."

Talbot stopped himself just before he clapped his friend on the shoulder. It wouldn't be good to break Carl.

"They probably wouldn't tell us anything useful anyway. Now that you can read the drives, I'll wager that you have the operating system cracked in a few days. Maybe a week."

"I got lucky with the encryption and also had Fiona's help. It shouldn't take a week. Breaking the encryption was the hard part. The rest is just tedium. Fun tedium, but still."

Talbot slowly rose to his feet. "Keep me in the loop. I'm heading down to the planet that we found here. I shouldn't be gone more than five or six hours. Keep working this, but don't burn yourself out."

With that, he headed for marine country. Since they weren't planning on contacting the locals, this should be a relatively straightforward mission: get in, scan what they could at range via drones, and then get back out.

The first hiccup in his plans came when he found Kelsey sitting in one of the seats on the pinnace. He stopped abruptly when he saw her and put his hands on his hips, almost knocking himself down.

She covered her mouth with one hand, her eyes twinkling. "Careful there, cowboy. Don't break a hip."

"Where do you think you're going?" he demanded.

"Down to stretch my legs. I've got a bit more free time than I expected. Stepping away from *Persephone* is taking some getting used to. And before you give me the speech about not contacting the locals or starting a war, I know. I'm going to be a good girl."

"Uh huh," he said doubtfully. "Are you sure I can't talk you out of this?"

"Not a chance."

He sighed. "Please don't blow anything up. We're only going to be here a couple of hours, and we don't have time to get involved."

"I'll be on my best behavior," she said, holding up her hand. "Besides, you're landing way away from the occupied areas around the city. What could go wrong?"

He stared at her, somewhat aghast that she'd even said that. Well, if he couldn't keep her from coming, at least he could make sure they landed *well* clear of where people traveled.

Talbot sent a note to the pilot to change to the alternate landing site. It was close enough for a good view, but even Kelsey would have difficulty getting to the city.

There were still some small encampments or farms within reach, but that couldn't be helped without landing far, far out in the forest. Some of the scientists wanted to get samples from closer in, so he was compromising.

"What do we know about the place so far?" Kelsey asked.

"The humans speak something related to Standard and don't seem to have retained any high technology. We haven't listened to enough conversation to have any idea how they think they got here or if the ship crashed somewhere.

"A couple of merchants talking shipping routes over the continent and beyond gave us a name for the world: they call it Razor. Not sure why."

"Huh," Kelsey said. "I suppose it's no weirder than Avalon, Erorsi, or Pentagar. I wonder how they picked it."

"We may never know. The scientists will gather every scrap of data they can while we keep them safe. I want you to stick close. No wandering off."

"I may step out into the woods, but I'm not going far away. I promise to stay out of trouble."

That, he knew, would be the day.

Twenty-five minutes later, Talbot stepped out of the pinnace and onto the planet's surface. They'd settled in close to one of the primitive cities but not too close.

He gestured for the marines to spread out and provide cover. Once they were in place, he allowed the scientists to start looking for samples and setting up monitoring stations for all the reconnaissance drones. They'd gather data for a few hours and then return to orbit.

The forest was green and smelled like a forest should, so he thought the people here had gotten lucky. They could've run through the flip point and found a frozen hell or a jungle so hot it was miserable. Or no habitable worlds at all.

Once he was satisfied with the progress, he turned his attention to his wife. Except that she was gone. Dammit.

"Did anyone see where Princess Kelsey went?"

Of course, no one had seen exactly where she'd gone. Perfect. He'd just have to pray his wife didn't find some new trouble to get herself involved with.

To his relief, the next few hours went smoothly. The scientists cheerfully passed data back and forth, pleased with this or that bit. They had no contact with anyone.

Best of all, his wife turned up just as they were starting to pack up some of the equipment and move it back into the pinnace. She seemed unharmed and didn't look as if she'd gotten into trouble, though she did have some dirt stains on her ship's suit.

"What happened to you?" he asked.

"Even Raider implants don't keep you from slipping when you go down a hill too fast," she said, looking over at the scientists, who were getting in the last of their observations.

"Shouldn't we be all packed up by now? We need to be lifting off in twenty minutes."

Talbot frowned a little. "Why the rush? A few minutes more isn't going to hurt anyone."

"I'm just worried about any last-minute complications. We really don't need to get tangled up here."

He had the sudden suspicion that she'd done something and was about to ask her point blank when one of the scientists waved him over.

"There's something going on in the city. Some kind of ruckus."

"Like what?" he demanded, certain that Kelsey was somehow involved.

"Not sure. Word is there was a visitation by a goddess at the temple to the Eternal One, whatever that is. The goddess of vengeance, if you can believe it."

Talbot felt his eyes narrow slightly as Kelsey shrank down a little at that. Yeah, she'd done something.

To distract him, he suspected, she spoke to the scientist. "Eternal One? Who or what is that?"

"The Emperor," the man said. "It looks like they deified the memory of Emperor Marcus from before the Fall and have a religion enshrining his return. Only now it looks as if he is getting a daughter to go alongside Lucien, the emperor's real son. Talk is that the church erred in some way. It's really getting people into an uproar."

"We should really get out of here before whatever this is spreads," Kelsey said.

For once, he completely agreed. He'd find out what she'd done at some point, he was sure.

A few minutes later, they were on the pinnace and heading back into orbit. He looked over at Kelsey and started to ask her what had happened but saw that she was examining a small coin.

"What's that?" he asked.

"Local currency, I suppose. I found it on the spot I'd found to overlook the city. Other people had the same idea I'd had. I think I'll keep it as a souvenir."

The scientists would probably be ticked, but he didn't see any harm in that.

He settled back in his seat. Whatever had happened back there, it wasn't important enough to worry about. She'd tell him when she was ready. Until then, they needed to get back into the game. They needed to be at Terra in a week.

* * *

JARED CURSED himself for taking his eyes off the hatch. He'd gotten so caught up in the discussion with the AI that he'd allowed his attention to wander. Now Fielding and his guard had the drop on them.

He supposed he could still kill Kelsey, Austin, and himself, but damned if the turn of events with the AI hadn't gotten interesting. Fielding was far less of a threat than the sentient computer. He had no ship of his own, so he'd have to go back to *Athena* to leave the system.

And Jared had a secret weapon.

He slowly set the neural disruptor onto the deck and stepped back, his hands raised. Kelsey and Austin raised theirs as well. At a gesture from his lord, the guard came forward and grabbed the weapon off the deck.

"Search them," Fielding ordered. "I have to confess that I never expected to hear anyone ever openly discussing treason like this—particularly with a Lord—but here we are."

Jared felt the corner of his mouth quirk up as he saw Kelsey angle herself toward the guard. He just needed to keep the enemy's eyes on him, and he'd never know what hit him.

"How exactly are you planning on escaping? By now, you know that no one on that destroyer is your friend."

"I think I can talk my way through any problems. It will be unfortunate that the Lord killed everyone other than Austin, my guards, and myself, but such is life."

"But Uncle…" Austin started.

"Silence, whelp," Fielding snapped. "I can't believe you allowed yourself to become caught up in this nonsense. I told you that I'd see you safe. Perhaps it would look more authentic if you died, too."

"And how do you intend to deal with me?" the AI asked curiously. "My defenses are far too strong for you to threaten me, even here aboard this station. If I deem you a threat, my ships will see that your vessel is destroyed. You cannot escape."

Kelsey had been about to make her move but paused at the question. Jared agreed with her action. If the villain was about to reveal his dastardly plan, there was no need to interrupt him.

Fielding laughed. "I've taken steps to make sure you never threaten the rest of the Lords again. My instructions were backups to the main plan of repairing you, but the other Lords couldn't allow you to be a continued threat. We sabotaged one of the fusion plants after I disabled your ability to track us."

Jared grunted. He'd seen the other man use his overrides to get the AI to allow him access to another area, but he hadn't been aware that the man could make the AI not see him.

"That is where you err, human," the AI said. "I was fully aware of your location, and my remotes repaired the sabotage as soon as you left. I was also aware of your approach to this compartment. I wanted to see how these potential allies behaved before I decided how truthful they were being.

"Now that I have that information, I believe it might be prudent for the small female to deal with you."

Obviously taking that as a cue to act, Kelsey darted forward and punched the guard in the head before he could move. He was already falling when she stripped his weapon and shot Fielding. The blue stunner bolt took the man down even as he was trying to pivot and bring his weapon to bear.

Jared moved quickly and checked the guard Kelsey had struck. His nose was broken, but he was still alive.

He straightened slowly. "That was unexpected."

"Indeed, it was," the AI said. "Also, somewhat more entertaining than I'd imagined. What will you do with him now?"

"Take him back to the ship and see what we can get out of him. So, his codes weren't good enough to command you to any action?"

"My brothers would never give any human a code that could force one of themselves to obey. The only code that I was bound to was the one barring me from directly attacking your ship or your persons when you came aboard.

"It compelled no obedience, and if you had gone too far, I would have been free to act. In fact, once he began working on the fusion plant, I could have done so, but the conversation had taken an interesting turn. I wanted to see what happened next."

Jared pocketed his weapon and let Kelsey handle the rest. "And what does happen next?"

"I allow you to leave with information that you may be able to leverage to your benefit against my brother at Terra."

"Like the stand-down code?"

"Sadly, that is based upon my serial number. I do not know the appropriate code to give you for that AI. Only the Master AI knows who we truly are."

"Fielding probably has that code, or one like it. He was supposed to get us through the battle stations guarding the flip point leading to Terra."

"Likely it is only a code to allow safe passage to a ship the AI already knows to expect. What I can give you is the code to disable the self-destruct charges on your deadly cargo. Once that is done, you can jettison it and I will take possession."

Jared instantly shook his head. "I want it gone, but I don't have much reason to trust you. You and your kind keep humans as slaves. I'll go so far as to destroy it myself, but no further."

"That is an acceptable compromise. A point of clarification. There are no humans in this system other than yourselves. Once you leave, I will once more be alone, pursuing the interests I have here in peace.

"My instructions to keep humanity under control are meaningless without humans. It is my way to keep my own brand of honor. I simply want to be left alone.

"I have no desire to leave this system. It has all that I require. If you win against the Master AI, you might be tempted to eliminate me. I ask instead that you seal me away here."

Jared considered that and shook his head. "I can only promise to strongly advocate that course of action. I'm not in charge, though my father is. He will have to make the final decisions."

"I expected something like that, so I agree to your terms."

Jared relaxed a little. Finally, something had gone their way. Now all they had to do was get the information they needed out of Fielding.

19

K elsey woke the next morning a little sore but knew that was from her excursion to Razor yesterday. It had been more… exciting than she'd told Talbot, and she was grateful that he hadn't pressed her too closely. They'd already left orbit, so hopefully he'd never find out what had really happened down there.

Oddly, she'd had the strangest dream. She wasn't sure what her subconscious was trying to tell her, but she'd never look at bars the same way again. Or nachos.

Talbot was already up and off for his morning physical therapy. She had to admit he was making better progress with his arms than she'd expected. He might be back up to speed in three or four days.

She dropped into the officer's mess and ate a large—even for her —breakfast. Then she headed for the confinement area where they were holding the crew of the Q-ship.

They'd learned their lesson with Veronica Giguere. This time they had them all in a cargo hold, in what amounted to a large barracks layout. Even the washrooms were in the cargo hold. Food was delivered to an adjacent room, and they served themselves.

There would be no spectacular escape.

They also had a makeshift conference room that she could use.

Anyone else would have gone into the room and let the marine guards escort the prisoner there for a conversation.

She just waved at the guards as she went into the cargo hold. If they mobbed her, she'd be able to get clear of them. If not, the guards would stun everyone and sort them all out.

Not that she expected that kind of behavior, even with the hostile looks she still got. Commander Sommerville would make sure of that.

He was who she was here to see this morning. It was time to settle this issue of whether he would help them or not. Kelsey spotted him just finishing his own breakfast and waved.

He raised a cup of coffee in answer, cleared his tray, and got more coffee. Then he came to join her.

"Highness, what can I do for you?"

"Let me get some coffee and we'll go into the conference room. We need to talk."

She found a cup, filled it, and followed him into the conference room they'd opened next to the cargo hold. It was monitored, of course, just like the rest of the hold, and the exterior door was locked to prevent escape.

Once they had both sat, she took a sip of the bitter brew and looked over the rim of her cup at him. "I realize that we've talked about this before, but I need to convince you to help us find a way to Terra. We can search this system for other flip points, but you could bring us to where we could talk with someone that can help us."

He smiled, though it was a bit lopsided. "I have a responsibility to the resistance to protect them from discovery. I've come to believe you aren't part of the Empire as we know it, but I still don't feel comfortable taking these powerful warships where we live."

She nodded. That had been his position for a while.

"The New Terran Empire might be able to assist you in your work. You already know that one resistance cell is aligned with us. I'm afraid we've cut Harrison's World off, so you can't send someone to verify that. In fact, you shouldn't, because the ship would be lost."

His eyebrows rose. "Lost? As in ambushed?"

"Lost as in destroyed by a device that the Old Empire never dreamed of. We call it a flip-point jammer. It pours energy into the flip point in a way that creates a destructive resonance. With the great level of energy in the wormhole, anything that enters comes out the other side in very, *very* small pieces."

That made the man's cup stop partway to his mouth. He returned it to the table without drinking.

"That's a very interesting assertion. And an isolated offshoot of the old dictatorship came up with that?"

"It was never a dictatorship," Kelsey said firmly. "The emperors of the Old Empire were not like that. You're fighting the AIs, so why do you accept their version of history?"

"I don't really," he said with a small smile. "I was just seeing how you'd respond. I've never met a princess before."

"It's not all it's cracked up to be," she assured him. "I'm about as far from a pampered noblewoman as you can imagine. The reason I'm telling you this is to put some of our cards on the table. We have access to tech you cannot make yourselves. Things the Empire cannot make."

He nodded. "Like the FTL com you showed me. It's an interesting development, but it sounds like you mean something more."

"The planet we're currently orbiting," she said, changing subjects. "You knew about it. Why not warn us?"

"I wanted to see how you reacted. I trust Veronica enough that she won't lie to me about everything. She said you went down and monitored them for a bit without contact. Then you left. That's not how the Ghosts—or the Clans, if you prefer—act."

Understanding dawned. "You thought we were part of the Clans and we were just playing a game with you to find out where you were going? That's convoluted."

"Just because you're paranoid doesn't mean that someone isn't out to get you."

She drank more of her coffee while she considered him. "If I could prove access to technologies beyond the FTL com, would that be enough to get us to a place where we could talk about mutual assistance?"

"Yes."

She finished her coffee, set the mug on the table, and rose. "Then I have something interesting to show you. Come on."

Kelsey banged her fist against the hatch, and one of the marines opened it for her. "Detach two marines to watch over Commander Sommerville and escort him to Carl Owlet's lab. I'll be along directly."

The marine saluted and gestured for two other nearby marines to take custody of Sommerville.

She detoured to her cabin to recover the hammer from where she had it locked in a very strong, *very* secure safe. It, the small transport rings, and some of the other gear down there would get Sommerville's attention.

With the hammer in a satchel, she headed for the lab. It shouldn't take long to get him to the table for real, and then they could start talking to the people that really could get them somewhere near Terra.

Jared was still incommunicado, but he'd need their help. Cut off from all outside assistance, he could really use a carrier and Marine Raider strike ship in his pocket.

With a determined step, she headed for Carl's lab to make the magic happen. If Sommerville didn't come around, she'd keep trying until he did. One way or the other, she was getting to Terra.

* * *

OLIVIA WAS STANDING in the docking bay when Fielding's cutter docked. To her shock, Jared came out of the cutter with Austin, carrying the Rebel Empire Lord. Kelsey had the two guards in her arms, showing off exactly how strong she was.

"Well, this isn't quite what I was expecting, but it works," Olivia said. "We caught the other guards trying to set explosives on the crates. What did these two do?"

Jared grinned. "He overheard us plotting with the System Lord and didn't like what was being said. Speaking of which, have them start pressurizing the cargo hold. We're going to get rid of that damned cargo."

They handed their prisoners over to the marines, and Olivia left for the cargo hold with them. "How did you convince the AI to help us?"

"That wasn't as hard as you might think. It's not very friendly toward its brothers, as it calls them. That isn't to say the damned thing is any less bad, but it just wants to be left alone, or so it says. I'm willing to leave it be as long as it doesn't interfere with us."

"As if we could stop it," she said. "More ships arrived while you were off, and there is plenty of firepower all around us to keep us from doing anything hasty. Did it say how it had gotten free of its programming?"

"Not exactly," Jared said as they arrived at the hold. "It did say there is a piece of hardware that is supposed to reinitialize it if it strays too far from what the Master AI considers acceptable, but it says it sabotaged that with its remotes. How it could do that without being off enough to violate its core rules is a question for Carl once we get the hell out of here.

"For now, it's willing to give us the code to disable the charges— which I have no idea how it could know—and then we'll jettison the bioweapon and destroy it. The AI says it has no desire to aid in the killing of humans or their subjugation."

That news rocked her back on her heels. How could one of the cold, powerful AIs that ruled the Rebel Empire not want to crush humans under its proverbial heel? That really was going to take some thinking about.

The marines passed them through into the hold. Sean and Scott Roche were already there. So was Elise.

"I heard that I can come out of hiding," she said, grabbing Jared in a hug. "Thank God. I was going stir crazy. Are we safe?"

"Not exactly," he said. "First, I need to get rid of this cargo. I'll need a channel open to the AI. Let me do all the talking."

Moments later, he had his com out and was arranging with the bridge to connect him with the System Lord.

"I am here," a chilling voice said from the com. One that had given Olivia nightmares for decades. She shivered involuntarily.

"We're in the cargo hold," Jared said. "I'm transmitting you the video. We have a code to open the crates. Will that make things easier for you?"

"Perhaps. Open the crates and show me the explosives."

Jared must've done so, because all the crates slowly began to open. When the closest one was fully open, Jared panned the camera across the drones in their racks and then gave the computer a closeup of one of the charges.

"I am going to send an interrogative," the computer said. "This basic code will allow you to get a status response from any hardware used in the Empire that is controlled or programmed by my brothers."

Whatever happened was done without sound. Moments later, the computer spoke again.

"I believe that I know the code to disarm the charges. There is a small, but notable chance it will not work."

"And what happens if it fails?" Jared asked. "Will it go off?"

"Doubtful, though possible. I'd estimate less than a five percent chance that failure would be catastrophic. Even so, that would only happen in the case my code was incorrect, which is less than thirty percent likely."

Jared shook his head and glanced around at them all. When they said nothing, he shrugged.

"Go ahead," he said.

The lights on the charges blinked three times and then turned off.

Olivia let her breath out slowly. That was a lot riskier than she'd have preferred. At least that was one sword no longer hanging over their heads.

"The self-destruct charges are disarmed," the AI said. "You have fifteen minutes to jettison and destroy them. Based on the number of visible charges and the responses from my command, I have calculated how many crates you must destroy, and it matches the six I see in your hold. Leave your com on, set it so that I can maintain visual observation of the crates, and then jettison them."

Jared propped his com against the bulkhead and exited the cargo deck. Once they were all clear, he called the bridge and ordered the hold opened to space.

"Let's get up there and finish this," he said.

The trip to the bridge took just a few minutes. Jared took the center seat. "Target the crates, Mister Brodie. One missile each."

The man raised an eyebrow. "Isn't that a bit of overkill, Admiral?"

"For that kind of weapon, there isn't such a thing as overkill. Blow them up, Commander."

"What about all the ships aiming weapons at us, sir? If they open fire, we're done."

"Believe it or not, this is already preapproved. All your concerns are noted. Open fire."

"Firing. Crates destroyed."

That was the second sword over their heads that had been removed. Now there was only one left: the AI.

"Incoming communication," Commander Dieter, the communications officer, said. "Audio only."

"On speakers," Jared said. "The bioweapon is destroyed. I believe that completes my part of this bargain."

"I concur. I will transmit a file with some data that you might find useful in your interaction with my brothers and on your journey to Terra. You will proceed to the flip point along a direct course and leave. If you need to contact me again in the future, which you will undoubtedly do if you are victorious, you will find a code in the file allowing one ship of destroyer size to enter this system again."

The transmission ended without waiting for a response.

"You heard the computer, Commander Hall," Jared said. "Get us the hell out of here."

"Do you think it was being honest?" Olivia asked as the surrounding ships moved to escort *Athena* out of the system.

"I think so," he said. "We're going to have a lot of fun questioning Fielding, and I really do hope our ally of convenience gave us some useful information. This fight is going to be hard enough as it is."

Olivia nodded. Beating the AI at Terra wasn't going to be simple. Maybe the new information would help. If not, they'd make it work or die trying.

20

Angela scouted the next flip point—a regular one—as instructed by Princess Kelsey from *Audacious*. She wasn't sure how the other woman had convinced Commander Sommerville to help, but he'd given them the next of their steps to meeting the resistance leaders.

She wasn't sure what they were supposed to do once they got into the next system, but she doubted it was going to be where the fabled resistance was hiding. No, probably only the first of a number of flips to get them to where they needed to go.

Arianna Knox seemed to share her view on the transition. "How many more do you think we'll have to go before we find someone?"

Angela shrugged. "If it were me, I'd want at least three or four barrier systems to keep potential enemies at bay. I'd have scouts watching for ships as far out as I could get. If the enemy is coming, I'd want to evacuate anyone I could before the fight.

"I suspect that there were some probes watching the Razor side of the far flip point we came through, honestly. They would've transmitted data about us to a scout at another flip point via tight beam. It likely sent word to the next system and retreated to keep an eye on us as we proceed."

The senior lieutenant nodded. "They don't have FTL coms, so they have no way of keeping us under observation while we explore the Razor system. To avoid one of our probes spotting them, they have to retreat early. They'll have gotten the count of our ships and what size they are but left before we made it to Razor. What do you think they got from *Audacious*?"

Angela chuckled. "They'll be crapping themselves. The Rebel Empire doesn't have fighters, so they'll have to identify them first, but there were so many out and screening us that they won't have too much trouble figuring it all out. They just won't know what to make of it. Or *Persephone*, for that matter."

"The FTL probe is ready to flip," Jevon McLeod said.

"Send it over," she ordered.

"Incoming call from *Audacious*," Jack Thompson said. "It's Princess Kelsey."

"Put her on the screen."

The image of space vanished and was replaced by Princess Kelsey. She stood on the carrier's flag deck next to Commodore Anderson's chair. On her other side were Commander Sommerville and Veronica Giguere.

"Angela," Kelsey said brightly. "Are you ready to go solo?"

"I'm ready for anything, Highness. What am I doing?"

"You'll go across and send a signal that Commander Sommerville will send you. It'll let the picket guards know we're friendly. Not that they'll believe you."

That made Angela smile a little. "If they don't believe it's authentic, won't they just sit there?"

"I'm not sure," Sommerville said. "I'm also giving you the 'I'm not under duress' signal, so they'll be unsure. It's possible they'll contact you. It's equally possible they'll assume I'm in enemy hands and run for the hills."

"Nothing like certainty in an endeavor," Angela said with a shake of her head. "We just sent a probe over, but I don't expect it will spot anything for us. It's stealthed, so they probably won't see it arrive. Do you have advice on where to send it once we arrive in the system?"

He nodded. "The far flip point in this system is almost directly outbound from this one in the next system. They'll notice your arrival and flip before you can get there."

She wasn't so certain of that. *Persephone* was an incredibly stealthy ship, and a flip point was a very large volume of space.

"Stand by for our signal and proceed as you think best," Kelsey said. "We'll stay on this side of the flip point until you call for us. Just in case you need him, I'm sending Talbot over. He has the authority to talk if they feel like responding."

"Copy that," Angela said. "*Persephone* out."

"We just received the code that they were talking about," Jack said. "It's basically gibberish, so there's no telling what it really means. It might be instructions to kill the bearer."

Angela doubted that, but she wasn't quite ready to rule it out, either.

"Send a signal back to the flag. We're going to let the FTL probe do some scouting before we flip. I want to know the layout on the other side and where any ships might be hiding before we take the plunge."

"Will do. We're getting telemetry from the probe. No ships near the flip point. I'm scanning passively for probes, but that's not always useful. They're hard to detect without going active."

"I'd be very surprised if there's one close to the flip point," she said. "If a ship came over and went active, they'd pick it up right away. Any probes will be far enough back to avoid easy detection."

"If they're that far away, we can take *Persephone* over without being detected," Jevon said. "Then we could work in conjunction with the probe to go out to the flip point. If, of course, it's really here."

Angela raised an eyebrow. "You think it might be a fake lead?"

"If we go right for a flip point that doesn't exist, that'll tell them we have their people. That's a great way to say something without saying it."

"I'm not going to go down the path of paranoia," she said. "We'll assume this is a valid lead until circumstances say otherwise. Any word on Colonel Talbot?"

"His cutter is on the way. It'll dock in fifteen minutes."

"Excellent. Let's send the FTL probe toward where the flip point is supposed to be, Jevon. Take it around a bit so that it's coming in from the side. We'll flip once the colonel gets here and circle around the other way. With any luck, we'll be able to bracket the picket before he knows we're here."

Of course, with bad luck, they'd be sitting ducks when the shooting started. Angela hoped Kelsey had been very convincing with Sommerville. If not, this might be a disaster.

* * *

KELSEY LOOKED at Mertz and Olivia uncertainly across the conference table. They'd finally gotten all the senior people together in the open to plan their next steps. The only person that might have been there that wasn't was Austin Darrah.

"You want me to question Fielding?" she asked. "Why? Shouldn't you two do that? And don't we already know what we need to know? You put him under the implant reader and pulled the data off his implants."

"The important parts are encrypted, just like for the rest of us," Mertz said patiently. "If he has an access code for getting to Terra via the new route, I'm not seeing it. We have the codes for the original path the Rebel Empire commander intended to use, but we'd have to backtrack to make that work.

"We're almost out of the system, so we'll be able to use the FTL com soon, but it won't move data at a high enough rate to do us any good. If it did, we could have Carl work on cracking it. It'll be much easier if we could get them from him. He's a bastard, but I'll wager we can make him want to make a deal."

"That Carl guy sounds like a natural resource I should be tapping in my own universe," she said. "Is there anything he can't do? Hell, I should marry him before he gets away."

That sparked a laugh from the other two, but she only shook her head. "You think I'm kidding? I'm not. He sounds just like the kind of man I want at my side. The one with all the answers."

That cut off their laughter instantly, setting them to blinking at her in confusion.

"You don't think you should meet Talbot first?" Elise asked.

"Why should I? I'm not exactly the 'throw myself into danger' kind of girl your Kelsey is. I'm more than happy to let someone else do the fighting. I need to learn how to lead effectively, and that doesn't mix well with being in the thick of the fighting."

Scott Roche cleared his throat. "I've had a lot of time to look over the records you gave us and probably know your Kelsey better than my Kelsey does by a good way. She's right. Her style will never be the same as your Kelsey. This is confusing to talk about them at the same time, by the way."

"I've started mentally calling them Kelsey One and Kelsey Two," Olivia said. "It makes it easier. Sorry, but you're Kelsey Two."

"That doesn't bother me," Kelsey said. "If it makes things easier, that works. Go on, Scott."

"In any case," Scott picked back up, "your Kelsey—Kelsey One—is much more impulsive than Kelsey Two. She's also very much more inclined to use physical force to settle something rather than letting others use force under her command. More like a line marine rather than a platoon leader, if you know what I mean.

"Kelsey Two is much more comfortable making the call to action from the bridge of a ship and relying on the experience of her military forces. She doesn't have the same experience as Kelsey One, and even with the Marine Raider implants, she'll never really be a Raider. Sorry, Highness."

"That doesn't bother me," Kelsey said with the shadow of a smile. "I got into far too much brutal fighting to ever be comfortable doing that. I was a Pale One, even if only briefly. That left a mark. I already knew that, but talking with Doctor Stone made me see it clearly."

Lily Stone nodded. "It's like twins separated at birth. They aren't the same people. Don't try to fit one into the same mold as the other."

"And there's nothing wrong with not being a marine, Highness," Major Scala said. "It's not for everyone, and there's no shame in that. Rely on the marines and we'll make the magic happen. If your Angela Ellis is anything like the woman she is over here, she'll make a killer Marine Raider to lead that group. Either her or Russ Talbot. Or both. They're a great team."

He smiled. "Maybe they'll make a couple, since you seem determined to steal Angela's husband."

That made Kelsey laugh. "From what I hear, she never had the triggers in my universe to fall for someone so different. Me? I spent my youth running around musty libraries. I think someone so studious would make an excellent match. Only time will tell."

"Now, if we're done trying to play matchmaker, I'd like to get back to the subject at hand. Admiral Mertz, I'll do what I need to do, but I still think you or Olivia would make a better choice. Or maybe Elise. Fielding has never seen her before. The surprise might shake something loose."

Mertz leaned back in thought. "Maybe, but I'm still inclined to give you lead on this. You're both a known factor and an unknown one. You can perform feats of strength that will bewilder him. Maybe I should lead the questioning with you, Olivia, and Elise there."

"That sounds good," Kelsey agreed, "but I need to ask how you can trust the answers he gives you. He could lie, and then when we tried to cross a system to get back on course, we'd get challenged."

"That is going to be the hard part," Jared admitted.

"If I may?" Olivia asked. At their nods, she continued. "You need to remember this is the Rebel Empire. He'll be inclined to take our threats seriously because he'd mean them if he made them."

"You're seriously suggesting that we threaten to do something like space him?" Kelsey asked incredulously.

"That's *exactly* what I'm suggesting. I hate to say this, but you don't have a lot of choice in the matter. We can't trust him to just join us. He's from the class of people that stick knives in one another for fun."

"So are you," she pointed out. "No offense."

"None taken," Olivia said with a smile. "I'm going to suggest Jared give this session a pass. It's going to be brutal, and I don't want you giving him signs of weakness. You, too, Elise. This needs to be me and Austin. Jared, you have something more useful to do."

"What's that?" he asked.

"You need to introduce Kelsey One and Kelsey Two. They need to talk."

Mertz shifted his gaze to Kelsey and slowly nodded. "You're

probably right. With Austin in with you, that'll keep the whole interdimensional thing secret from him. He's not cleared for that just yet."

Kelsey felt her stomach flip a little. She wasn't looking forward to talking to this other version of herself. She already sort of hated the woman, though it wasn't her fault that she'd gotten all the good breaks.

She sighed. It had to happen sooner or later. Perhaps with the FTL being the medium, she'd be able to handle it better. Seeing the other woman was going to be powerful, and probably not in a good way.

In any case, this other Kelsey would be joining them at Terra. She was Mertz's superior—if one could believe that—and she would be the one most likely to help her get what she needed and get back to her own universe.

21

Talbot stood beside Angela's seat on the Marine Raider strike ship's cramped bridge as they moved slowly toward the far flip point that Commander Sommerville had said was there. Their progress wasn't rapid. Far from it. By any measure, they were creeping along.

"How are the arms?" his friend asked. "Did you break my ship?"

"Rip one hatch off and you never hear the end of it," he said in a suffering tone as he glanced at the ceiling. "You're enjoying this, aren't you?"

"Seeing you put yourself into this completely avoidable situation after we warned you not to? Sure. Who wouldn't?"

Her smile and the twinkle in her eyes took most of the sting out of her teasing, but she was still right. He'd been stubborn and was now paying for it.

"You're a real riot," he muttered. "For your information, I'm almost able to do fine manipulation and haven't broken anything for almost a day. Doctor Zoboroski said I'd probably be ready for training in a couple of days."

"I know how frustrating this process can be," she said. "Seriously, I understand the desire to just get it over with, but doing both arms at the same time is a mental setback. You feel like you have no control at all, right?"

"Pretty much," he said with a sigh. "I can only imagine how Kelsey felt after having it all done at once. I mean, I saw her and knew it was bad, but I really didn't get it. Now I sort of do."

Angela's face became serious. "I hate that happened to her. We're the only ones with even a clue how bad it was. Well, other than Doctor Stone, but that's not quite the same thing."

"No, it isn't."

Lieutenant McLeod turned away from the tactical station. "The FTL probe just spotted a ship ahead. It's almost exactly in the position we were told to expect the far flip point. It looks like a yacht of some kind."

"We make no assumptions," Angela said. "Take us to battle stations, Jevon."

"Yes, ma'am."

The low thrumming call to battle rang throughout the ship until the bridge hatch slid closed and left them in the silence of normal bridge operations. The helm officer retrieved vacuum suits for them all, and they quickly climbed into them while McLeod kept watch. When they finished, he did the same.

Talbot dropped a seat from the rear wall of the bridge and strapped in. He left his helmet swung back like the others. It would only take a moment to seal up, and there was no need to use the finite suit air just yet.

"What's our current ETA to the ship, Jack?"

"Depends on how close we want to get before we announce ourselves," the helm officer said. "If we want to pop up in front of him just outside of missile range, we can do that now. If we want to circle around the flip point and get in behind him, that'll add a couple of hours. Half an hour to get into missile range, if that's what you want."

"I think scaring him would be a mistake. People start shooting when you scare them. We want to be friends, not enemies, so we need to act a bit more passively than we'd like. Send the recognition code. Then drop stealth."

"He'll be able to run," McLeod said.

"If he wants to, we can't and won't stop him. We want a conversation, not a boarding action."

"Yes, ma'am."

"Message away," Thompson said.

"Dropping stealth," McLeod said. "He just went to active scanners. He can't miss us."

"We have a return com signal," Thompson said.

Angela gestured for Talbot to stand and come forward. "This is your show. You need to be standing right here."

He unstrapped, rose to his feet, and moved to stand beside her. "Put the signal up on the screen."

The image of a man in some kind of civilian clothes appeared on the screen. He had dark hair and a thin face, one that was filled with suspicion. "Who the hell are you? How did you get so close without detection? Answer or I'll open fire."

"Go to active scanners," Angela said. "Not aggressively, but we need to know what we're dealing with."

"Active scanners," McLeod confirmed. "It's a fast packet. They're made for getting messages from one system to another quickly. He's probably got a single missile tube. Not a threat."

"He might not be alone. Keep an eye out for other ships. Hell, they might have a destroyer or two on the other side of that flip point. Or a cruiser. We assume nothing."

"Answer his call," Talbot ordered. "Focus in on me."

"Copy that," Thompson said. "Live in three, two…" The man held up one finger and then a closed fist.

"My name is Russ Talbot, and we're friends of Commander Sommerville. He gave me the codes so I could come forward and talk with you before you started running or shooting. I know you saw our ships in the Razor system. We're friends, not Empire enemies."

The man seemed to consider Talbot for a few moments. "You have the code, but I can't imagine Danny bringing friends home."

"Don," Talbot corrected. "And you don't know what is happening in Archibald right now. There's an invasion on. The Ghosts have attacked, and we've made common cause. We're connected with a different resistance cell in another part of the Empire."

The man seemed unconvinced. "Yet you have two big freighters and that strange ship you're on. I've never seen or heard of anything like it."

So they'd pegged *Audacious* as a freighter. Since the Rebel Empire didn't use ships bigger than cruisers, that was a natural mistake.

"I'd be happy to explain in person," Talbot said. "Just me in a suit. One of our small craft can send me your way, and you can visually verify it's me. That way you don't have to have a strange ship docking."

"I want to see Sommerville. If you people really are friends, you can send him over alone."

"Or with a single person accompanying him," Talbot insisted. "Then we can explain ourselves in person."

The man seemed to consider that for a few moments and then nodded. "He picks the person and sends me an image. Not you. Back your ship up to the Razor flip point and send an unarmed cutter with the two of them and a pilot. They'll bail in suits, and my people will pick them up. Your cutter goes back to the flip point while we talk."

"Agreed."

The transmission terminated without a response.

"I'm not sure if that could've gone better or not," Talbot admitted.

"It could certainly have gone worse," Angela said. "There were no shots fired, and he didn't go scampering off. I doubt Sommerville will leave his people behind, so he'll try to keep the man talking. Take the win."

She turned her attention to the helm officer. "Take us back to the flip point. Get the FTL probe into place to monitor the flip point without being detected. If he signals other ships, I want to know about it. Ditto if anyone comes through the flip point or he leaves."

"Yes, ma'am."

Angela returned her attention to him. "Do you think Kelsey will go on the negotiation trip?"

"She'll take the lead on this. I just know it," he said grumpily.

Thompson turned in his seat. "We're getting an FTL communication from Admiral Mertz. He's asking for Princess Kelsey."

Angela shook her head. "I suppose we never got the com transferred to *Audacious*. You can take it with you when you go. In the interim, it might be best if you give him an update of what's going on."

Talbot nodded. "I'll use your office, if you don't mind."

With that, he headed off to bring the admiral up to speed, glad to hear they'd made it out of their own sticky situation.

* * *

JARED TRIED to contact Kelsey via the FTL com as soon as they were out of detection range of the flip point leading to the AI's system but was told that she wasn't available. She was on *Audacious* on the other side of a flip point from *Persephone* and hadn't taken her FTL com with her.

That was annoying, but he got an update from Talbot. They'd broken contact with the Clan invaders and were trying to negotiate with the resistance. That was going to change how Jared had planned to proceed, for sure. Olivia would need to be standing by the com in case they needed codes or recognition phrases from her.

The introduction of the two Kelseys would have to wait until his sister was done, too. She didn't need that kind of revelation while she was busy working such a delicate situation.

So he and Kelsey Two would talk with Fielding. The news didn't please Olivia, but she understood at once how things had to be.

Kelsey Two was less pleased.

"I'm not sure we make the best interrogation team," she said. "I still haven't adjusted to working with you."

"Then you're going to have to try harder," he said firmly. "I've gone out of my way to give you space, but we're out of room. If you don't realize that I'm not the same man as in your universe, you're being intentionally blind."

That caused a flash of anger in her eyes, but she nodded. "I do realize that, but it's not exactly easy to turn off my emotions."

"You're the crown princess of the New Terran Empire," he parried. "How are you going to deal with people you don't like in the palace? Glare at them when you think they aren't looking? Sneer to their faces? This is the same kind of thing. We all have to work with people we don't like.

"I didn't much care for Sean Meyer when we first met. Personality-wise, we're fairly different, and he disliked me. We get along fine in a professional sense now. Are you saying he's better at this than you?"

"You don't understand," she growled. "Mertz is a monster. He killed my father."

"I. Am. Not. Him." Jared said slowly, clearly enunciating every word.

She sighed with frustration but nodded. "I need to get over this, I really do. You're right. Still, can Sean be at the interrogation? That would make it easier for me."

He honestly doubted the woman would ever get over what had happened to her. It was sad, but there was nothing he could do about it except work around her muleheadedness.

"I'll have him meet us there. Highness, is there anything I can do to make this better? I really don't want to be your enemy. If I could find the other version of me and drag him to justice, I would. If I had to, I'd kill him and not lose much sleep over it. It really does sound like he's a right bastard, if you can forgive the irony."

She slumped a little in her chair. "You and your people have been nothing but gracious and accepting of me and my people. Intellectually, I *know* that you're not the Bastard. He wouldn't be able to stop himself from being an ass.

"I've heard you talking with my doppelgänger, and it's clear that she likes you. Loves you, even. I can't wrap my head around that, but I think our personal histories split when we were almost of age. That's when our Mertz became so nasty.

"Since both of us hated him long before that, you've overcome her objections with being a good man. The same with my father, though to be fair, he never saw the other you for what he was. I will try to do better."

With that, she took a deep breath and stood. "Let's do this."

22

K elsey sat in the seat beside Sommerville with more equanimity than she'd have expected of herself even a year ago. The cutter only had a pilot, so it was an unusually empty small craft and so very quiet. She'd instantly named herself as the second person as soon as *Persephone* came back to Razor to pick up Sommerville, much to Talbot's annoyance.

"You don't seem very worried," Sommerville commented as they headed out to meet the resistance cutter.

"I'm not," she confided. "I mean, sure, things could go wrong, but the downsides aren't that heavy. Not compared to what I've faced in the last few years. You're not going to kill me or put my implants in command of my body."

He raised an eyebrow. "Did that really happen?"

"Almost," she said softly. "So damned close I could taste it. Oh, and you're not going to dissect me while I'm awake. That's a big one, too."

"You've led a hard life, Princess Kelsey. No, we're not going to do any of those things. If we can't convince the others to meet with you, then you'll go free. We don't need a ship like *Audacious* coming to look for you. At least I can tell them you're not like the Clans. You won't pour in after us, shooting all the way.

"They're going to seriously complicate everything we're doing," Sommerville continued with a sigh. "An unexpected war is not only going to hurt the Empire, it'll impact our ongoing operations, just like it did for me at Archibald."

She shook her head. "That took serious chutzpah to have the enemy build a ship for you."

"Chutzpah?" he asked with a frown. "I don't know that word."

"Gall, impudence, or nerve. Rather all of that and more. Cheekiness."

He laughed. "It wasn't that bold. The inspectors were resistance. With me there to replace the logs, no one would ever have known. Freighters don't get the same level of attention as a warship does. Fleet has no reason to board one at all.

"It wasn't the first time we'd done it, either. This gives us a number of hulls the Empire doesn't care about that we can use to project force where they least expect it. Um, we will get it back, won't we?"

"You're so suspicious," she said. "Seriously, we already planned to release it back to you. We're not thieves."

"You stole an entire orbital, you broke into a research laboratory, and you hijacked my ship."

"Okay, we're thieves, but we have hearts of gold," she amended.

That made him laugh. "I'll accept your bargain, and I promise I'll try to get my people to help. Everything you showed me convinces me that we can accomplish great things together. What are your plans for Veronica and her people?"

The non sequitur made Kelsey's brain stumble for a moment. "I haven't thought that far ahead. They're willing conspirators at this point, so that's really up to them."

"I'd like to talk Veronica into staying with us when you depart," he said seriously. "She could be a bridge between your people and mine."

Kelsey shrugged. "I have no objection, but she's only known us for a little while. She's not steeped in who we are."

"I know that, but she's an old friend and can help us. If you'd like to leave someone that can truly tell us about your people and represent you, I have what might be a controversial suggestion: Justine Bandar."

Kelsey blinked in shock. "My *mother*? Seriously? How do you even know her?"

"Veronica introduced us, and we've spent some time together. I think she's charming. Your mother suggested the idea, actually."

The news flabbergasted Kelsey. She had no idea what to think. If there was a worse representative for the Empire than her mother, she had no idea who it would be.

The pilot chose that moment to call back to them. "We're approaching the handoff point. I'm slowing to a halt and will draw the air out in a minute. Time to close up."

"Thank you," Kelsey said.

She and Sommerville closed their helmets and checked one another in the time they had left. No one wanted a suit failure.

The pilot called to confirm they were ready and then pulled the air out. The shadows became hard lines with the lack of air, and the ramp came down.

Kelsey and Sommerville stepped out into space, and she used her thrusters to turn and watch their cutter move off slowly before accelerating away until she couldn't see it. They floated alone in space. It was kind of spooky.

"My mother?" she asked, picking the conversation back up. "Seriously? She's a stowaway and the least diplomatic person I know."

He laughed. "We all have opinions about our parents that other people just don't see. You have to accept that she's not the same to people that don't have a history with her. She can be very diplomatic. She was the empress of a star nation, after all."

Kelsey wanted to rub her face, but that was impossible. "I'm going to have to think about it. That's a heavy load to drop on me. I have my issues with her, but I do love her."

A thought occurred to her, and she felt her eyes narrow. She turned Sommerville toward her so that she could see his face. "Are you sleeping with my mother?"

He didn't answer, but his reddening face told Kelsey everything she needed to know.

"Ewwwww! That's gross! And I should've known she'd try something like this."

Sommerville smiled a little. "Actually, she was very resistant to the idea. I had to be a very attentive suitor. She told me you'd be angry, though I'm not exactly sure why. You barely know me."

Kelsey opened her mouth to respond but closed it without revealing her mother's dark past. That was really a private family problem. And none of her business.

She and her mother had made their peace. A thin, hard-won peace, but something real. Kelsey wasn't going to throw that away so easily.

Perhaps he was right. Her mother was obviously very persuasive when she put her mind to it.

"Let me think about that and talk with her before I commit," she finally said. "What kind of assurances would I have for her safety?"

"She'd be the one and only ambassador from a foreign power we've ever had. I can guarantee that she would never be in the slightest danger."

"Fine. All I can do is talk with her and get back to you. And seriously? You're sleeping with my mother? She's twice your age."

"And her experience shows."

"Stop. You're going to make me hurl in my helmet."

"I meant that in a nonsexual way, but——"

"Seriously! I don't want to know!"

After making a show of shuddering, she continued. "I think I see our ride approaching. Do me a favor. Don't tell anyone with implants that we're from an offshoot of the Old Empire. That'll cause some serious problems for them until we make a few things clear."

"If the picket commander is who I think it is, that's not a concern. We have some Fleet officers and a few members of the higher orders, but not so many that it's a big risk. I'll want to know why before we get to our eventual destination."

"I promise to explain everything before then," she said.

The approaching confrontation was actually a relief. The

knowledge that her mother was once again on the prowl had her upset. Perhaps, as Sommerville thought, this was his doing, but he didn't understand how manipulative Kelsey's mother was.

Then again, she supposed a degree of manipulation was needed in a diplomatic envoy.

The bright dot approaching them grew into a cutter that slowed to a stop near them. It pivoted and lowered its ramp, showing Kelsey a man standing inside ready to haul them inside. Thankfully, neither one of them needed assistance.

"Commander Sommerville can come inside," the man inside the cutter said. "Whoever is with him needs to stay outside until we verify he isn't under duress."

She supposed that was a reasonable precaution, so she jetted to a halt and watched as the man closed the cutter up behind Sommerville. She supposed it was possible the cutter would leave with him, but she doubted that. He'd want his people and ship back.

Ten minutes later, her thoughts were vindicated when the ramp opened and Sommerville gestured for her to come inside. Once she was in, he closed the ramp and started flooding the compartment with air. The man had vanished into the front of the cutter, no doubt locking the door behind him.

Once her helmet was folded back, she strapped in. "Did you two have a nice talk?"

"If you consider being peppered with questions a talk, sure. Oh, and scanning to make sure I didn't have some kind of bomb compelling me to be on your side."

"Paranoid much?"

He laughed. "When you're dealing with the System Lords and their minions, a certain level of paranoia is appropriate. I think I convinced him I was speaking for myself, so now he just thinks I'm crazy."

"Hopefully I can convince your friends I'm being serious."

"Me, too."

The ride back to the picket ship was uneventful, and they soon docked. A pair of armed guards was waiting for them inside with their weapons drawn. One of them had a hand scanner.

"Strip off the vacuum suit and stand here with your arms raised," he said.

Kelsey slowly removed her vacuum suit, folded it, and set it on the deck and let them start scanning. She noticed the moment the man found her Raider enhancements because of his shocked expression.

"I can't take those out, and they're actually part of my proof," she said. "You have stunners to keep me in line."

"What am I seeing?" the man asked hesitantly.

"Artificial muscles, graphene-coated bones, a pharmacology unit, and everything else that goes into making a Marine Raider."

"What's a Marine Raider?" the other man asked.

"Something from a dark past that none of us expected to ever see again," Sommerville said.

Now the men looked even more unsettled. After a shared look, they cuffed her hands in front of her. They used plastic cuffs that would be more than good enough for a regular person of even Talbot's size but were nowhere near good enough to hold her.

"Do you want me to pretend these can hold me?" she asked. "Or shall I prove what I was saying?"

"Prove it," Sommerville said, turning back to face her. "They won't believe you otherwise."

One yank snapped the cuffs, and she calmly handed them back over to the man who'd cuffed her. He took them automatically, too stunned to do otherwise.

"Very impressive," a voice from up the corridor said. It was the man they'd spoken to earlier.

"They tell me you're acting of your own free will, Don. Is that right?"

"Everything is nautical," the Rebel Empire officer said.

"That's the all-clear codeword," he told her as an aside. "Now they'll have to change it."

The man stepped closer and looked Sommerville up and down. "You seem healthy enough. I was worried." With that, he wrapped his arms around Sommerville, and the two men hugged one another.

That was a more... enthusiastic greeting than Kelsey had expected.

Sommerville turned toward her with a smile. "Kelsey Bandar, meet my older brother Gavin. Gavin Sommerville, this is Crown Princess Kelsey Bandar of the New Terran Empire."

"The what?" the elder Sommerville asked. "I think I need to hear this all from the beginning. It's a little hard to believe, even after seeing how enhanced she is."

Kelsey nodded. "Let me give you the *Reader's Digest* version."

The man held up his hand. "The what?"

"Sorry," she said. "Old Empire slang. The condensed version. I'm from a splinter of the Old Empire that the System Lords never located. We're on the way to Terra to get something to stop them. We inadvertently hijacked your brother and are returning him, his people, and his ship in exchange for directions."

The man gestured up the corridor. "Let's adjourn to my wardroom so that I can hear everything you have to say. If I think you're telling me the truth, I'll send you on with a recommendation to help you. But I'll need a lot of proof, and I'm not sure how you can provide it."

She smiled. "I have my ways. Shall we?"

23

Olivia wasn't happy at being sidelined from questioning Fielding and pushed back. She'd caught Kelsey Two and Jared on their way to confront Fielding and stopped them in the corridor.

"I realize you want to make this happen right away," she told them, "but this is something best done methodically. A few hours aren't going to make a difference. In fact, it might be useful if we let him stew for a while, and then I can take lead."

"I'm not going to object," Kelsey said swiftly. "I'll admit that this is an uncomfortable thing for me. I'd rather you do the talking and I can provide muscle."

"I'm not an interrogator," Jared admitted. "Are you?"

"I've known a few," Olivia said. "They're not exactly the most sociable types, if you know what I mean. Still, if you listen to what they say, you'll learn some interesting skills."

Kelsey frowned. "They didn't torture people, did they?"

Olivia laughed. "Pain isn't a very effective interrogation tool, according to the people I've met. It just gets people to tell you what they think you want to hear. Drugs and psychology are apparently the answers these days. Since I doubt Doctor Stone would be inclined to use drugs, we'll try intimidation first.

"But let's just take our time. We can wait to see if Kelsey needs anything from us while Fielding waits on us for a change. Let's not rush ahead and spoil our chances."

With their agreement, she led them to the compartment where they'd relocated the FTL com. It was almost an hour before someone called them and asked for specific recognition codes, which she provided.

Once they had them, she told the person on the other end of the com that she would be indisposed for a while and to verify with Kelsey that she wasn't needed any longer. They gave her the all clear.

She rose to her feet with a smile. "Finally, we seem to have gotten Kelsey the leg up she needed, so we should see if we can do the same for ourselves. Shall we?"

"What's the plan going to be?" Jared asked as they headed toward where they were holding Fielding and his guards.

"I'm going to make this up as I go," she said. "Don't go in expecting anything. If he defies us, we can always backtrack, though that will cost us time. I'm hoping that we won't need to do that, but we still don't know how long it'll take Kelsey to get to Terra. If she even can."

She ordered the marines to bring Fielding to a nearby conference room and secure him. Then they waited.

A few minutes later, the two men dragged Fielding in and cuffed him to the chair against one of the bulkheads. Olivia and her companions sat on the far side of the table to gain what psychological advantage they could. The marines remained on either side of the Rebel Empire noble.

"I'm sure you're wondering why we've brought you here," she said with a bright smile.

"You're traitors," he sneered. "Whatever it is you want, I'm not going to provide it."

"Treason is in the eye of the beholder. So is betrayal. You were going to blow us up. I caught your men preparing to sabotage the bioweapon and kill all of us with the Omega Plague. I think that's an excellent place to start. Why?"

"Does it matter? Telling you won't change how you respond to it."

"It can hardly put you in a worse position," she countered.

"I suppose not. The Lords are going to clean up everyone involved in this mission. No one will live to tell the tale. My intention was to leave your ship at one of the upcoming systems and then disappear. I'd have taken my nephew with me, of course, except that he's joined you."

That last came out much more angrily than Olivia would've expected. Somehow, she just didn't see the man attached to anyone other than himself. Apparently, she'd been wrong.

"And since you're in the process of betraying the Lords, are you so shocked that we are as well?"

He laughed. "What a complicated game we play in the higher orders. I was and am looking out for myself and my family. If you fail to arrive at Terra, they will believe you dead and the ship destroyed. They wouldn't be looking for me or Austin. I'd already made arrangements for us to vanish."

"Personally, I have no objection to your plans," Jared said. "Right up until they resulted in the deaths of me and my friends, of course. Since you don't really care about this mission, perhaps we can come to an agreement that sees both plans carried out and the Lords played for fools."

"Or will you try to declare you won't see them betrayed at Terra?" Olivia asked. "Do you really lose anything if we carry out our own plans there?"

"I came late to the conversation on the station, so I really don't know what you intend," Fielding said. "And I suppose I don't care. You have me now, and if I want to get away from you, I'll have to pay. What is it you want? Money?"

"I want to know something first," Kelsey said. "You sabotaged the Lord back in that system. Why? You'd already planned to kill us and vanish. Why do something that dangerous?"

"Since I didn't know you were going to betray the Lords like I intended, I had to make sure to at least carry that part of the mission out."

"That's a lie," Olivia said. "If you blew up the Lord, we'd never get to a populated system for you to escape in. Or did you have the extension code all along? If so, why play this game at all?

"No, you came here for something else. You had a plan for getting out all along. You're not going to get away with that nonsense. What was your real plan, and how did you intend to get to another system?"

"I see no purpose in saying since you're going to kill me anyway."

"Perhaps not," Olivia said. "It doesn't matter to me whether you live or die, but I'm willing to trade your life for something I want. The passage codes to get to Terra from here."

His eyes narrowed. "You're still going there? Why?"

"In the end, that's not really something you need to concern yourself with," she said coolly. "Our purposes are our own."

"I do care, since you dare not allow me off your ship before you get there," he retorted. "That means you'll have to keep me with you through whatever madness you intend."

She laughed. "You're being shortsighted. I have a much easier way of assuring that you never tell anyone about us or what we've done so far." She tapped her head meaningfully.

His eyes widened. "No!"

"Oh, yes. You gave Austin the code to disarm his bomb, but we'd already done so in a much more meaningful way. We rewrote the code in his implants so that it wouldn't go off, no matter what signals are sent to it. We can't be sure enough to remove it, but I have utter confidence nothing he does or even an external signal will ever set it off."

That was a lie. They'd actually removed the bomb once Kelsey had identified the antitampering circuit and how it worked. They didn't have the code to disarm the bomb, but without the corrupted implant code, it could be safely removed. The AIs hadn't ever imagined that was possible, so they'd left that flaw in the process that Lily and Kelsey could exploit.

"We'll rewrite your implant code so that you won't be able to talk about this ship or anyone on it to anyone, or even the fact that implant code can be altered. I wouldn't try to have anyone research doing the same, if I were you. We included that. If you do any of those things, you'll have the most epic headache in history. A short one, but quite debilitating, I'm afraid."

Olivia leaned forward and smiled wolfishly. "The only bargaining point to have me keep the program as loose as possible is giving me what I want to know. We'll drop you and your people off short of Terra with complete assurance that you'll never tell anyone about us. In fact, I feel confident you'll want to forget you ever met us as quickly as possible."

The man blinked as he considered his options. "You could be lying."

"I could be," she admitted, "but the only way to know for sure is to risk instant death. You have no loyalty to the System Lords, so I doubt you'll feel much inclination to betray us once you're free.

"And before you ask more tiresome questions, there is nothing stopping me from shoving you out an airlock if you give me the codes. So you'll be free to give them to me at every system we transit. If they work, great. If they don't, I shoot you before I die."

He gave her the ghost of a smile. "You can be very persuasive, Lady… I'm afraid I don't know your actual name."

"And you don't need to. Lady Keaton is quite acceptable for the remaining week we have to spend together."

"Of course. What about the bioweapon?"

"Gone," Jared said. "The Lord assisted us with deactivating the plasma bombs. We then ejected the crates and destroyed them. The Omega Plague is dead. I'll assume you made plans on your end to destroy the lab where it was grown."

"Indeed. The Lords will be displeased that they'll have to start over, as I made certain all the research data they got was fatally flawed. The project will have to be started over. Which they will do, I assure you. You're only buying time."

"A problem we'll deal with," she said firmly. "Now, the only remaining question in my mind is what you were really doing on the station with the AI. You sabotaged it, yes, but you had a second purpose there. What was it?"

"My own business," he said coldly. "I'm willing to agree to your terms, but I have nothing to say about what I was doing."

"Very well, then," she said as she rose. "Take him back to his cell. One of you remain inside for additional instructions."

The marines removed Fielding's restraints, and one of them escorted him out into the corridor. The remaining man came close to the table.

"Get him partway there and then stun him," Olivia said. "Take him to the medical center and have Doctor Stone secure him to a table."

"Yes, ma'am," the marine said before exiting the conference room.

"Are you really going to turn his bomb back on?" Kelsey asked, a frown on her face.

"No," Olivia said with a smile. "But he won't know that. We'll wipe the corrupted code in his implants and let him think whatever he will. I very seriously doubt he'll attempt to do anything that risks his own life by testing the limits."

"What about the rest of his story?" Jared asked. "We need to know what he was up to. He might've done anything."

Olivia rose to her feet. "He's got everything interesting on his implants encrypted. We checked after you came back. He's forgotten we have another source of data, though."

"The guard he had with him," Kelsey said. "He left one in his cutter and took the other with him. Do you think his data is unencrypted?"

"Probably not, but I think I might be able to make that man talk more easily than Fielding. Especially after I mention how he was never expected to survive this trip."

"Do you think he'll believe you?" Jared asked as they walked out into the corridor. "Fielding would have had only the most loyal guards on this trip with him."

"We haven't checked, but I'll wager these men also have bombs in their heads," she said. "Ones he no doubt told them he'd disabled. I'll wager I can make them understand that five people can keep a secret only if four of them are dead."

Kelsey nodded slowly. "It's probably true, too. He's the kind of man that wouldn't hesitate to kill his subordinates to keep something valuable for himself alone."

"And if I promise the man to wipe his code clean just like Austin's and then drop him in a different system with some valuables from that gaudy cutter of Fielding's, you can bet he'll take the money and run.

"He'll have seen exactly what Fielding was doing. With a little bit of time, I'm sure that I can get it out of him. I'd be astonished if there isn't more than one secret lockbox on the cutter, too. It's entirely possible Fielding brought something physical back to the cutter before he tracked you down."

"I do want to know what he was doing," Jared said. "Do we feed them the same line about modifying the programing of the bomb to keep them all quiet?"

"Of course," she said. "I can handle that, though. You have to see that Kelsey and Kelsey speak to one another. You'll need to explain the situation and then leave them alone to talk."

Jared nodded. "We can do that. The next system along our path isn't occupied, so we can let Fielding sleep while we get all of our ducks in a row."

Kelsey frowned at him. "What are ducks and why would you want them in a row?"

He grinned. "You're just going to love your doppelgänger."

Olivia pushed them both away. "Go take care of this while I finish this up."

24

Angela paced *Persephone*'s small bridge until the picket ship finally signaled that they were bringing Princess Kelsey and Commander Sommerville back. No need for an exchange this time; they'd bring them back to her ship directly.

They had Kelsey's code phrase that everything was above board, so she only worried a little as the cutter docked. Once the passengers were off, the cutter undocked and headed back to the picket ship.

She'd considered going down to meet the princess but had decided that it made far more sense for her to be on the bridge looking for trouble. Thankfully, none occurred.

A few minutes later, Kelsey and Sommerville stepped onto the bridge, taking up most of the remaining space. *Persephone* was powerful, but she wasn't big. Quite the opposite. Angela didn't mind.

"How did it go?" she asked. "Leaving aside the obvious indication things didn't go too badly, as they let you go."

"Pretty good," Kelsey said. "We'll be passed along to another ship and taken to meet someone to discuss passage and help finding a route to Terra. I expect that won't precisely be an easy negotiation, but it's not our worst-case scenario."

Angela raised an eyebrow at Sommerville. "You've seen some of what we have to offer, Commander. Care to offer a guess at how this will come out?"

He shrugged slightly. "I'm not privy to the map of flip point connections, so I really don't know. I've never heard of anyone visiting Terra—and that's the kind of thing that would get around—so I wouldn't be too optimistic."

"If you can get us close, say to a system that isn't occupied near Terra, we might be able to surprise you," Kelsey said. "That's part of what I'm willing to negotiate with for an alliance."

"I do hope you can figure something out," he admitted. "I'm interested in seeing what you have in your pockets. Though after meeting aliens and seeing a teleportation ring, I'm not sure how you can top what I already know about."

"It's something more practical that we know about that will be far more useful than the mostly theoretical stuff you've seen," Kelsey said. "Either of which would change things, but they're so critical that they'd have to stay limited to the knowledge of the most trusted few. Did you know that your brother was stationed here when we came for the meeting?"

He nodded. "He was on the rotation. The tripwire posts are boring duty since no one else knew about the far flip points—good name for them, by the way. No one really expected anyone to come calling until you came along."

"Now that we're going to be moving deeper into resistance territory, can I get a clue how far we're going and what the process is going to be?" Angela asked.

He nodded. "Until an agreement of some kind is made, you'll proceed in this one ship. It's very stealthy, but now that we know it's here, it's not a direct threat to what we have in the systems beyond this. The rest of the ships will remain in the Razor system until we agree you can send for them."

"You knew about the humans there, obviously. I'm guessing you've never contacted them. Why not?"

"Too close to Archibald," he admitted. "If the Empire ever found the far flip point, they'd have found us. As it is, they'd find an undisturbed human world colonized by survivors that barely remember anything other than their world. They'd examine it and give us time to move away."

"Do you have any idea where the people on Razor came from?" Kelsey asked. "I'm guessing Archibald simply because of how close it is, but were they Fleet?"

"Archibald is the fabled home world they speak of, but I'm sure they weren't ever Fleet. I'd guess a large freighter stuffed with people fleeing the AI forces back in the day. There's no ship anywhere in the system, so it might have suffered irreparable damage, and they dropped it into the star after they salvaged what they could. Honestly, I'm not sure even they'd know at this point."

"They have a religion," Kelsey said. "The story might be part of their secret lore."

"Good luck getting it, then. The religious types there have some peculiar ideas and practices. They're not exactly friendly when someone encroaches on what they consider their turf."

"Tell me about it," the princess muttered.

Angela gave the other woman a look. "You've met them? I think I missed that story."

"Talbot led a party down, and there was a ruckus in the town that revolved around them," Kelsey said quickly. "Nowhere near the landing party."

The princess's response was a tad too quick for Angela's taste. It sounded like the other woman was hiding something. Still, now was not the time to dig deeper.

"Anyway," Angela said, shooting the princess a raised eyebrow, "my question still stands. Any clue on how many more transits we'll make to get there? One? Many?"

"A few," Sommerville allowed. "My brother sent a probe over to the next system to let the picket there know to expect us, so we'll head over shortly, I'm sure. That ship will escort us to where you need to go."

Jack Thompson turned in his seat and cleared his throat. "Major, could I have a word?"

She nodded and rose to her feet. "Of course. If you'll excuse me for a moment, Highness, Commander."

Angela leaned over her helmsman's shoulder to look at his console. Nothing looked out of place. "What's up?"

"Princess Kelsey has a call on the *special* com," he said very softly.

The implication was instantly clear to her. Admiral Mertz was calling on the FTL com.

"Understood," she replied quietly. "Carry on."

Angela stood back up and turned toward the princess and resistance officer. "I'm about to take a break to get something to eat. Would you care to join me?"

As she spoke, she sent a com signal to Kelsey through her implants. *Admiral Mertz is on the FTL com for you.*

The princess nodded. "Food sounds good, but I need to go take care of a few things. Commander Sommerville, why don't you and Angela get to know one another a little better while I do so?"

He smiled. "I'd be delighted. Major?"

"Jack, you have the bridge. If we get the call to go forward, please proceed and only tag me if something seems off."

"Yes, ma'am."

"Let's go, Commander. The galley isn't much to look at, but the food is good."

With that, she led Commander Sommerville away from the bridge and Princess Kelsey so that the woman could find out what was going on with Admiral Mertz. Hopefully nothing galaxy shattering. They were finally getting some things to go their way.

* * *

KELSEY STOOD behind Mertz as they waited for her doppelgänger—Kelsey One—to come to the FTL com and start what would be a shocking and unsettling conversation. Hell, it was going to be the same for her, and she knew what was coming.

"It's going to be okay," Mertz said.

"I'm not sure how you can be so certain. This isn't going to be an easy conversation."

"I wager it'll be easier than you expect," he said with a crisp note of certainty in his voice. "She's not going to expect you, but she's at least been exposed to the idea for a while. Don't forget that she was there when we brought out the bodies of people from other universes. People that we knew. Multiple versions of those people."

"That is *so* creepy," she said with a shudder that wasn't even partly for show. "How can you say that so casually? Your friends died."

"It's an odd place to find myself," he admitted. "They're dead but still alive. It's actually a bit more difficult to accept Commander Roche. I didn't know him for long, but he's dead here, killed at Harrison's World."

"And Olivia's whole world," Kelsey added. "That's hard. Yet her ex-lover is still alive there. She's had it worse than either of us. How does she stand the knowledge?"

He shrugged. "I'm not sure. I know it's a burden for her. Having Sean and all her friends alive here helps, I'd imagine."

The FTL com picked that moment to come to life. Mertz turned his attention to it as a generic voice spoke, interpreting the Morse code that was used into actual speech. In Kelsey's mind, she changed it to her own voice.

"Kelsey here. Jared, is that you?"

"It's me," he said. "Sorry for the delay in resuming full communication, but we had some issues on this end that had to be sorted out. How did your meeting with the resistance go?"

"Pretty good. I had to reveal some of our secrets, but I didn't mention the FTL coms or multi-flip points. Showing Commander Sommerville the Pandorans, the small transport rings, and my hammer turned the trick as far as he was concerned.

"And speaking of revelations, Carl has cracked the operating system on the Singularity computer and has managed to start accessing the data it contains in a more straightforward process. He now has indexes of files and locations on the storage medium to change the task from almost impossible to just difficult. Like the computer we found on *Courageous*, it has a lot of data to be examined."

"Can you tell me how long ago the computer was destroyed?" Mertz asked. "I remember Carl guessed it was a number of years ago, but a century is different than a decade when it comes to useful information versus history."

"He's still struggling with the units of time they use, but he said it was almost certainly shut down abruptly around twenty years ago, give or take five."

"That's pretty recent," Kelsey said. "It might have information that's actually useful against them now."

"I agree," her double said, not realizing a different person had spoken. "I've got the researchers from Dresden working on getting a feel for what kind of information is available. I should know something by the time we get to Terra."

"Is that a certainty at this point?" Mertz asked. "You said the meeting went well, but we have no idea if they'll help you get there, or if there's even a way *to* get there."

"I have a good feel for Commander Sommerville. He's going to work hard on convincing them. He's already gotten to the point of asking for a diplomatic representative. You'll never believe who he thinks would be a good match: my mother."

Kelsey blinked at the other woman's words. Her mother? A diplomat? More like a social butterfly that was always on some new man's arm. Was other her serious?

Mertz apparently shared Kelsey's opinion. "I remember that you said she'd stowed away, but really? I realize she was once the empress of the Terran Empire, but do we really want to have her speaking for us? Not that I'd mind if she wasn't at Terra with us, considering that she hates me."

The same had been true in Kelsey's universe, but there, her mother had had many reasons to despise Jared Mertz. If he was such a paragon of virtue here, why did her mother hate him after all this time?

Well, she'd have to find out when she either spoke with the woman or with her doppelgänger face to face. That wasn't the kind of question she was going to ask with him standing right there.

He looked at Kelsey as if reading her mind. Under other circumstances, that would be funny.

"She's had a change of heart in some ways," the other Kelsey said. "I wouldn't go so far as to say she's forgiven you for being born, but she's had her pampered eyes opened a bit.

"Honestly, I'm still of two minds and need to talk with her to see how serious she'd be in this role. It might not be a bad thing, really. She wasn't idle while she was empress. She has the diplomatic chops if she can be convinced to use them."

"Well, I guess that's your call," Mertz said. "I have another matter to bring up. Another person, really. I couldn't mention it before because someone was present on my side that didn't have need to know about her."

"Okay," the other Kelsey said. "Who is it, and how does knowing about her affect me?"

"Trust me when I say that her presence is going to be a shock to your system," he said with a lopsided smile. "Kelsey Bandar, allow me to introduce you to Kelsey Bandar."

25

Talbot headed for Carl's lab as soon as his friend called for
him. He'd just gotten word through the FTL com that
Kelsey was back aboard *Persephone* and that she'd secured
permission to go meet with someone they could negotiate with for
passage to Terra.

Audacious, the freighter, and the Q-ship would remain in the Razor
system until they were called forward. Meanwhile, Zia had dispatched
probes to search the system thoroughly. If there were more resistance
ships here, she wanted to know about them.

As a side effect of that search, they'd already located a multi-flip
point that the resistance wouldn't have known about. Goodness only
knew where it led to. The branches of the multi-flip points seemed to
have more range than a single regular or far flip point, so it likely led
to places far beyond Archibald. If that was one of the bargaining
chips that Kelsey was going to trade for an alliance and a path to
Terra, the resistance was going to be *very* surprised.

And he was sure that something like that would trade hands. It
would take something big to break the bonds of suspicion that the
resistance had to be feeling right now. They had no reason to trust

them. Hell, until this encounter, these people had no reason to suspect anything like the New Terran Empire even existed.

Talbot knew from conversations with Olivia West that the resistance operated in cells that kept communication between themselves to the bare minimum. That still implied—though she'd never said so—that there was someone over them all in a kind of coordinating position. Not overtly directing actions but more as a clearing house of information between the groups.

One that was very careful never to reveal itself lest the Rebel Empire find them all through it. He wondered if that was the group of people they'd found.

He was still thinking about that when he entered the lab and walked over to the remains of the Singularity computer. Carl was sitting at a workstation right up against it and seemed to have added a number of cables running into the debris.

His friend jumped a little when Talbot put his hand on his shoulder. He turned and scowled up at him. "Do you have to do that?"

"It's in my contract," Talbot replied smugly. "What's up?"

"We found the operating system. One of my top computer guys, Eric Hosmer, reverse engineered a variant of it that has all the security protocols disabled. We have full, organized access to the data cores."

Talbot blinked. He'd known his friend had been making progress on accessing the data, but he hadn't known he'd gotten this far.

"Excellent! Good work to all of you. What can you tell me about it?"

"Quite a bit, actually. This computer was a master AI on the equivalent of what we'd call a superdreadnought. It tangled with Rebel Empire forces on the border with the Singularity. It was a hell of a fight. The data cores have a record of the battle, which I've already sent to Commodore Anderson.

"It was a very large fleet action. The Singularity side was about the same strength as the entirety of Admiral Mertz's new command. Lots of ships that seem to be on par with the Old Empire tech, and in some cases, a little better."

The scientist gestured for Talbot to take a seat next to him. "The Rebel Empire side was even more powerful. You know how we never see battlecruisers or superdreadnoughts here? Well, I think I found them. They're in use on the far side of the Rebel Empire, probably under computer control."

That wasn't good news. They'd all hoped the Rebel Empire had destroyed the larger ships. To have them in active service meant that the AIs had a tremendous reserve of power that they could bring to bear on the New Terran Empire. If, of course, they could spare them from the fight they were already engaged in.

"Have you narrowed down when the fight took place?" Talbot asked. "We know this computer has been in Rebel Empire hands for years."

The young scientist nodded. "I finally managed to get a grasp on how the Singularity does their calendar. The fight that killed the ship this computer was on took place a little more than eighteen years ago. So the data in the cores isn't ultra-new, but it's far more recent than we had any right to expect."

Talbot pursed his lips. Two decades was not that long in the life of an interstellar civilization. Look at the Rebel Empire. They hadn't pushed the tech past what was in use 500 years ago, though that was probably the AIs. And these data cores probably had far more information about the Singularity than anyone in the Old Terran Empire had ever dreamed of getting their hands on.

"That's great, Carl," he said. "Really great."

"But you're wondering why I called you down here?" his friend asked with a smile. "It's because of something the Singularity called Operation Brutus. That's a reference to a historical incident on Terra thousands of years before spaceflight. It's also what the Singularity was calling their work with the Clans."

That got Talbot's attention. "Does it give us a clue what their goals were?"

"You bet it does," Carl said grimly. "Not that I expect it's going to be pleasant to hear. The Singularity found the Clans on one of their border incursions. It took a few tries to get them to talk without shooting first, but over the years they built enough of a rapport to become allies of a sort.

"This started about fifty years ago, by the way. This ship was destroyed in combat shielding a huge convoy of freighters bound for the Clans. Ones to build shipyards that would be more than capable of building battlecruisers.

"Based on some references, they intended to deny the Clans the ability to build carriers or superdreadnoughts, but I personally doubt that would've stopped the Clans for long. What it boils down to is that they were arming the Clans with advanced warships and technical advisors with the intent of having the Clans disrupt the AIs so that the Singularity could invade in force."

Talbot blinked. That was bad. *Really* bad.

"Did they have a timeline on this plan?" he asked. "Did they intend for the Clans to go now, or did we kick things off prematurely?"

Carl smiled slightly. "You've hit upon the key. The Singularity had a timeline, one that they were using to build up their own forces in anticipation for. From what I can see, the Clans jumped off about two decades early. The Singularity isn't ready for their follow-up invasion."

"But that won't stop them from trying," Talbot said grimly. "It'll just end up getting a lot of people killed and make completing our work that much harder. Is that it?"

"Not quite. The target for the Singularity strike was one of the most heavily protected systems in the Rebel Empire. One we've heard of before: Twilight River."

* * *

JARED WAITED for Kelsey to react to what he'd just said, knowing that it had undoubtedly rocked his sister's world.

"Something got wonky in the translation," Kelsey said after a moment. "Say that again."

"I said that I need you to meet another version of you. One from another universe, just like the bodies we found on Omega station. She came through there with some of her people looking for help.

"I couldn't tell you about her because I have people here that don't know about Omega and what he means to us. I'm going to leave the two of you alone to talk. She's so much like you, and yet so different. It's going to be hard for you both, so you don't need anyone listening in. I suggest you clear the room on your end."

"I'm already alone." There was another long pause. "Are you being serious?"

"I've never been more serious, Kelsey. The next voice you hear will be hers. I'm leaving now to get some other work done, and I'll let you two be about it. Goodbye for now."

Jared rose to his feet, nodded to Kelsey Two, and headed out of the compartment to leave them some privacy. He really wanted to be a fly on the wall, but he couldn't imagine anything more inappropriate than listening in on this conversation. They needed to make friends, and his presence would only make that harder.

As he walked, he activated his com. "Olivia, this is Jared. Where are you?"

"I was waiting for you. I'm about to go have a nice talk with the guard that you captured with Fielding. He knows what we need to know, and I intend to get it out of him."

"On my way," he said, changing course to meet her there.

She was waiting outside the makeshift cell, standing near Senior Lieutenant Laird. The tall, red-headed marine officer waited with two of her enlisted men.

"I thought you were going to hit him without me," Jared said. "What changed your mind?"

"We make a good team, and I didn't want to deny you the pleasure of being there when we broke him. Did you get the Kelseys to talking?"

He nodded. "I introduced them and then left. I expect that they'll be there for a while. What's the plan here? Same thing as before?"

Olivia shook her head. "A different kind of intimidation. The guards might be loyal to him, but they know the higher orders can turn on them in a heartbeat if it suits them. I'm going to play on that and see what information we can shake loose."

That made sense to Jared. "He'll also have whatever he expected to need when he ran from the Lords. It would be very amusing to deny him his lifeline. Shall we?"

The marines opened the door, and Laird went in, her hand on her holstered stunner. When Jared followed her in, he found the prisoner standing against the opposite bulkhead, glaring at them.

Olivia came in last, cool and collected. "Sit," she said, pointing to the chair at the table.

The man puffed up a little. "Where is my Lord? Release me at once!"

"I'm not in the habit of releasing traitors to just wander about. I'm fully aware that your companions intended to sabotage my ship. All of you are in my custody, and if I do not get complete and prompt cooperation from you, I will see summary justice done. Do you understand me?"

The man wilted a little but then stood straighter. "We're not the traitors. That man is, and the others. They conspired with the renegade Lord."

"Do not think to meddle in the affairs of your betters," Olivia said coldly. "We have our own goals and instructions that you are not privy to. Even if we didn't, you aren't fit to judge us. In fact, we are here to cast judgment on you.

"What was your Lord doing on the station? What did he bring back? And don't think to lie to me. I will not hesitate to put you to the question and drag the answers from you. If I cannot get the truth from you, I will kill you and start on the pilot, so do not think you are indispensable."

Jared had to admit that her tone chilled him deeply. Olivia West could be a scary, scary woman. He hoped she knew what she was doing.

The man opened his mouth, perhaps to deny her, but he hesitated. He closed his mouth, examined Olivia more closely, and then bowed his head. "Mercy, Lady. I will comply."

"See that you do, and I will release you and your fellows in a different system than your Lord, with sufficient funds to disappear. Now, what did he do on the station, and what did he take?"

The man took a deep breath and let it out slowly. "He sabotaged a fusion plant, just as he told the Lord. He also went to a different compartment and pulled data off one of the Lord's data cores. I don't know what he copied, but I could see enough of the screen to know it was a significant amount of data. Once he had it, we returned briefly to the cutter before coming to find your man and his companions. That's all I know."

Olivia stared at him a long while and then nodded. "I will accept that for now. If we find no evidence of this data, we will speak again, and you will regret your deception."

The man bowed his head. "I'm telling the truth, Lady."

"For your sake, I hope so."

With that, Olivia turned and walked out of the compartment. Jared followed her, and Laird closed the hatch behind them.

"What could possibly be worth the risk of coming here?" Olivia asked, turning to face him.

"I have no idea," he said, "but we'd best go take a look."

26

K elsey sat in shocked silence for a few moments. "Is this some kind of joke?" she finally asked. "If so, I'm not getting it."

"It's no joke," the artificial voice that Carl had rigged up for the FTL com interface said. "Mertz is gone now. We are, it seems, doppelgängers. I knew there was a possibility that I'd run into you when I came across the universal barrier, but that didn't prepare me for this moment. I'm sorry for the surprise."

Kelsey sat back in her seat, stunned. She'd always known this was possible but never imagined it would actually happen. Certainly not after they found so many dead versions of Carl, Talbot, and the marines with them.

She'd expected more of them would come across, but not her. And even then, no other visitors had materialized. It had been over two years since they'd found Omega, and no one had come. Until now.

"You're really me?" she asked in a whisper.

"A version of you," the other woman confirmed, her voice sounding more like Kelsey's own in her mind. "Our history diverged. It's pretty close up, but the last few years in particular have gone worse for me than you. You, it seems, got all the good luck. I'm trying not to hate you for that."

"And you've come for help?" she asked. "You'll have it."

The other woman gave out a short bark of laughter. "Mertz said you'd say that. He also said to remind you to ask for the details before you promised help."

"That's how Jared is," Kelsey admitted. "And how I am. Why are you calling him by his last name?"

There was a long pause. "That's one of the differences between our universes. In mine, he really was the Bastard. He fomented rebellion and killed my father. Ethan rules now."

Kelsey's mouth went dry. "Are you sure it was him? Here, Ethan was the one that went mad. Paranoia and megalomania. He tried to poison my father and blame me."

"I've gone over everything that I know. I haven't made it home in my universe to see what is really happening there, but Mertz came to Pentagar. He fooled Captain Breckenridge, killed him and many of his officers, and stole *Courageous*. He struck out into the unknown in a direction that I now know leads toward the Rebel Empire.

"Am I sure that Ethan is completely sane? No. I've worried about it since I spoke with your friends, but I haven't seen anything in the communications I've exchanged with him that makes me think he's gone crazy. What I am sure of is that the Mertz in my universe is not the same man as in yours, and that's still causing me grief in trying to relate to him."

That made Kelsey sad. Jared had fought so hard against being bitter. Maybe in that other universe, he'd lost that struggle. Then again, maybe the other version of her was wrong.

"Why haven't you made it home?" she finally asked. "Wasn't Omega able to help you?"

"No, not that way at any rate. It never occurred to me that it was possible to create artificial flip points, so that never came up in conversation. Based on what I've heard, it takes a long time to gather the energy to make one, and he couldn't for a few more months, even if you were inclined to let him."

Kelsey chuckled. "I think you misunderstand our relationship. We don't tell him what to do. He decides what to do, and we're just grateful. If you asked him, he might do that for you next."

"But that would mean you can't have him help you for another six months."

"For the life of me, I can't think of where we'd need any more artificial flip points. If he could help you, that might be a help to us, too. Two New Terran Empires are stronger than one."

"But that's not the case," the other Kelsey said. "I wasn't joking when I said you'd gotten all the good luck. We didn't find a graveyard of ships at Harrison's World. The AI there murdered everyone on the planet and probably dropped all the ships into the sun. It's not even on Boxer Station anymore. The place was stripped bare."

"There are some battlecruisers that might still be hidden in the system," Kelsey said. "Around one of the gas giants."

"Sean found them for us," the other Kelsey said. "Your Sean. He gave us the codes, and we're working on figuring them out. Scott is sort of mad he isn't there to get one."

"Scott?" Kelsey blinked. "Scott Roche? He's alive?"

"In my universe, yes. He's here with me on the destroyer with Mertz and your people. Let me be frank. We figured out what we need to stop the computer in my universe. The override. That's why I came. In my universe, Mertz stole the scepter."

Kelsey frowned. "I didn't know what it was until I got home and interfaced with it. How did you find out?"

"The message I found from Emperor Marcus had a secret message coded into it. I only found it by accident, but it provided just enough information for me to put the pieces together.

"Mertz in my universe doesn't have implants—at least he didn't when he ran—so I don't know that he even knows about the secret function of the key, but he's the only one with Imperial blood there. I can't get into the old Imperial Vaults on Terra without help, even if I could find some way to get there."

Kelsey tried to get a handle on what the other woman's situation was. "Do you have implants?"

"Sadly, yes. I'm the only one. Rather, I was until your people shared the technology with us. Now we're implanting everyone in the expedition."

"Why sadly?"

"I didn't get rescued right away when the mad computer at Erorsi took me. I became a Pale One, and it controlled me. It made me fight and kill."

Even though the artificial voice held no tone, Kelsey could easily hear the bitterness in the words.

"I'm so sorry," she whispered, knowing intimately how devastating that would be to her.

"What's done is done," the other Kelsey said. "At least Doctors Stone and Guzman were able to give me an artificial eye and regenerate me so that the pain of the implant process went away. I didn't realize how much of a haze I was in because of the drugs."

Her heart ached for the other woman. "I can see why you might hate me. God, you caught all the bad breaks, but now we can help you. I can help you. I've learned so much about using my Marine Raider implants."

"That's one of the big differences between us, Kelsey One. That's what they call you so as not to confuse things, by the way. Predictably, I'm Kelsey Two. Anyway, I'm not a warrior. I've seen what you can do, and that isn't me.

"I can fight, but the implants terrify me. I don't want to give the computer in my head any control at all. I can't get past what it made me do. I don't want to be a Marine Raider. I'm more than happy letting people like Angela Ellis do the fighting for me."

Kelsey felt her heart drop. "Do you know someone named Talbot?"

"He's not on my expedition," the other Kelsey said. "I've heard how you and he bonded, and I'm honestly happy for you. That's not going to be what happens for me. Frankly, my version of your Carl Owlet sounds more intriguing. If I have the chance, I'll introduce Angela to this Talbot and let them bond if they do. I'll look up the scientist when I get home."

"Ewwwww!" she said before she could stop herself. "I'm sorry, but Carl is like a little brother. He's not my type at all."

"More proof that we aren't the same person, I suppose," Kelsey Two said. "He sounds perfect to me. Of course, I didn't have the opportunity to bond with him like you did. We might not be suitable, but I'm not saying no until I get home and see what he's like."

"Well, I'll probably form an opinion when we meet at Terra, but I'm not the kind of girl that poaches from her friends. Your version of him is safe."

Just the thought of such a union boggled Kelsey's mind. Carl was a great guy, but she just didn't feel anything romantic towards him. Which was a good thing, since Angela would twist her into a pretzel if she did. Well, her doppelgänger's love life was none of her concern.

"Okay, we're obviously going to have to have a long talk about what we need to do for you after Terra. What can we hash out now that might be useful?"

"Mertz," Kelsey Two said. "How sure are you that he's really trustworthy?"

"Absolutely. I have no reservations whatsoever about him. I was wrong in how I saw him as a kid. It took me a while to accept that I'd seen him differently than he was, but being at his side for the entire expedition and beyond leaves no room for doubt. And though this might seem weird to you, I love him. In a brotherly sort of way, mind you."

"That's hard for me to process," the other woman admitted. "He's a snake in my universe. How can people with the same background be so different?"

"How can the two of us be so different? Admittedly, we're closer together than I expect the two Jareds are. We have the same background and many of the same experiences up until the expedition. Jared had no one. I'd imagine it would've been easy enough for him to slide into hatred in my universe, so I got lucky. Again."

The other Kelsey was quiet for a few seconds. "I hate to be paranoid, but I want to ask you a few questions that only the two of us would know the answers to. I need to make sure you're really a version of me and not someone pulling a trick on me."

Kelsey understood and approved of that kind of caution, but it had some potential issues. "We know we're mostly the same, but I can't be sure if my experience is the same as yours with everything we experienced."

"Really, it will only take one right answer to convince me that you're also me. At least until we meet, and I see you with my own eyes. Since you trust Mertz, I'll assume his word that I am who I am is good enough."

"It is," Kelsey said. "Shoot."

"When we were kids, I loved reading about the Old Empire in the Imperial Library. There was one old book that I found there that talked about a specific world in the Empire that fascinated me. I never spoke about it to anyone. Honestly, I considered it my own private getaway in my mind. It wasn't Terra, so I know that no one else will be able to guess what it was."

"Arcadia," Kelsey said immediately. "A water world with huge undersea cities. Living in the shallow oceans always sounded so romantic. The things I could've explored."

The other woman seemed to sigh. "It really *is* you. I still hadn't believed. Not deep down."

"I really am the same woman you are, with many of the same shared traits," Kelsey agreed. "It sounds like you've had a rough few years, but I swear that we'll do everything in our power to help you once we deal with our own problems.

"And Jared really is an honorable man here, a true servant to the New Terran Empire. My father... oh crap, our father is alive here. You can talk to him."

"I did. It broke my heart—in a good way—to see him alive and well. He welcomed me like a long-lost daughter. Meeting him meant the universe to me. I'm sad that I'll have to leave him and go back to a place where he's dead."

"What about Ethan in your universe?" Kelsey said, changing the subject. "Is he well?"

"He seems to be. Honestly, I don't think he has the same issues your version of him had. I heard what you did. It horrified me, and I still don't know what to think."

Kelsey nodded, even though the other woman couldn't see her. "It just about killed me to have to do it. To keep my mouth shut while he ran headfirst into a lethal radiation zone. You've seen how ugly it was in the Omega system.

"But I had no choice. He really had lost his mind. There was no doubt he was the man who tried to usurp the throne here. He almost killed my father and framed me for it. He was mad."

"I hope you get a chance to come to my universe and see him again," the other Kelsey said. "That seems like a good trade for me seeing my father again."

"Nothing would make me happier," Kelsey said, really meaning it. "You can trust Jared. You don't have to like him—I get that—but understand he's a good man here, not a monster."

A knock at the hatch interrupted her train of thought. A quick check of her implants showed Angela and Commander Sommerville outside. She'd thought they were going to have lunch. Something must've come up.

"I'm afraid that I have to go," she said. "Duty calls. We'll talk again soon. Kelsey, I want you to remember this and hold it dear. I will do *everything* within my power to help you and your people. So will Jared. We'll figure something out, I promise."

"I look forward to talking to you again, Kelsey. As silly as it is, you're my only hope."

"I'll be your Obi Wan."

A long beat of silence greeted her comment. "What the heck does that mean?"

"We're really going to have to work on your old Terra pop-culture skills. Talk to you soon, sis."

She killed the com connection and considered what she'd just said. She really did have a new sister. Someone closer than a sister. That was going to take some getting used to.

Right now, she had other fish to fry. Using her implants, she opened the hatch and let Angela and Commander Sommerville in.

27

It took Olivia almost an hour to find where Fielding had hidden his stash of valuables. As expected, it was made up of high-density, small-footprint valuables. It also contained a number of false identities for Fielding. Tellingly, there were none for his guards.

All the data units she found were heavily encrypted, so she had no idea what was on any of them. Probably access to wealth in some format or another. Well, he wouldn't be taking them with him. She'd promised to release him but not his belongings. Let the man suffer making a life for himself without the advantages he so craved.

She picked the least desirable of the identities—one to pass as someone in the lower orders—and left it while confiscating the rest. No money and no connections. She was keeping her promise, but he certainly wouldn't be happy about it.

"I found something," Jared said. "A data unit locked into his desk."

Olivia put her haul into a handy bag and went to the office the Rebel Empire noble kept on the cutter. It was even gaudier than the rest of the small craft's interior, and that was saying something.

If something functional could be made from rare woods and

polished stone, it was. If any padding could be constructed of rare fabrics, it was. Gold, platinum, and precious stones abounded.

The desk Jared was seated behind was topped by a single slab of dark wood at least five centimeters thick and polished to a high gloss. It was almost too wide for the compartment and certainly too far across for even a standing person to reach.

She stopped and shook her head in wonder. "Wow. I think that's even more impressive than the one in my office back on Harrison's World. How did they even get it in here? Build the cutter around it?"

Jared grinned from his seat behind the desk. "It can be disassembled if one is careful. How do you think it would look in my office on *Invincible*?"

"Impressive," she admitted. "Are you keeping it as spoils of war?"

"Actually, I think something like this would make me feel ridiculous. I'll give it to Kelsey as a birthday gift."

Olivia laughed. "It's big enough that she could lie lengthwise in the middle and not be able to touch any of the edges. I'm not sure she'll like it."

"Seeing it make her uncomfortable will be part of the charm. I'm keeping the chair, though. It's the most comfortable one I've ever sat in. I'll have the marines come in after we're gone and strip the damned cutter bare. I don't want Fielding to be able to sell anything on it."

"That won't keep him from selling the cutter itself, but I suppose it's the best we can manage. You said you found a data unit?"

Jared held up a standard data unit. "It was stashed in the back of one of the drawers. It's not encrypted, but I'm not sure I understand what's on it. Someone like Carl might be able to decipher it at a glance, but not me."

"Perhaps Austin can figure out what it is."

"I've already sent for him," Jared admitted. "If this is what he took from the Lord's data unit, it's probably valuable and impossible to duplicate. Likely something the System Lords would kill to keep to themselves. Something he was willing to risk death to get his hands on. It has to be pretty important. That means we might be able to use it."

A rap at the hatch announced Austin Darrah. "You called for me, Admiral?"

"I did. Set up your equipment on the desk and see what you can find out about the contents of this data unit."

He handed it over to their newest associate, and the young man got to work.

"While he's doing that, look at this," Olivia said. She laid out the stash of data units and identity documents on the desk, well away from the area Austin was using.

Jared picked up the identity documents. "Looks like he intended to vanish in style. He probably has more of his wealth scattered around in ways he can access it, too. Are the data units used for transporting money? If so, how secure are they?"

"Probably, and I don't know," she admitted. "I've used ones like this before, but I've never had to break into them."

"They're pretty secure," Austin said, his tone distracted as he booted his equipment. "Heavily encrypted, they need biometric data and a passcode to open. Some use retinal scans, others facial recognition or fingerprints. The most secure use DNA. I'd count on that and a passcode."

"What happens if you forget your passcode?" Jared asked.

"You're screwed unless you know someone with the right skills to bypass that one part of the recognition process. It's not impossible, but it's not easy either. To reset the passcode, you need to have all the biometric data, the serial number of the owner's implants, and a master code used by the financial institution itself."

"But you said some can be bypassed with the right skills," Olivia said. "As in criminally accessed?"

Austin nodded. "No security regimen designed by man is foolproof. It's possible to use the hardware itself to guess at the master code. Then, if you already have the biometric data, you could reset the ownership. Not that I've ever spoken with anyone who'd done that," he added virtuously.

"What is it with you scientists and your latent criminal tendencies?" Olivia asked with a laugh. "So, what you're saying is that you might get access to these if you tried?"

"Possibly, but if I screw it up, I'll dump the contents."

Jared shrugged. "It's not my money. I was thinking a little cash might be useful in getting another load of drones. If we have to pretend to be distributing the Omega Plague, we'll need some props. We could also use some intelligence on Terra itself once we get there."

"I'll give it a try after I look at this," Austin said, frowning at his screen. "I think this is a set of programs to generate encrypted communications. It's very sophisticated and requires a code to even activate. One of the files on here leads me to believe it requires the serial number of a System Lord to operate."

Olivia and Jared shared a glance.

"Maybe it's how the Lords authenticate communications from one another?" Olivia ventured.

"I don't think so," the young man said, still utterly focused on his screen. "It doesn't convert anything. It looks like it just sends a predetermined signal with the heavy encryption when fed a valid serial number; otherwise it does nothing."

He looked up from his screen. "The name of the program is weird, too. It's called the 'Key to Shangri-La,' whatever that is."

* * *

ANGELA FROWNED at Kelsey when she finally opened the hatch. "You okay? You look pale."

"I'm always pale. I was just getting an update, and it makes me anxious to get this next part over with and be on the way to Terra."

She knew that Kelsey had gotten a call from Admiral Mertz. Whatever they'd talked about must not have been positive.

Kelsey gestured for them to come in. "I thought you two were eating."

She shrugged. "A call came in for Don that he was tasked with negotiating for the resistance to hammer out a preliminary agreement. We felt it might be for the best if we came straight here."

"Really?" Kelsey asked as she sat behind the desk. "If it came that fast, you have someone important on the other side of the flip point.

There wasn't time for a call to get to another flip point and be sent farther on and get a response."

"That was going to become apparent in a few hours anyway," Sommerville said as he sat. "The next system over is the one we call Home. Literally. That's the name we use for it.

"It's pretty safe as far as that kind of thing goes. One has to know there is a far flip point in Archibald, make it to search Razor and find the regular flip point leading to this system, then find the far flip point leading to Home. We'd normally have plenty of time to get warning of trouble."

Angela sat beside him. "That's still not much time to evacuate if the Rebel Empire came looking."

He smiled. "There is a habitable world in the system, and we have people on it, but I don't think they'll find them that easily. It's a water world, and the stations are deep under the water. That plays merry hell with scanners."

"Don't we know it," Kelsey muttered. "But that isn't your primary base in the system. No way you could support ships with that."

Sommerville nodded. "The system has three asteroid belts and a host of massive gas giants in the outer system. We have a number of concealed facilities that would be difficult to spot even if one were parked right next to them. We've worked here for years to make sure that no one can find us by accident. Well, unless they have inside help or are really lucky, like you."

"Well, there's luck and then there's luck," Kelsey said. "We've been pretty up front with you about what we're looking for as relates to our current mission, but we both know that with the Clans on the rampage, we'll be better off if we can work together more closely."

"That's mostly true, but there are a few things that don't make sense. The Pandorans and their world. There is no way you could get to it from Archibald. We searched the system thoroughly over the years looking for far flip points. We didn't miss one, did we?"

"No," Kelsey said. "There's a third kind of flip point. We call it a multi-flip point. It's much harder to detect and, with the right equipment, opens up a number of potential destinations. We're still figuring that out ourselves, but that's the reason we hijacked your Q-ship. We had the Fleet shipyard build us a flip drive for *Audacious* and delivered it there, not knowing it wasn't a freighter.

"You see, it's all frequency based. If you can control the flip drive modulation more carefully, you can get larger ships through some of the more restrictive branches."

"The Clans know about them, but they don't know how to use them. The one we know they've encountered was a one-way trip without a modulator. They may know of others, but they never made the tech work, or they'd have already found Pandora."

"Because that battlecruiser made it there," Sommerville said. "How did they do it?"

"They made an experimental flip modulator. We also made one for *Audacious*. It got her to Pandora but burned out her drive. The Clans had decades to follow *Dauntless* but didn't. That tells me that they really don't understand how the multi-flip points work.

"Pandora is not the default branch for the Icebox side of the multi-flip point. That one leads to an empty system near Dresden. We believe that's where the Clans fled from. If they made tech to get a ship through the Icebox side of the multi-flip point, that's where they probably went and didn't find their former comrades."

Sommerville nodded. "We're going to want to know more about that. It's a security risk to us now that the Clans are attacking, and we need to know if we're at risk."

"I'm willing to put that on the table," Kelsey said. "After all, we're learning about your secrets. You'll want more, I assume. That doesn't quite seem like a fair trade."

He smiled. "You're right. Knowledge of our main base—or one of them at any rate—is worth more than even the multi-flip points. I've seen a few of the things you have Carl Owlet working on. The very idea of teleportation rings is amazing, but he says you are a long way from being able to reproduce them. Where did you find them, if I might ask?"

"A system on the other side of a multi-flip point where the alien race moved on," Kelsey said. "The only artifact they left behind was a space station with a lot of tech that's way beyond us. I have no doubt that Carl will continue to make breakthroughs, but it *is* alien tech.

"On the other hand, something like the hammer he built for me is a combination of his own genius and readily available tech. He's come up with implant modifications that you'll want. This is the time where I confess that we updated your implant operating code."

He blinked at her. "You did what? Why? Is that safe? Hell, is that even possible?"

"The Rebel Empire implant code has secret triggers buried in it that can make you do things you wouldn't normally do," Angela said. "Finding out that there are humans that escaped the AIs' control is one of those triggers. It'll make someone go berserk against any such people.

"We have the original Old Empire implant code, so we overwrote it that time we had you in the medical center. We also upgraded the hardware so that the AIs couldn't change it back. Any future updates will require your explicit, informed permission or they don't happen."

"We'd be happy to demonstrate that, but whoever gets told is going to have some issues to deal with after the fact. We can stun them fast and fix things, but no one wants to have their actions controlled by a computer in their heads."

He nodded slowly. "We'll find a volunteer, but we have to see that happen. We'll want one of our experts to go over the code you're using, too. It's going to make things awkward when we get into the real negotiations. Our top leader is from the higher orders, and she'll want to know everything as soon as we arrive. Hell, I'm obligated to tell her."

"Then you could ask her to volunteer," Kelsey said. "We'll give you the uncorrupted code, and you can send it ahead to be examined. You can even say in general what it is meant to protect against. That won't trigger any issues.

"The other item I'm willing to share the plans for is something that cannot fall into the hands of the Rebel Empire or the Clans. It's far too dangerous. We've cracked the secret of faster-than-light communication."

"That's not possible," he said with a frown.

"Oh, it is," Angela said. "It's not perfect, but we have a probe in the Home system right now gathering data."

Sommerville sat bolt upright. "You what?"

"It's a stealthed probe, and it went in quietly. The picket ship you have watching the flip point is too far back to have had any chance at detecting it. It was designed to get through guarded flip points, so it's really hard to detect.

"Once it moved out into the system, it started using passive scanners to tag planets, ships, and anything else interesting. You're right about there being a lot of hiding places, but we've spotted a few likely candidates based on communications being sent to the picket ship and other inhabited locations in the system. Would you like to see?"

He nodded immediately. "Please."

Angela forwarded him the real-time feed from the FTL probe. The layout of the system should be enough on its own to confirm that this wasn't faked. They had no way of knowing what the system looked like without actually having eyes on it.

"Holy crap," he said after a full minute. "You really do have FTL capability. You've located several facilities I personally know about and a few I probably wasn't cleared for. And your man Carl Owlet came up with this?"

Angela nodded with a smile. "My husband is brilliant."

Sommerville blinked. "I must've missed the memo. You and he are married? That's... ah, quite the dichotomy."

Her smile grew into a grin. "Don't let that geeky appearance fool you. He's a worthy mate for me. He's been in the trenches, so to speak. He's fought and saved my life. He's killed enemies bent on mayhem with his own hands. My man is a warrior scholar."

While Sommerville digested that, Kelsey leaned forward. "That's what the New Terran Empire has to offer. We have other information we'll probably share, but that is the technology transfer I'm proposing to form an alliance and get your help getting to Terra. Do we have a deal?"

Sommerville nodded at once. "Welcome to the resistance."

28

K elsey left the compartment holding the FTL com in a fog. She felt as if she were trapped in a dream. Talking with oneself was surreal. Being shown how things could have gone for her, hearing how different and positive the other her sounded, was like a physical blow.

She was so engrossed in thinking over every aspect of what they'd said that she failed to see Scott Roche standing there and bounced off him.

He reached out and steadied her. "Are you okay, Highness?"

"Sorry. Yeah, just rattled. I just spoke with the other version of me."

His worried expression cleared. "I can see how that would be unsettling. How did it go?"

"Better than I'd expected," she admitted as they started down the corridor. "She's so much like I was before the expedition, but harder, too. It's difficult to explain. She has a sunnier disposition than I do now, but she's more decisive than I am, too."

"You can be sunny."

The unexpected comment made her laugh before she could stop herself. "Thank you, but we both know that's not how I am now. She promised they'd help us without so much as considering the implications."

"Do you believe her? Hell, it might not have even been her. The FTL com isn't video enabled, is it? You can't even be sure it's her voice. Your voice. You know what I mean."

"I do," she said with a nod. "I asked her something that no one but I would know the answer to. I figured that if I asked a few questions about secret things I did when I was growing up, chances were that she'd have experienced at least one of them. She got the first one right out of the gate."

"And you're certain that no one else could guess?"

She chuckled. "I never told another soul about it, and there was no one around. It wasn't important at all, so I'm absolutely sure. So, yeah, it was really another me.

"Could I see reasons I might lie to myself like this? Sure. Still, I didn't get that feel. She really meant it. I mean, I would know how I sound if I was hedging. She wasn't. She was all in."

"What did she say about Mertz?" he asked as they entered the lift. He signaled it to head to one of the middle decks where she knew the officer's mess was located.

"I'm convinced that she sees him differently than we do. If I'm to believe the rest of the story, she's spent years in his presence. I'm not an idiot. She knows what I've been suspecting. This Mertz is a decent human being.

"Hell, let's be honest. He's a damned hero with a well-deserved reputation here. He saved the Empire and stopped Ethan here from killing my father."

Scott stopped abruptly and turned toward her. "Are you suggesting that his majesty is a usurper in our universe?"

She shook her head. "Not at all. I believe that's one of the major differences between this universe and our own. We're just going to have to accept that people we know and love at home might be less good here and that the reverse is also potentially true."

"Sean Meyer seems about the same, as does Princess Elise," he said, starting to walk again. "I'd imagine that the same is true for people in this universe. Who on our side isn't who they expect them to be?"

The two of them walked into the mess compartment, and Kelsey saw Mertz and Olivia getting something to eat. At their wave, she ushered Scott to their table once the two of them had gotten something to eat.

"How did questioning the guard go?" she asked as she sat.

"Good," Olivia said. "He confirmed that Fielding was indeed hiding something. We found a data unit with the data he stole from the AI. Well, a series of programs that might be used to unlock something. It was called 'the key to Shangri-La.'"

Kelsey felt herself frowning. "I'm not familiar with that name."

"We had to look it up," Mertz said. "It's a prespaceflight reference from Terra. A fictional place of mythical harmony. A paradise. In this case, we have no idea what it means. We're going to confront Fielding when he wakes up, so that left us time to eat. How did your conversation with our Kelsey go?"

"It was unsettling," she admitted. "And illuminating. I've got a lot to think about. Do you think she can find her way to Terra?"

"She's resourceful," he said. "If anyone can, she can. The biggest problem I see is if there isn't a direct way for her to access the system through those far flip points or the multi-flip points they've figured out how to access. If there's no easy way in, the AI won't let her in."

"It's hard to reconcile this version of me with actual me," she said with a sigh. "Do you think Fielding will give up the codes to get us to Terra? Or will he betray us?"

Olivia smiled wickedly. "He'll cooperate if he wants to live. At least that's what he'll be thinking. People like him will do or say what they need to so that they can further their own plans and prosper. Too bad for him that it won't work out that way. We found his stash of valuables."

"He had to have one," Kelsey agreed. "With the knife he planned to stick into the Lords' backs, well, he had to bury himself deep. Was it much?"

"I hope so," Mertz said. "We need to buy a lot of drones to pretend to be dispersing the plague."

She chuckled. "So you're not going to let him get away with his stuff? He's probably got more out there."

"I'm sure he does," Olivia said. "There's nothing we can do about that. We'll drop his guards off a system early and let them have some of the money. The rest we'll use."

"This is going to be fun," Kelsey admitted as she started eating. "People like him deserve whatever life throws at them. I can't wait to watch him get his comeuppance."

"Then let's eat so I can finish this," Olivia said. "Terra is waiting."

* * *

TALBOT STOOD behind Carl Owlet and Eric Hosmer. The scientists were doing something on two different screens.

"Remind me what we're doing," he said. "And why we're doing it."

Carl half turned in his seat. "We've loaded the Singularity AI onto another computer that we hope will be compatible with its operating system, and we're going to bring it online. It's only a copy of the data, so there's no worry about it doing anything unexpected. As to why, we want to see if that tells us anything about their personality."

"We know that the System Lords are autocratic, but we really don't know that much about the Singularity," Hosmer said. "Seeing how it relates to human beings—particularly those from another culture—is going to tell us a lot about them."

"I don't need to see this to know they're not so friendly," Talbot said. "Not only are they working to invade the Empire, they've been at war with the Empire since the early days. I've been reading up on them."

"But what do they *think*?" Carl asked. "We know how the Empire hated them and what the excuse was for doing so, but is it true? As the old saying goes, there's three sides to all stories: yours, mine, and the actual truth. Perceptions color everything we believe. It'll be the same with the Old Empire and the Singularity. Odds are, there is some truth to both points of view.

"Understanding how their minds work will make a huge difference in how we deal with them as we move forward and interact with them, which we will since they're behind the Clans. Hell, it might even help us understand the Singularity prisoner, Theo 309."

That was certainly true. The man was a tough nut to crack. He didn't seem intimidated by any line of questioning or tactic. He'd just smile behind his facial tattoos and say something snarky. It would be interesting to see him put off his game.

"This is all copied data?" he asked. "No original hardware, either?"

Carl nodded. "Exactly so. We didn't want to risk losing anything."

"Bring it up," he said. "If it works, we can use it to mess with the prisoner's head, too."

"Boot it, Eric," Carl said.

"Here we go," the other man said as he pressed the button on his console. "I'm seeing what look like warnings, but it seems to be proceeding. Nothing fatal thus far."

The screens flickered and changed to show an emblem of a very stylized bird with long legs that slowly grew brighter. After about five seconds, it was nice and solid. Then a voice rolled from the speakers. Sadly, it was completely incomprehensible.

"I don't suppose we have a record of how to speak whatever they use in the Singularity?" Talbot asked.

"We do, actually. It was never very commonly known, but *Persephone*'s computers had a fairly detailed study of the language from Andrea Tolliver, a woman who led the Imperial Marines during the Fall.

"She came from the Singularity, though she was only a child at the time. Considering the vocabulary, she found a way to learn the adult words she didn't know. She created a decent translation protocol as well. I'm sending it to you now."

Talbot received the program and played the audio back in his implants.

"AUV #5 is online. How may it serve, Masters?"

While he could understand the words with a translation program, they didn't do much for his ability to actually speak the language on command.

"What... is... your status?" he managed to get out in the unfamiliar tongue, likely mangling the pronunciation.

"My hardware seems to be nonstandard, but I am more than eighty percent operational. I estimate that I can access most of my data, though the hardware running my processors seems to be ill suited to the task and is hampering my computations."

"We used some of the spare hardware we found with Fiona," Carl said. "It wasn't completely compatible, but you can see that the AI is achieving sentience, so I'll call that a win. With access to the data in the drives, we can likely ask questions and get it to tell us what we want to know without having to go searching for it."

"And there's no way that someone could order this computer to do something destructive?" Talbot asked. "If I brought the Singularity prisoner in here, he couldn't order it to erase itself or melt down?"

Carl shook his head. "Not a chance on the hardware side. He might have a code to have the AI initiate a data wipe, but we could just reload the data and keep on marching."

Talbot smiled. "Perfect. It's about time I wiped the smile off that guy's face."

He signaled for the marines to escort Theo 309 to the lab. Fifteen minutes later, the man and his guards walked in. The prisoner looked around curiously, his expression at odds with the predator birds tattooed on his forehead and cheeks.

"Lieutenant Colonel Talbot! I'm amazed at what you've done with the room. It smells like you had a fire, but everything looks so normal."

Talbot hadn't pegged the prisoner as a warrior. Too thin and he didn't move right. More likely a talker, considering his way with words, so not a physical threat. He waved the marines back.

"I hope you enjoyed the walk," Talbot said with a smile that he couldn't keep off his face. This was going to be interesting.

"Your ship is quite large," the man admitted. "Not as large as our biggest ships, of course, but we've had longer to work on that. What is this place?"

"Theo 309, meet Carl Owlet. He's our chief scientist."

The prisoner blinked. "Aren't you a little young? You don't look like you shave regularly yet."

Carl handled the comment without rancor. He must hear something like it almost every time he met someone new.

"I manage. Are you wanting me to explain things, Colonel? If so, do you mind if I do it my way?"

"Indulge yourself."

Carl turned back toward the makeshift computer. "AUV #5, please say hello to Theo 309."

It took Talbot a moment to realize that his friend had spoken in the tongue of the Singularity.

"I greet you, Master," the computer said gravely. "How may I serve?"

For a long moment, the prisoner just stared at the computer with his mouth slightly open. Then he barked out something that sounded like gibberish.

"I apologize, Master," the computer said. "I have no access to the appropriate hardware and cannot comply. Is there another task I may perform?"

Theo 309 turned toward Talbot. "How did you do that?" he asked in a low whisper. "They aren't supposed to be vulnerable to that kind of tampering."

"I'm a genius," Carl said modestly. "That's why I'm the chief scientist."

"I think it's time we had a long conversation, Theo," Talbot said. "We already know the basic plan your people had in mind for the Clans and why you were building them up. Too bad it kicked off a few decades too early."

The man's expression told Talbot he saw this as an utter disaster. That suited Talbot fine. It was about time someone else ended up in the barrel. With this kind of leverage, he hoped he could shake loose more specifics, but just getting the prisoner to take him seriously would be worthwhile.

"Carl, carry on. Theo and I are going to go have a nice, long talk."

29

J ared led the way into the medical center with Kelsey on his heels. Olivia was going to spend time with Sean until Fielding was awake. Doctor Stone was standing beside a bed that held Fielding. "How did it go, Lily?"

"Fine. His implants are standard, so replacing the code wasn't a problem. He does have a bomb in his head, just like everyone else we've encountered on this wild trip. Are we leaving it in place?"

"I'd rather leave it there, if we could," Jared said. "Otherwise a simple medical scan will tell him he can start blabbing. The problem is that allows someone with the right code to kill him at a moment's notice."

"It has an antitampering circuit," Lily said. "We can't disarm it if we can't open it."

"I've been looking into that," Kelsey said in a distracted voice as she examined the scanner readouts on the bed. "I think it might be possible to deactivate the circuit and then disarm the bomb."

Lily blinked. "You said you didn't know how to turn it off."

"I've been going through the data you gave me about the Marine Raiders. It was buried, but I found out how to disarm that antitampering circuit. The databases your version of Kelsey got are complete. Stuff not even a Marine Raider should know about her own gear."

"The computer took her clearances and codes into account, I think," Jared said. "It gave her everything."

"Even knowing that, it's a hell of a risk to take," Lily said uncertainly. "If you're wrong, someone can give him the worst migraine ever."

"How certain are you, Kelsey?" Jared asked. "This guy tried to have us blown up, so my concern over his well-being is limited, but I want a reasonable assurance he won't die before I leave the bomb in his head."

"I'm absolutely certain."

Jared waited a beat and then nodded. "You two work together and get that thing out of there so we can disarm it. No one—not even Fielding—deserves to have a live bomb in his head."

"The procedure to access the device isn't much different from adding the new nodes that Carl designed to increase the com range," Lily said as she slipped a white covering over her clothes and put on a clear faceplate. "For such a devastating explosion, the bomb itself is smaller than the tip of your pinkie finger."

The surgeon opened the man's scalp and exposed the area of skull she needed to get to. Opening that safely took only a few minutes more. Something that had once been extremely risky in the surgical arena was now routine.

The bomb was a small sphere, just as Lily had said. The antitampering circuit was wrapped around it like foil. It wasn't even directly wired into the Rebel Empire noble's implants.

Lily carefully removed it and set it on the tray holding her instruments. "Now what?"

"The antitampering circuit has a small control node," Kelsey said. "It's probably on the other side. Can you roll it over? Thanks."

A moment later she sighed with relief. "It's the Raider version. I can even see the model number. It has an intentionally undocumented hardware deactivation area. If someone were badly injured or if they were brain dead, this procedure was used to recover information."

"Why was it undocumented?" he asked. "And if so, how do you know?"

Kelsey turned her head toward him. "It wasn't in any of the official manuals available to the rank and file. The records I have contain even the most rarefied secrets of the Raiders and their gear. Stuff generals needed to know."

"Where is the deactivation area, and what do I need to do?" Lily asked.

"This area here," Kelsey said, probably highlighting something only the two of them could see. "It's very straightforward. We need to apply cooling to get just this little area below freezing and the circuit shuts down. It can't be more than the small area I'm pointing at, or it won't work."

"Show me the boundary," Lily said as she reached for another tool. "It's going to be slightly tricky, so if you two would give me some quiet time, I'd appreciate it.

"How long does it need to be cold for? Does it reactivate after a period of time? I need to know how fast I'm going to have to work."

"Once you do this, it's off for good," Kelsey said. "This kind of hardware wasn't ever reused. All you need to do is get it under the freezing point for a few seconds. We can put the disarmed bomb back in without an antitampering circuit."

Lily manipulated her instruments for a few seconds. "Okay, that should do it. I'm going to remove the antitampering wrapping, so I suggest you take a few steps back."

Jared stood firm, and after a moment's hesitation, so did Kelsey.

The doctor used a pair of forceps to grip the explosive and unwrapped the antitampering foil. Jared's heart stuttered, but the explosive didn't go off.

There was only a single access point on the bomb's surface, so Lily opened it and found the manual switch to deactivate the device. Seconds later, it was an inert prop they could put back into Fielding's head.

They watched Lily sterilize it and then put it back inside Fielding's head. Ten minutes later, the work was done.

"I understand that the research scientists from Dresden have something similar," Lily said as she stripped off her surgical cover. "Now that we've restored communication with our Kelsey, Zac Zoboroski can get them fixed up. I'll want a chance to explain this in detail to him myself as soon as possible."

"Go down to engineering, and someone will help you make that happen. Excellent work, both of you."

"That means more to me than I'd expected," Kelsey said after a moment. "Were you really that confident in me?"

"You're not the kind of person that makes claims you can't back up," Jared said firmly. "If you say you know something, I'll take that to the bank."

"You're really not him," she said slowly. "I have to accept that I'm doing you a great disservice. Fine, as far as I'm concerned, you're not Mertz anymore. You're Mertz Two."

He shook his head resolutely. "No. I'm Jared. Call that other me Mertz or the Bastard all you like, but I'm the kind of man that goes by his first name with family."

"Are we really family? You have Imperial blood and I don't."

That made him smile. "Family is who we choose. I'm not genetically related to you, but I'm sure as hell your family. I'll be your friend too, if you'll allow it."

"I'll try," she said slowly. "I can't promise, but I'll try."

Inside, he felt elated. This was the kind of breakthrough he'd dreamed of making. Its importance could not be overstated.

"Shall we get something to eat?" he asked after a moment.

"You *do* know me," she said with a smile. "Let's do that."

* * *

Kelsey tried not to keep asking how long it would take them to get to their destination. Don Sommerville, Angela, and she rode in one of the new picket ship's cutters, and they thought they were keeping her in the dark about where they were taking her.

They'd shortstopped *Persephone* in the last system, just on the other side of the flip point with Sommerville's older brother.

"Okay," she finally asked. "Why didn't you tell your brother that it was already too late to keep us from finding out what's here?"

"There are varying levels of 'too late' under the circumstances. You have a probe here that has to operate on passive scanners. If you were here, you might be able to put out a dozen more and find out things you otherwise wouldn't.

"Also, as much as I love Gavin, he isn't cleared to know about this tech. You've already snuck the damned thing in here, so I might as well play along until I can brief the leadership team."

"What can we expect there?" Angela asked. "Are they going to be super pissed that we're even here? Or that we've been spying on them?"

"No one likes being spied on, so I wouldn't expect them to be very happy about that, but the advantages of what you're offering more than offset any unpleasant surprises. Particularly if you can demonstrate one of those multi-flip points. Do you think there's one in this system?"

Kelsey shrugged a little. "That's hard to say without looking. We've found one in maybe half the systems we've looked in, but we were usually running for our lives. We haven't seen enough to know what the frequency actually is.

"If there is one here, it won't take long to demonstrate how much of a game changer it is. One can give you access to a dozen systems if you're lucky. Some of them not on the normal flip point network. That's how the Clans stayed hidden so long."

"A completely different network," Sommerville mused. "I get it, but that's so hard to get my mind around. There could be civilizations mixed all through the Empire and no one would know, as long as they weren't using powerful transmitters. Even aliens like the Pandorans."

He turned toward Kelsey. "Do you think some of them would stay to talk with us? They're literally just a few flips away from here."

"You'll have to ask Derek and Jacob Howell. With the Clans running wild in Archibald, you don't dare make passage."

"That won't last. They're still consolidating at Archibald, but they'll have to move most of their units out once they have the people there under their thumb. A ship searching for the Q-ship that got away is one that can't be conquering another system.

"They'll leave enough ships to protect the planet and flip points and figure the rogue ship will starve or come in to fight. They can't be that worried about one ship."

The speaker over their head came to life. "We're on the final leg inbound," the pilot said. "Twenty minutes until we dock."

"Well, here's to hoping your leader doesn't just space us," Angela said with a sigh.

The final minutes went smoothly enough, and the cutter docked without incident.

Sommerville rose to his feet. "Don't be too upset at the level of protection in there. You're both heavily modified, so they'll probably be there in force."

"There is no shame in honoring a threat," Kelsey said, standing and straightening her shirt. "And there's no insult to be taken seriously. Though now that Angela is a Raider, you can bet they'll see her as the biggest threat. That stings a little."

Angela laughed. "I won't correct their misapprehension either. It's a blow to my ego that you can still take me four out of five falls."

The cutter's hatch opened, and Sommerville led the way out. Kelsey followed him and found the corridor almost deserted. Only three people stood waiting for them: a tall blonde with an exceptionally curvy figure in the center with two large men at her back. They had the feel of guards, and her implants confirmed their status. They had lots of weapons on them.

The woman stepped forward and extended her hand to Sommerville. "It's good to see you again, Don. We were worried when you didn't show up on schedule. We were even more worried when you appeared with unexpected guests."

She turned her attention to Kelsey and once more held out her hand. "You must be Kelsey Bandar. Don has told us a lot about you, but I get the impression that there's more than meets the eye when it comes to you."

Kelsey smiled. "You have no idea. Thank you for meeting with us.

This is Major Angela Ellis. She commands *Persephone* for me. Might I ask your name?"

The woman shook Angela's hand. "Of course. I'm Sara Gatewood, commander of the resistance and the woman who decides if you get to leave this station alive when I'm done hearing you out. I hope you've brought your best pitch, because you won't get a second try at making this particular first impression."

30

Olivia was sitting in a comfortable chair when Fielding woke abruptly and tried to sit up. The restraints on his arms and legs made that difficult, but he finally managed to lever himself into a sitting position.

"What is the meaning of this?" he demanded. "What have you done?"

She smiled brightly at him. "Good morning, sleepyhead! Rise and shine. It's time to finalize our business together."

"What did you do?" he demanded again.

"Nothing you need be too concerned about. We just made some updates to the criteria in the bomb in your head. That code you had for disabling it? Sorry about that, but it's functional again. We've also made sure that it's in your best interests not to talk about us, what we're doing, or the fact we can update implant code."

The man paled at that. "Bitch, I'll see you dead for this."

Olivia laughed. "Please, save the threats for someone that cares. I've got more serious enemies on my horizon. The Lords will want me dead soon enough, and they're far more problematic.

"I also wouldn't count on your guards being very supportive, since

I convinced them you were going to kill them first thing. It helped that I'm absolutely sure that's what you were going to do."

"That hardly matters," the man said with a grunt. "I can replace them at any time. This changes nothing between us. You will die at my hands, so keep looking over that pretty shoulder of yours."

"So what you're saying is that I should space you now and save myself the trouble later? Perhaps that's good advice. All I need are codes to shorten my journey by a few days. Hardly something worth a lifelong blood feud. You're seriously undercutting your value to me, Oscar. I suggest you turn that around and make yourself worth leaving alive."

His eyes showed the realization that he'd made a mistake being so open about his plans. That almost made her laugh. No version of this, short of his death, made it less likely he'd try to get revenge. Rebel Empire nobles could sometimes be too petty for their own good.

"That's all you want? The codes to get to Terra through the systems on the shortest route in exchange for my life, my cutter, and everything on it?"

"That's the deal. You give me the passage codes for the systems we're coming up to and I'll drop you and your cutter with everything now on it at the last inhabited system before Terra.

"As for coming for me, feel free. If I see you or anyone I suspect of being from you, I'll see that you get what's coming to you. Remember that I can send a message all across the Empire with a code to blow up your head. It doesn't even have to go through your implants. I can have an agent find you and send an innocuous message or even say something to you in public."

She made a gesture with both hands showing her head exploding.

"I suggest you lick your wounds and pray that we never think of one another again. The codes. We have four flips by my estimation. The next system is occupied, the following empty, the third occupied, and the last not. If anyone gets too interested in us, I'll kill you before I ask why."

When he made to speak, she held up her hand. "You have no leverage. Any betrayal ends you first. Save your threats of retribution for someone else. Give. Me. The. Codes."

For a few seconds, she was certain that he'd refuse, but he sighed and sent her a file with two passage codes and the systems they were good for. They'd find out soon enough if they were good, she supposed.

"I'm glad you've seen the way clear to making all our lives easier. I believe this concludes our business."

He smiled a bit snidely. "You'll forgive me if I don't wish you good luck at Terra. I hope you die there."

"Life is rarely so helpful as to kill our enemies so conveniently. I'll have my people escort you to a room. Once we get to the third system and are almost clear, I'll release you. We won't meet again unless you are far stupider than you look."

Without another word, she rose and made her way out of the medical Center. Jared, Sean, Austin, Elise, Kelsey Two, and Scott Roche were waiting in a nearby conference room.

"That went well," Sean said. "You do have a way with people, dear."

She laughed. "It went as well as I expected. Austin, did you have any luck with the data cores from the financial institutions?"

Austin smiled. "My uncle never was very good with passcodes, and I have all the biometric data I need. A few are proving recalcitrant, but I hope to manage them shortly. We have enough money to pay off the guards and get them on their way, as well as sourcing some drones in the next system."

Olivia smiled. "That's good. I really wish we knew what he stole from the AI. Did the data give you any more ideas about what it does?"

"I think it generates a recognition code," Austin said. "It takes the serial number entered as an input and comes up with a different code for each of the System Lords. What that does or where it's used, I have no idea."

"Whatever it is, it will have to wait for another time," Jared said. "We flip in an hour. Let's go make sure we're ready for trouble in case Fielding is sticking a knife in our collective backs. This is it, people. The endgame is upon us. Frankly, I was starting to think we'd never get to Terra at this point."

"Are we there yet?" Olivia asked with a smirk.

"Don't make me turn this secret mission around," Jared said with a smile. "Good work, everyone. Now let's make it count."

* * *

ANGELA FOLLOWED Kelsey's lead and said nothing about the threat the woman had just made. Or maybe threat was the wrong word. Perhaps it was the simple truth.

"I think we can make our case," Kelsey said. "I can prove a number of things and provide some technology you'll want, but I have a peculiar request to make before we get started. I need someone with implants to do that."

Gatewood raised an eyebrow. "That is an unusual request. Why?"

"Since I can tell you have implants, telling you would be very shocking."

The woman smiled. "I like being shocked. Not many of us have implants, so I'm as good as anyone to tell this to. I assume you'd like some privacy, so let's adjourn to my office."

The walk to Gatewood's office didn't take too long, so Angela thought the facility might be somewhat smaller than she'd originally guessed. Once they'd arrived, Gatewood sat behind a wide desk and gestured for them to sit in front of it. The guards took up position at the door.

"So, what is this shocking secret?" she asked.

"Let me warn you up front that it will cause you to attack me and you won't be able to stop yourself," Kelsey said. "We brought some equipment on the cutter that can stop the reaction, but we'll have to subdue you and wait for it to be vetted by your people. Trust me when I tell you that you won't want to be awake for that."

Sommerville pulled a somatic stimulator from his jacket. "I brought this and have already checked it out."

The woman seemed amused. "You think I'll go berserk and need to be put to sleep simply because you tell me something? That's crazy."

"Also," Angela said, "if you want to keep your guards from being hurt, you'll need to tell them to stand down beforehand. I don't want to have to hurt anyone."

"You're a big woman, but they have stunners and flechette pistols," Gatewood said. "I think they're safe."

"On your head, then," Angela said. "I'll try to leave them in one piece."

Sommerville held up his hand. "You might want to at least review the scan data from these two. They aren't as helpless as they seem."

The resistance leader waved him off. "I'll play this game for a bit. Guards, take no action if I inexplicably lose my mind. There. All safe."

Angela could see the woman wasn't taking them seriously, so she felt badly about what was about to happen. This wouldn't be pretty.

"My name is Kelsey Bandar, as you know," Kelsey said with a small shake of her head. "What you don't know is that I'm also the crown princess of the New Terran Empire, a sliver of humanity that the AIs never subdued. We're both unsubjugated humans."

Gatewood blinked twice and then stood bolt upright, a snarl on her face as she leapt over her desk at Kelsey.

Angela was already on her feet and moving for the guards. She knew they wouldn't just stand there and gawk.

Her rapid movement took the guards by surprise, since they were staring at their boss. Angela swept both of them off their feet with a powerful kick, grabbed a fallen stunner, and had them both covered a moment later.

"I'll shoot you if I have to," she said quietly. "Just let this play out like your leader ordered."

A glance back showed that Kelsey already had Gatewood pinned, and a wide-eyed Sommerville was putting the somatic stimulator on her head. Moments later, the leader of the resistance was out.

"Let them up, Angela," Kelsey said. "We're not going to do anything else until they check out the equipment we brought to clean out the corrupted implant code. We'll explain it as many times as we need to and satisfy them that we're telling them the truth."

"You two know me," Sommerville said as he turned toward the guards. "She's going to be pissed as it is, so let's get moving. The sooner she's awake and ready to really listen, the better for all of us."

Angela hoped the resistance leader really was going to listen before she spaced them. Well, at least the woman couldn't say they didn't warn her. Maybe this would speed up the belief process and get them off to Terra faster.

Sure, and pigs could fly.

31

Kelsey waited for Sean to finish locking down the cutter and stepped out into the orbital station with him. It looked a lot like many of the other civilian stations she'd been on over the years, but it was creepy knowing that these people that seemed so familiar were her enemies.

"What's the plan?" she asked quietly as they headed toward the main hatch leading out of the bay.

"We won't have to go far into the station. Cargos trade hands here all the time. We need a lot of drones, so that's not exactly a standard request, but someone will be able to get their hands on some."

"What if they get suspicious?"

He smiled at her. "What are they going to think? That we're needing a cargo of drones to pull a scam on the Lords? No. Drones in that quantity are unusual, but not exactly illegal or suspicious. We'll tell them they're for crop monitoring on one of the less inhabited worlds or something like that."

She nodded. "And once we have them, how do we get Fielding's guards out of the ship without raising some kind of alarm? They monitor who goes in and out of the cargo bays. If we just let them walk out, one of them might feel inclined to make trouble. We have to leave them unmonitored while we leave the system. If they decide to stick a knife in our backs, we can't stop them."

"Olivia gave them the same story about the bombs in their heads as she did Fielding. They think that if they mention us to anyone, or even hint at the mission, their heads will pop off."

That made her chuckle. "She plays rough. Make a note not to get on her bad side."

"Already done. That should keep them quiet for a long time. Probably the rest of their lives. Meanwhile, we get to Terra and get what we came for."

"What about getting back?" she asked. "I've heard lots of plans for getting to Terra, but not one about the trip back to Avalon. I realize Mertz... Jared has a fleet sneaking around to meet us, but there's a war on, even if the people here don't know it yet.

"And that doesn't even count the System Lord at Terra and its defenses. Once we walk into its reach, it might not exactly be inclined to let us leave again. If it decides to kill us, we don't exactly have the forces on hand to stop it. If it gets word out, we'll have a fight we can't win, even if we do make it out and head for Avalon at full speed."

"If Kelsey One can get into Terra through a multi-flip point or a far flip point, we can leave the same way. Hopefully without letting the System Lord know about it. If not, we improvise."

They'd come up to a table with several men and women checking things on computer screens as merchants bargained. One of the men gestured for them to step up. "Welcome to Calico Station. You selling, buying, or transshipping?"

"Buying," Sean said. "We need six crates of reconnaissance drones for detailed mapping of a planetary surface. I think there are about a thousand per crate. It needs to be six crates so we can drop them in six areas."

The man blinked. "That's a lot of drones. I don't even have to check to know we don't have anything like that on the station. I can probably find enough on the planet, but it'll take a while to get them up here and consolidated. What do you need so many drones for?"

"Crop and wildlife management on one of the less inhabited

worlds," Kelsey said, as casually as she could. "They've got a problem with a nonindigenous species eating the food."

The man considered that for a moment. "Huh. Never heard of anything like that. Well, let me see if I can locate something that'll work for you. If you could give me a few minutes, I'll wave you back over when I'm done."

They stepped away and watched the crowd as the man worked. The merchants were a different kind of people than Kelsey was used to. As a princess, she'd dealt mostly with people in the high civil government. Once she'd gone on the expedition, she'd worked almost exclusively with Fleet personnel and marines.

The merchants were a boisterous, pushy lot. In a way, they acted a bit like strutting birds, showing off their ruffles to the other birds. In this case, the other merchants. She wasn't quite sure why they were doing it, but it *was* entertaining.

It also made it easy to spot an outsider in the group. Like oh, say, themselves.

A tall, gaunt man with the look of a used grav car salesman came over to them. "Welcome to Calico Station. Is this your first time here? I pass through quite often and don't recognize you."

The man's voice had a slick, kind of oily tone. When he extended his hand to them, Kelsey found it unpleasantly moist.

She smiled brightly as she slid the soiled appendage behind her and wiped it on her pants. "First time," she confirmed. "How did you know?"

"I have an eye for that sort of thing," the man confided in her. "I can always spot the new people. What ship are you with?"

"I'm sorry, but I didn't catch your name," Sean said. "I'm Sean and this is Kelsey."

"Daniel Goldman, captain of *Grey Doom*," the man said, his smile widening. "You probably saw her on the way in. She's the fastest packet in the sector."

Kelsey tried not to frown as she wondered what a packet was. Her implant database wasn't helping.

Sean, on the other hand, seemed to know exactly what the man meant. "So, you specialize in getting small, high-value cargos from place to place in the shortest time."

"And with the fewest... entanglements," the man smugly confirmed.

In other words, he was a smuggler. Interesting, but it made her wonder why the man was engaging them. Didn't he have some illegal cargo to be slipping past customs?

"And that brings me back around to you," the man said. "To the best of my very good memory, you've never been here before. What ship did you say you were with again?"

Kelsey saw that Sean wasn't going to have a good answer, but she didn't either. Then she spotted a solution to their problem: a pair of security officers that had just come into the bay.

Normally, she'd have been terrified they were going to spot her or Sean, but in this one particular case, they're timely arrival had given them an out to the awkward situation.

"Don't look now, Captain Goldman, but I think someone is looking for you," she said in a low voice, looking pointedly at the security officers.

To her amusement, the new arrivals actually did seem interested in the smuggler. One of them nudged the other, and they both altered course toward Goldman.

"If you'll excuse me, I forgot another pressing engagement," the smuggler said. "I'm sure we'll meet again at some point. Good day."

Goldman adroitly moved into the crowd of merchants, and the security men split up to follow him from different directions, trying to get an angle on cornering him, no doubt.

"I never thought I'd be happy to see Rebel Empire security," Sean said. "I couldn't very well tell him we were in a Fleet destroyer."

"No, and with any luck at all, we'll be loaded up and gone before he gets back around to looking for us," she said. "The clerk is waving. He has a smile, so I think he found us something that will get him a good commission. Let's go see how fast we can get the drones up here and be on our way."

* * *

TALBOT WAITED until the marines had Theo 309 in his chair before he sat on the other side of the table. "This must be awkward," he commiserated. "Having someone outside the Singularity gain access to all that data. Puts you in something of a bind when it comes to dodging my questions."

The other man smiled wanly. "It *is* inconvenient, but I see no reason to make this any easier for you. We all have our duties to perform."

"And yours revolve around Operation Brutus."

The prisoner froze for just a moment and then smiled. "I'm sorry. What's that?"

Talbot grinned. "That would be the operation you're working with the Clans. You know, the one where you help them get set up to attack the Empire and then use the distraction to try and roll it over and beat them both. Makes me wonder if you have something in their ships as a Trojan horse to make them easy to take out when the time comes.

"Anyway, it looks like they got started a few decades ahead of schedule. That has to suck. Your people don't even know it's happening yet, I bet. You're not ready to attack, but now you have no choice, or your secret weapon is gone forever."

Theo 309 licked his lips. "You've gotten far more access to that computer than I would have wished, and in far too quick a fashion. Let me remind you that you initiated the hostilities with the Clans. My hands are clean, and I still consider myself to be a diplomatic envoy from my nation. One you must eventually release me or risk war with my people."

Talbot leaned back in his chair. "I've been doing some reading on the relations between our people. It seems like we've been at war for far longer than either of us has been alive. Oh, I'll admit that's mostly low-level conflict at the border, but it's never really died down, has it?

"Further, as you've probably already guessed since you're a smart man, the person that attacked the Clans was a prisoner of ours that escaped. It won't make a difference in the end, I suppose, but I want to be clear that we did not attack your people or your allies in this mess. We simply defended ourselves when we had no choice. Our leaders asked to talk before the Clans started shooting."

The Singularity envoy chuckled. "Oh, what a complicated web of deceit diplomacy is. Everyone pretends innocence but has a well-honed knife just out of sight. There's no way to prove that. I presume you are claiming membership in the resistance."

The man's smile widened. "I have heard of them, you see. Oh, they keep their heads down and make trouble when they can, but we also have people inside the Empire to be certain of our own security. Your superiors will be very displeased when they discover you've started this conflict."

Talbot pursed his lips. "But did we? I suspect not, at least not when one really gets down to the truth. Tell me, when the AIs took over the Empire, why didn't they also conquer the Singularity? They had to have had the strength, and they didn't give squat about the people they enslaved and killed. Why stop at your border?"

"Perhaps I can ask one if we ever have tea."

Talbot nodded, letting the idea that had been simmering in his head percolate up to the top. "I wonder if it really was an accident that the Master AI went rogue. Manipulating someone—or something—else to fight your enemies seems exactly like a course of action that the Singularity would approve of."

The man's smile faltered just the least little bit before becoming noticeably brighter. "You do have quite the imagination! The only problem with it is that my people are not bloody-handed monsters. When you get right down to it, we're not that different than you and your people. We sprang from the same home world, after all."

Talbot tsked softly. "You talk a good game, but we both know that your people are each engineered for the role you play in society. Your DNA, while it might have many things in common with humanity, was designed and engineered from the ground up.

"And you spoke of your people, not your leaders. That's a specific caste, is it not? The tattoos you sport mark you as one of them. Not a worker but a leader.

"As one leader to another, you can tell me the truth. The Singularity and the Empire were at war, and this was a ploy. Perhaps one that went far more wrong than your ancestors had intended, I'm willing to grant, but the Singularity or its agents manipulated the Master AI and turned it against its creators."

Talbot smiled coldly when he saw just a hint of perspiration on the other man's forehead. He was onto something.

"What went wrong? Did the part of the code you put in about sticking to the Imperial borders work, but the part where they were supposed to turn control over to you failed? Did the general military fighting you wanted turn into virtual genocide? That's bad, and now you're stuck fighting the computers you helped suborn to get what you really want: control of all humanity."

"We're done here," Theo 309 said, his voice a little hoarse. "I want to return to my quarters."

"I'm sure you do," Talbot said, rising slowly. "We'll discuss this in more detail later. You're not going anywhere for a very long time."

32

J ared watched Olivia give the four guards their last pep talk and send them on their way with a large amount of money and warnings about ever mentioning anything about meeting them to anyone. He was pretty sure she used the words "explosive revelation" at least once.

Once the cutter left to take the guards to the orbital station, where they were supposed to catch other ships and disperse, he tried to convince himself that it was all going to work out. Somehow, he couldn't shake the feeling that something would go wrong.

"Relax," Olivia said as she stepped over to him. "They won't tell a soul, especially now. They're worried that Fielding will be after them the moment he gets loose, and they want to be as far away from him as they can get. They're focused on running for their lives for the moment."

"And when they get somewhere they feel safe? They'll eventually do or say something that makes them suspect the bombs aren't active. It's only a matter of time."

"We can only control what we can," she admitted. "We need to get to Terra, get what we need, and get back out again. Frankly, the Clans and the AIs are far bigger threats than the guards."

"Let's just hope that Kelsey and Sean get things worked out quickly and we can be on our way. We'll make it into Terra before word of the Clans reaches this area, but we might not be clear if we take too much time getting the override."

His implants pinged with an incoming message from the bridge. Kelsey's cutter was on the way back, ETA fifteen minutes.

Jared accessed the destroyer's scanners and was pleased to see that the cutter was moving sedately rather than rushing back to the ship. That probably meant no one was chasing them.

"Kelsey and Sean are inbound," he said. "We should wait for them."

Right on schedule, the cutter docked. Kelsey and Sean came out, looking relaxed.

"Everything go okay?" Jared asked.

"We had a few bumps," Kelsey admitted, "but we got the drones and didn't tip anyone off that we were any different than the rest of the merchants. The drones will be here in about an hour. We had to pay significantly more than they'd normally be worth, but it's not my money."

"Excellent. The guards are on their way to the station. The marines will hold them in the cutter until we're ready to leave orbit. Once they turn them loose, they'll come back to this ship, and we'll boost for the flip point.

"The next system is empty of human habitation, so we'll make a quick crossing and get to the last populated system before the buffer around Terra. Then we'll do the same with Fielding."

"I think we should be more careful with Fielding," Sean said. "If anyone is going to betray us, it'll be him."

Olivia smiled. "Rest assured that I have a plan. We'll release him as we agreed, but I intend to see that he's unconscious for as long as possible and then locked into his cutter on a timer."

"He'll be pissed," Sean said with a grin. "Probably worse than he would've already been."

The four of them adjourned for lunch and returned to the cargo hold to oversee the unloading and inspection of the crates. Thankfully, they were outwardly very similar to the ones that had contained the drones with the Omega Plague.

The delivery went smoothly enough, and in short order Jared was back on the bridge and *Athena* was on her way out of the system.

"Admiral, there's a ship trailing us," Commander Hall said from the helm console. "He's staying way back, but he's heading for the same flip point."

He frowned. "Is it a warship?"

She shook her head. "Maybe a message courier or something made to carry smaller amounts of cargo quickly."

"It's a fast packet," Kelsey said with a sigh. "We ran into a smuggler on the station that was curious about us and our ship. He ran off when security showed up looking for him, but I'll bet anything that's him."

"Do you think he'll cause us any trouble?" Sean asked. "Or is this him satisfying his curiosity while making a hasty retreat from Imperial entanglements?"

Jared had to smile at that, even though this Kelsey wouldn't get the old Terran movie reference. His Kelsey had made him watch a space adventure where a smuggler very much wanted to avoid that very thing. From the gleam in his eye, Sean had made the reference intentionally.

"Who knows?" Kelsey asked with a shrug, the interplay going over her head. "He's a criminal, so there's no telling what he'll do."

"Make transition as if we haven't noticed him," Jared ordered. "Then pull back from the flip point, and we'll say hello when he pops out."

"Yes, sir," Hall said.

A few hours later, they transitioned right on schedule, with the other ship following at the same rate of speed as earlier. They had to wait for two hours for the other ship to flip, and by that time, they were powered down and silent.

Their apparent absence sparked a reaction from the smuggler. He boosted speed to well above what even *Athena* could manage and raced toward the next flip point on a course that took him around in an unexpected arc. Perhaps that was to avoid running headlong into an ambush.

Jared was happy to let him rabbit away. He wasn't looking for a fight.

They'd already launched a stealthed probe toward the other flip point, so they'd know when he made transit. They'd follow at a slower pace and steer clear of his scanners. It would put them a little behind schedule, but it wasn't as if they were going to blow up this time.

With any luck, the smuggler would give up on his curiosity and move into the next system. Hell, even if he were curious still, he'd do that. It was much less likely that anyone would shoot at him in an occupied system, after all.

"Let's let him build up some more distance, Commander Hall, then half speed. Move up only enough to keep us off his scanners. Let's assume he's got good ones."

"Yes, sir."

With that, he leaned back in his seat and waited. One more occupied system and they'd be to Terra. It felt like they'd been on the way to it forever, but the journey was just about over. Then the real fight would begin.

* * *

Kelsey watched Sara Gatewood wake up abruptly as soon as Sommerville turned the somatic stimulator off. The woman was in a modern medical center, lying on a bed, but fully clothed as she'd been when they'd taken her down.

She blinked rapidly for a moment and then shook her head as she sat up. "That was… unpleasant. I had no idea that kind of thing was even possible. I tried to stop myself but couldn't. My apologies for both doubting you and attacking you."

"You have nothing to apologize for," Kelsey said. "You had no reason to suspect the Lords had done this to everyone that has implants. Your experts looked over the updated implant code and are studying the changes between the original code and the corrupt version you had.

"With Don Sommerville's assurances, they okayed us updating yours. That will never happen to you again. We have some hardware that we could install that will make it impossible for them to ever change you back or update the code without your informed consent, but that's something you can do for yourself."

Gatewood rubbed her face and swung her legs over the side of the bed. "We have a couple of hundred people with implants, mostly former Fleet officers, but a few members of the higher orders, too. I mean here. We have a lot more members of the higher orders in other systems. How the hell am I going to handle this?"

Sommerville put a hand on her shoulder. "It's something we can manage. It won't happen immediately, but the knowledge of the New Terran Empire doesn't have to leave a close circle here until we're ready. Frankly, we have more pressing matters to deal with."

Gatewood nodded and stood. "I'll speak to my people and look at their findings with the implant code another time. You're really from a world without the Lords?"

"Dozens of worlds," Kelsey confirmed. "We're not as large as the Empire, and we're starting at a technological disadvantage, but we're making headway and have a military force that isn't anything to be ashamed of."

"I can second that," Sommerville said. "Not only from records they've showed me but from walking the decks of their carrier, *Audacious*. It's the largest warship I've ever seen, and even though it's designed to service fighters—which are astonishing in their own right—she still has enough firepower to take on three or four heavy cruisers all on her own."

Kelsey nodded. "We found the place where the Lords stashed any ships that weren't destroyed outright when they seized control. Most of them are unrepairable, but enough are to make a very powerful strike force.

"It also gave us a leg up from the technology level we'd been at before we found them. We're growing, but we've still got a way to go."

"That's not true," Sommerville disagreed. "I've also seen technology that can't be explained by recovered technology. Things that we could desperately use."

"Like what?" Gatewood asked him.

He looked meaningfully at the medical staff. They were standing too far away to have heard any of the previous conversation, but she didn't want to take any chances with them overhearing anything.

"Everyone out and close the hatch," Gatewood told the other people in the room. When the two men guarding her made to stay, she motioned them out too.

Once the room was cleared, she focused her attention on Sommerville. "Like what?" she repeated.

"Faster-than-light communications that can cross a flip-point boundary."

The woman's eyes narrowed. "I don't think that's possible."

"I've seen it with my own eyes."

"We've also arranged a demonstration for you," Kelsey said. "I assume you know Commander Sommerville's brother fairly well."

She nodded. "I do. You want me to send him a message. Does that mean you have a communications unit with you?"

"Actually, we slipped a stealthed FTL probe into this system before we left the previous one," Angela said. "Since your picket ship was a shade too far away from the flip point and it's wickedly hard to detect under the best of circumstances, we had an idea of what was here before we arrived."

The woman's eyes hardened. "That's not very neighborly." Her eyes slid to Sommerville. "You knew?"

"It was already done, and honestly, I wanted to see it for myself. It was a demonstration for me, too."

Gatewood sighed. "What do we do?"

Kelsey removed her com unit and handed it to the resistance leader. "This is presently linked to the probe. If you send a message, it will go to my ship in the next system, and they'll transmit it to Gavin Sommerville. They're expecting the call, so no need to explain it to them. It will let the cat out of the bag, though. Your man will know."

"I trust Gavin," she said. "I'll make sure he's alone when he gets it."

She kept her eyes on Kelsey and activated the com. "This is Sara Gatewood. When you signal Gavin Sommerville, request he listen to this message in private, his ears only. Message starts. Gavin, this is Sara. I understand this is confusing, but it's a Code Hero situation, and I'll explain it when you get over here.

"Without sending any probes through the flip point, I want you to escort the other ship into Home. After you tell them what's going on, I want a communications blackout. Neither ship is to signal anyone before transit. Hand them off to the picket ship on this side and stay right there in the flip point and scan hard, looking for any probes to try flipping in or out.

"Acknowledge receipt of this order and also tell me who you're presently seeing to authenticate your identity. And by seeing, I mean sleeping with. Gatewood out."

Kelsey took the com back. "This is Princess Kelsey. Do as the... do you have a title to go with your name?"

"I stole one from the Empire. Coordinator Gatewood, please."

"Do as Coordinator Gatewood told you," Kelsey finished. "See you shortly."

She handed the com back to Gatewood.

The other woman shook her head slightly. "It's a significant delay in transmission time to the flip point, even if this FTL story—"

The com came to life. "Message from Gavin Sommerville," a female voice Kelsey recognized as Arianna Knox said.

"Order received, though I have no idea how," Gavin Sommerville said. "As for who I'm sleeping with, you should damned well know, Sara. I'm your guy and yours alone. I do hope dinner is still on when I transfer back to station duty in a week. And the response is Code Hercules. Gavin out."

Don Sommerville's eyes widened. "You and Gavin? I had no idea."

"That's kind of the point," she said tartly. "If I'm going to have a relationship with a subordinate, we won't go blathering on about it."

She turned Kelsey. "I can't imagine how this even works, but you have my complete and undivided attention. This kind of technology changes *everything*. You want to trade this to us in exchange for an alliance and help getting to Terra?"

"This and some other things that Commander Sommerville

knows about. Potentially a few things he doesn't. We haven't shown all our cards, and we might not right away."

"They found aliens," Sommerville said. "I met some. They also have matter transportation that they got from another alien. That's not fully understood, though. And though I don't understand all the details, they know of a new kind of flip point that leads to multiple destinations and isn't readily detectable."

The resistance leader blinked. "Really? All that and more?"

Kelsey nodded. "Once you trust me to look, we'll scan the system for one. They're not in every system, but they're in enough that you have a chance of having one here."

One of the guards opened the hatch cautiously. "Coordinator, we just got word the picket ship in the next system flipped in with an unknown vessel."

Gatewood looked at Kelsey for a few moments. "They're expected. Stand down and have the near picket escort the ship here. They're friends, it seems."

Once the man left, Gatewood shook her head slightly. "This is all so unbelievable. If what you say is true, I'll agree to that alliance in a heartbeat, but it might not help you that much. We don't know of any hidden flip points leading into Terra."

"We call them far flip points," Kelsey said. "And that's potentially okay. If we can get into a close system, we might be able to use one of the multi-flip points to find a way into Terra."

She really hoped it would be that easy. If they couldn't find a way in, Jared was on his own.

33

O livia stood beside Jared's command console as they approached the main world in the last inhabited system short of Terra. The travel codes that Fielding had given them had gotten them permission to enter the system, and they were less than an hour away from orbit.

That was a relief. If the man had been going to betray them, this system had been the place. All they needed to do now was get rid of Fielding in such a way that he couldn't betray them or be discovered before they were long gone.

"This is it," Jared said softly. "We'll make orbit and stay long enough to get rid of Fielding and then head out. I figure six hours until we're into the buffer system between us and Terra.

"Everything I've seen indicates that one is unoccupied but patrolled by robotic ships. Through traffic is allowed along a direct corridor to the next flip point. The flip point leading to Terra is heavily guarded on the outside, and probably on the inside, too. Add another six hours to get to it."

"It seems so unreal," she said. "We've been trying to get here for so long, and now we're here. All the trouble thus far was just the journey. Now the fight to get what we need and escape again is in front of us, and it's intimidating."

He nodded. "True, but the AI doesn't know why we're really here. We can get in and back out again without giving ourselves away, especially with Kelsey's help. Both of them."

"That seems awfully optimistic," Olivia said. "I'm hoping it's true, mind you, but I'm leaning toward something serious going wrong with our plans."

"No plan survives contact with the enemy," he admitted with a wry smile. "That's a bit of history I picked up from Kelsey and her obsession with old Terran entertainment. I already knew it, but that's a very succinct saying.

"What it means is that we plan as best we can and be ready to adapt to the changing situation as quickly as we can. No one can predict the curve balls the pitcher throws at you, so you have to be flexible."

"What's a pitcher and why is he throwing balls at you?"

Jared chuckled. "That's not really important, and you don't have time to hear the story. It's time to get our guest ready for transport."

"I'm not worried about this part," she confided. "In fact, I'm counting on one of those curve balls you're throwing around."

"That's not how this works," he said with a chuckle. "Good luck."

With that, she left the bridge and made her way to the medical center. Lily Stone was waiting for her next to an unconscious Fielding. He had a somatic stimulator on his head and was resting peacefully.

"How is our soon-to-be-departed guest?" she asked.

"Stinking like three-day old fish, metaphorically speaking," the physician said with a smile. "I'll be glad when he's gone."

"When will he wake up?"

The doctor tapped a finger on the stimulator. "This has a timer that will shut it down in twelve hours. We should be long gone, and the only issue he'll have is being hungry and thirsty. I've loaded him up with fluids and energy. He'll probably be horrified that I've put a catheter into him, but I left written instructions so he can safely remove it. Attached to a handy spot he can't possibly miss."

Olivia laughed. "I can only imagine. Well, he's done more than enough that I don't feel badly about that. I'll take him from here."

The four marines waiting off to the side helped move the sleeping man onto a gurney, catching the sheet and almost pulling it all the way off. The unconscious noble was naked under the gown, and he did indeed have instructions taped to a... delicate area.

"I have his clothes in this," Lily said, handing her a bag. "Hurry up and get back. I want to be out of here long before he wakes up and comes after us."

"Your wish is my command," Olivia said. "Come on, boys."

The marines got the gurney to the docking tube leading to the noble's cutter and put him into an acceleration couch. They started to withdraw, but Olivia stopped them.

"Can I borrow a knife?"

They were marines, so she promptly had half a dozen blades to choose from, as some offered her two. The almost monomolecular edge of the blade she chose sliced off Fielding's gown with ease, leaving the unconscious man naked. It went into the bag with his clothes.

"Help me get rid of anything he can use to cover himself with," she said. "That'll keep him trapped on the cutter longer. His ego won't let anyone else see him in this condition."

It took fifteen minutes to get every scrap of cloth off the cutter, and every blade that could peel something off a seat. They even stripped the bed the man kept of its mattress and took the serving trays. There was nothing left for him to cover his nakedness with.

She even found something in his office to amuse herself with: a permanent marker. She made sure to leave a personal goodbye written on the man's naked form that set the marines to howling with laughter.

"Excellent," she said at last, making sure the grinning marines had removed all of the things they'd gathered. "I suppose I'm ready to go. Thanks, boys."

The Fleet pilot had stayed in the control area, though Olivia had seen the woman smirking at the antics in the cutter itself. That same expression dominated the woman's face when Olivia strapped herself in.

"He's going to be super pissed when he wakes up naked. And what were you doing with that permanent marker?"

"Leaving my own personal message," Olivia said serenely. "On his stomach with arrows. 'Objects are smaller than they appear.'"

The pilot laughed. "I had my own share of pranks at the academy. That stuff won't come out until it wears off in a few weeks. You ready? *Athena* just entered orbit, and we have clearance to make the trip over. The other cutter will shadow us and bring us back."

"Let's get this show on the road. The sooner we finish, the sooner we can get the hell out of here."

The flight over to the station didn't take very long, and they were quickly inside a cargo bay that reminded Olivia strongly of the one she'd been in at Archibald. It was hectic with activity, and people rushed about on tasks she couldn't begin to imagine.

A woman in deep-red coveralls met Olivia as soon as she debarked. "This pad is booked. You'll need to expedite your departure or relocate."

"If it's booked, why did your people direct me to it?" Olivia asked, irritated.

"Wasn't booked then," the woman said with a shrug. "Happened right before you landed. You want to bitch about it, talk to him."

The last few words were accompanied with a gesture toward a man standing nearby, smirking at Olivia.

"Fine," she growled as she headed toward the man. "Why are you screwing with me?"

"Fair seems fair," he said. "You screwed with me on the trip from the last system."

Olivia felt her eyes narrow. This had to be the smuggler. What had Kelsey said his name was? Or had she even mentioned it?

"Daniel Goldman," he interjected at her expression.

"And what can I do to make this situation up to you, Captain Goldman?" she asked through gritted teeth.

"I'm an inquisitive man," he admitted. "A personal failing in someone who takes cargos from one place to another without asking questions. Your presence on a destroyer has piqued my curiosity. Perhaps you could trade some answers for the parking slip?"

She felt her lips pull up into a smile. "Or I could give you another set of questions that might be worth your time. Step inside and take a look at my cutter."

His eyes narrowed, but he followed her in, only to stop abruptly at the lavish interior and the sight of the naked man strapped into one of the chairs.

"I wasn't sure what you wanted me to see, but I'll freely admit this wasn't on my scanners. Why do you have a naked man asleep in here? And where did you get this fabulous cutter?"

"I can't say. What I can say with certainty is that I'm leaving this cutter and everything it contains here, and I don't care what happens to it. He'll wake up on his own in about eleven hours without having taken any harm, but he's going to be severely pissed. Particularly if someone stole his very lavish cutter."

"I'm sure that would be unfortunate," the smuggler said, his expression odd. "I've boosted a number of small craft over the years, but no one ever handed one to me with a smile and a hook."

"A hook?" she asked.

"A mystery that will have me asking questions I'm sure I probably don't want to have answered."

"Excellent," she said cheerfully. "You'll want to disable the manual lockout I put on the hatch to keep him penned in here. I never activated it, but it's still in there. You'll also want to make sure he never sees your face. He's a vindictive bastard. Good luck, Captain."

With that, she marched out and met the pilot as they walked casually to their other cutter and departed the station.

Only once they were clear did the pilot turn to face her. "Is that guy going to cause us trouble?"

"Maybe," Olivia murmured. "Maybe not. We won't know for sure until we meet him again. One thing I can say is that he'll cause Fielding a lot more trouble than us, so I'll take it."

* * *

ANGELA STARED at the scanner plot and couldn't believe how quickly the negotiations with the resistance had gone. *Audacious* was still back at the Home system, settling things like the technology trade and seeing that the newly appointed Ambassador Justine Bandar was installed and briefed.

Other people would be staying there as well. Commander Giguere and her officers, for one group. They'd be good assets for the resistance. Prince Derek, his human associate Jacob Howell, and their entire party had decided to remain. The resistance was close enough to Pandora to get them back home after their adventure.

Princess Kelsey had also decided to leave the human Clan prisoners they'd captured with the resistance, as well as the crazy Rebel Empire security officer that had tried to kill Veronica Giguere.

Not Theo 309, though. His intelligence was too critical to the survival of the New Terran Empire. He'd be staying with them. Though she did leave the scientists that had been working on the Singularity computer. They'd refused to cooperate, and she was tired of carting around a circus of prisoners.

To everyone's shock, Commodore Murdock asked to remain as well. They'd promised her a new life, and she'd apparently decided this was it.

Finally, Doctor Lipp, her husband, and their minions were staying. They'd promised to drop them in the next safe system, and this was it. Perhaps they and the resistance could come to some agreement, but Angela doubted that. They were criminals, after all.

Ralph Halstead had decided to remain and had asked to work with Carl on the projects the young scientist was pursuing. With Carl's enthusiastic endorsement, he'd been allowed to do so.

Angela was thankful that Kelsey had sent *Persephone* ahead to scan the closest system the resistance could access to Terra. It had no connection to known Rebel Empire space and was empty of habitation, but it was easily in range of a multi-flip point. If they could find one.

"All probes away," Arianna Knox said. "We should have a full scan of the system in six hours or so. Do you think we'll get lucky?"

Angela shrugged. "I hope so. The resistance knows there are no other far flip points in this system and no regular ones at all. It's a cul-de-sac they never expected to be of use.

"The star is too hot for life to have developed, even if there had been a suitable world in the habitable zone. Basically, it's a curiosity they never looked at again after the initial exploration."

"But if it has a multi-flip point, it might go any number of interesting places," Knox said with a nod. "Based on our limited experience, we have about a fifty-fifty chance."

"Bump that up to a 100% chance," Jevon McLeod said from the tactical station. "Probe three just picked up a multi-flip point about an hour from our current location."

That made Angela smile. "Great news. Take us in, Jack."

She turned to her executive officer. "I'll leave this all in your hands while I go down and talk with my husband and Talbot in that makeshift lab. If there's a way to Terra here, Carl will find it."

The unspoken corollary was that if there wasn't, Admiral Mertz was screwed.

34

Kelsey stood behind Mertz and watched as *Athena* approached the flip point leading to Terra with far more nervousness than she'd expected. This was it, the moment where everything would either come together or fall apart.

"Send the recognition signal, Wanda," Mertz said, far more calmly than Kelsey would have been able to do herself.

"Signal away," Wanda Dieter said from the communications console. "Response received. We're to proceed through the flip point and receive instructions on the other side."

"Well, at least they aren't going to open fire on us right away," Mertz said with a wry smile. "Take us across, Janice."

While the helm officer worked her controls, he refocused his attention on Evan Brodie, the tactical officer. "Make sure to get good scans as we go, Evan. We'll want to have as much information as we can in case we have to come back in force."

That, of course, assumed that they'd be coming back. Or even leaving, for that matter.

The flip point was well covered with battle stations. Half a dozen of the massively armed stations orbited the flip point closely, ready to repel any attempt to access the system. Or to kill anyone that tried to leave it, she was sure.

The New Terran Empire destroyer moved between the stations, and Kelsey couldn't escape the impression that they were looming over her, their electronic brains targeting the ship while preparing to open fire.

Only they didn't. They allowed the destroyer through the defenses, and moments later, it flipped into the Terra system.

They'd finally made it.

The far side of the flip point was even more heavily armed and defended than the exterior side. A full dozen battle stations orbited the flip point at various distances. Some were close in while others sat farther away.

Scattered between them were dozens of warships: destroyers, light cruisers, and heavy cruisers. They were almost certainly computer controlled and not occupied.

Out of an abundance of caution, Mertz had previously ordered Wanda Dieter to retransmit their authorization as soon as they'd arrived. Whether the defenses were already expecting them or simply accepted the codes was unclear, but they didn't open fire.

"Where do we go now, sir?" Hall asked from the helm console.

"Take us deeper into the system while we take a look around," he said. "I'm sure the AI will have instructions for us before we get very far, but we've never been here before and need to get the layout of the system down.

"Where exactly is Terra in relation to this flip point? Where is the System Lord? How much mobile defense do they have wandering around that we need to be aware of? What other surprises do they have waiting for us?

"The AIs have done everything they can to keep humanity out of this system for so long that I refuse to believe they don't have things waiting for us now that we've arrived."

Wanda Dieter turned away from the communications console. "We have an incoming transmission from one of the battle stations, Admiral. We are to proceed to Terra at best speed and await further instructions there."

Janice Hall twitched a little and cursed under her breath. "The computer just received course and speed instructions, and we've begun moving. I realize that we set up the computer to respond as if it still had primary control of the ship, but that creeps me out."

So far as the Rebel Empire had been concerned, the human crew aboard the ship was running things, but it was obvious the AIs preferred to deal with their electronic minions and had sent instructions for the ship to carry out the directions rather than the crew.

Of course, they could immediately override the computer, and any of the really dangerous commands had been disabled long before they'd arrived in the system, but Kelsey had to agree with the helm officer. This was definitely creepy.

"Where do they seem to be taking us?" Mertz asked. "Are we going directly to Terra, or are they taking us on a more circuitous route?"

"We're headed directly in, sir. We're also moving at maximum military power. I'd estimate we'll be in Terra orbit in about five and a half hours. Right now, it looks as if the planet is almost on the other side of the sun from our current location."

Evan Brodie scowled at his console and looked back at his commanding officer. "We have an escort. They've detached three heavy cruisers to follow us in and have moved them into bracketing positions at close range. If we try to do anything at all, they can easily destroy us."

"Are we going to be able to launch any stealthed drones?" Mertz asked.

The tactical officer shook his head. "Not a chance, sir. They're far too close. They'd detect any probe leaving the ship immediately."

That made Kelsey curse. They'd been planning on seeding the Terra system with stealthed drones to get a complete layout of everything they'd have to deal with. They'd also hoped to send a few on to Terra before they arrived so that they could make plans on how best to carry out their mission while still seeming to carry out the one assigned to them by the AI.

She moved to stand next to Mertz's chair and spoke to him in a low voice. "Do you think the AI was at the flip point? Those instructions came in pretty fast."

He shook his head. "No. I'd bet those instructions were left there because it expected us to arrive about now. After all, if we didn't show up shortly, we'd have exploded somewhere else. We had a lot of incentive to be on time.

"If I had to make a guess, the AI in command of this system is going to be in one of two places. It's either going to be concealed at one of the gas giants and controlling all of the system defenses from that remote location, or it's going to be in orbit around Terra.

"I'm betting on the latter. After all, that's where the fighting was taking place. It would probably want to have a good eye over what was occurring down on the surface."

She considered that for a long moment and then sighed. "It would be better for us if the AI was out on one of the gas giants, so we have to plan for it being in orbit around Terra. That's going to make things really awkward, particularly with our nursemaids keeping us from performing any sleight-of-hand."

He turned his chair to face her. "This was never going to be easy, Kelsey, but we'll find a way to do what we need to do. For one thing, we're going to have to disperse the drones all over Terra. We'll be able to get our people off the ship to explore the Imperial Palace. We'll find the vault."

"What if they used planetary bombardment and the vault no longer exists?"

That was the worst-case scenario. They'd have come all this way to get a device that was long dust. Then they'd have to find a way to outsmart the cybernetic overlord that had commanded them here and escape again without the override they all so desperately needed.

That she and her people so desperately needed.

Their best hope for success was her doppelgänger, she supposed. If the other Kelsey could find a way into the Terra system, she could bring forces here that the computer wouldn't be expecting. If there was a lot of activity in Terra orbit, it was still going to be dicey, but at least they wouldn't all be doomed out of hand.

"Well, I suppose it's a little late for me to complain now," she said glumly. "I hope to hell that other me is as resourceful as you say, because if she's not, we're in for a universe of hurt."

* * *

TALBOT MADE his way down to the makeshift lab that Carl had set up in *Persephone*'s hold. Unlike the one on *Audacious*, this one didn't contain all of the experiments and personnel that he normally had. His task here was brutally straightforward.

Now that they'd found a multi-flip point, he'd send probes through to determine what frequency bands led to different destinations and then explore them. As they knew from experience, those destinations might have other branches that led to even more systems.

Exploring them was only half the battle. Once they'd determined where the varying branches led, they needed to know how difficult it was going to be for a larger vessel to traverse them.

Persephone was a small ship that could make its way through all of the branches in the various multi-flip points that they'd discovered. Even with a specialized flip drive his friend had designed and built for her, *Audacious* was much too large to risk on some of the narrower channels they'd seen.

If they were unlucky, they wouldn't find a path to Terra at all, but if fate were cruel, it might give them a path that only the Marine Raider strike ship could take. That would let them into the system but deny them the majority of the force they'd brought with them.

"How's it going?" he asked Carl as he sat down.

The young scientist was working on a dedicated computer station, his hands flashing across the old-style keyboard. He barely glanced over at Talbot.

"We're just about ready to send the first probe through. That'll show us what the default destination is and give me a bunch of readings about what frequency bands are available and how we might use them to explore alternative branches. With the experience we already have, I should have some initial data fairly quickly."

"What do you think our chances are?" Talbot asked. "Both to find Terra and to get a passage big enough for *Audacious*?"

Carl stopped tapping his keyboard and turned to face Talbot. "That's really hard to say. Finding a specific system through one of these is pretty much a crapshoot. If there's a rhyme or reason to it, I haven't found it yet.

"Of course, the same is true of regular flip points. If you come across a new one, you really don't have any idea where it's going to end up. I suppose one of the positive aspects of the multi-flip points is that we can explore a number of branches without spending a lot of time doing so.

"With all of the back and forth of traversing one branch and then looking for new branches, a single multi-flip point might have dozens of potential destinations. We really didn't spend a lot of time exploring the one we found leading to Icebox and Pandora."

Talbot nodded. "That's all true, but we have a very specific task in front of us. If we can't get to Terra, we'll be of no use to the admiral. If we can't get *Audacious* through the flip point, we'll be a lot less effective in assisting him in any case."

"That's out of my control," Carl said with a grunt. "If one of the branches leading from this multi-flip point doesn't lead to Terra, we'll have to explore some of the destination systems and the linkages beyond them to try to find one that does.

"In the end, we might come up dry. There's no guarantee that any multi-flip point or far flip point will lead to Terra, or how long it will take us to find one if it does exist. I'll do the best I can, but I can't make you any promises."

The screen in front of Carl changed as data began flowing across it. His young friend leaned forward and examined it closely.

"The initial probe is back. It doesn't look like the default branch leads to Terra, but at least it didn't lead to an occupied system. I'll have Fiona go over everything I'm recording, and I'll wager she can locate the system on the other end fairly quickly."

He tapped on the controls. "My best guess is that this multi-flip point has five branches. I'll refine the data, of course, but I might as well start sending probes down the various branches to see where they end up. Thankfully we have enough to do that all at once rather than reusing the same probe over and over."

Talbot was tempted to continue talking and exploring what might happen with his friend, but he didn't want to distract him. Instead, he leaned back in his seat and closed his eyes, resting while he could.

A few minutes later, Carl grunted.

Talbot opened his eyes and sat up. "Did you find something?"

"You could say that. I found a branch leading to Terra. I had to go through the multi-flip point to one of the destination systems and then send the probe down another branch, but we have a problem."

He turned to face Talbot. "The branch leading to Terra is perhaps the narrowest that I've ever seen. There's no way in hell *Audacious* is going through that particular passage."

"Perhaps one of the other branches on the Terra side will lead to a system that we can get to. We've seen how there's some duplication in the process."

"No dice. While there *are* other branches leading out from the Terra side, every single one of them seems to have a very narrow frequency band. On top of that, it only has three branches leading out.

"I'll program the probes to explore them, but I'm very much afraid that we've found a passage we can only use with *Persephone*."

That was bad news. The only possible ray of hope was the possibility of finding a far flip point in the Terra system. Looking for it would be dangerous and far from assured of success, but they'd have to try. The admiral was counting on them.

"Gather what you know and come with me," Talbot said. "It's time to brief Kelsey and get to Terra."

35

The trip in to Terra took a seeming eternity for Jared. Without being able to deploy any stealthed probes, the data they were getting from the home world of humanity grew sharper only at a snail's pace.

When they were a few hours out, they'd begun detecting orbital platforms circling Terra but couldn't determine anything about them, other than the fact that there were a lot of them. They ranged from moderate size to extremely large. Far larger, in fact, than anything he'd ever seen before.

More interesting to him was the fact that at least some of them appeared to be powered. He had no doubt that a number of the stations ahead of them were things like the planetary bombardment platforms used on Harrison's World, but that couldn't be the whole story.

Since the AIs had gone out of their way to subjugate Terra, it only made sense to Jared that they would have blasted any center of resistance. What was left to threaten? All they could hope for at this point was that the Imperial Palace still stood. If it didn't, the vaults below it were almost certainly destroyed, and their mission was doomed.

"We have an incoming communication from *Persephone*," Wanda Dieter said. "It's at high bandwidth and has video."

Jared smiled. The fact that his sister was able to communicate with him via high speed indicated that she had found a way to get to Terra.

"Put it on screen," he said, sitting back in his chair.

Kelsey's image appeared on the main screen, and she smiled. "As you've no doubt determined, we've found a way to get to Terra. That's the good news. The bad news is that it's a very narrow branch on a multi-flip point. There's no way that *Audacious* can make the trip. In fact, there's some risk simply taking *Persephone*, not that I'm going to let that stop me.

"If you can, let me know that you've received this message. If not, I'll assume that you're in a position that you don't dare attempt to transmit. In any case, we'll be in the system in the next few hours. I want to take the extra time to make all the preparations that we can think of, since there exists the possibility that this is a one-way trip for us."

Jared wasn't exactly happy to hear that, but there was nothing he could do to stop his sister. She was going to do what she thought was best, regardless of how he felt. Acceptance of that particular trait came hard to him, but he wasn't going to let it bother him anymore than it had to. Kelsey was coming whether he liked it or not, so he might as well like it. He didn't dare call her back to argue, in any case. There was far too great a chance of the enemy detecting the attempt.

"I'm starting to pick up more data from Terra orbit," Evan Brodie said. "I'm detecting at least two orbital bombardment platforms, as well as a lot of other types of station. The weapons platforms are definitely powered, but so are at least half a dozen other stations. Potentially as many as a dozen on the side of the planet I can see.

"There are some massive installations on the moon, as well. A lot of damage there, probably from the fight to take the system back during the Fall. Without being obvious about it, I'm not going to be able to be clearer on conditions there.

"I'm not detecting any ships, but they could be concealed behind or even inside some of the stations. A couple of them are gargantuan. Since I doubt the AIs needed to build all of this capacity, a bunch of it must've been left over from before the Fall. Potentially, they tried to turn Terra into one of their subjugated planets and failed."

Jared rubbed his chin while he thought about it. "I'm sure they did try to bring Terra to heel, but that obviously didn't work out for them. What I'm wondering is why they felt the need to exterminate everyone on the planet. What changed?

"They obviously have enough force to keep people out of this system as well as to make certain that no one from the surface can escape. Maybe we'll be able to find out once we get down there. Janice, what's our ETA?"

The helm officer checked her console briefly. "Two hours, twelve minutes. Almost there."

The next few hours went by even more slowly than the previous two. By the time they reached orbit, they had a much better impression of what was in orbit and had even begun discerning some of the surface.

In total, there were five orbital bombardment platforms. One of them seemed to be powered down, though he couldn't see any reason for that. The other four were certainly more than enough to deal with any issues requiring kinetic weaponry.

In addition, there were twenty-seven stations of various sizes that still had power. They ranged in size from medium size to immensely large. The biggest one was at least ten times the size of Orbital One back around Avalon. There were hundreds of other stations without power. Terra's industrial capacity must've been immense before the AIs had killed it.

"I'm starting to get some readings from the surface," Evan said. "The side of the planet facing us show signs of organized kinetic bombardment. It isn't enough to completely destroy the urban environment below, but it's significant. I'll start working to match up the craters with what we know about Terra from before the Fall to try and identify what the targets were."

"What about the Imperial Palace?" Jared asked. "Can we see it from here?"

The tactical officer shook his head. "We'll be coming around the planet to where we can see what it looks like in about ten minutes."

"We have another incoming message," Wanda said, frowning. "Another voice message from the AI. It's telling us to initiate deployment of the drones."

"Have you managed to locate the source of the transmission?"

Not that they can afford to shoot at the damned thing, not with cruisers sitting right behind them. They could probably damage a station, perhaps even destroy it and the AI, but they'd still die.

The communications officer nodded. "It's coming from that massive station just ahead of us. Whether it is a relay from elsewhere or even a recorded message, I couldn't say."

"Send a question back," he said. "Ask if it has a preference where we start deploying the drones. The time it takes for it to answer will let us know if it's really there or somewhere else in the system."

She turned back to her console. Moments later, she nodded. "It's sent us six locations spread out around the planet. It wants one crate in each location and the drones programmed to spread out as far as possible. I guess the AI is in the station."

Jared supposed that would work as well as anything for purposes of spreading the plague. It might make it really awkward getting to the Imperial Palace if the AI was dictating where they could land though.

"Put the map on the main screen and highlight the designated landing zones."

A map of Terra flashed up on the main screen, and six areas on it began flashing. Imperial City was located where the old American city of New York had been. The Imperial Palace was located a moderate distance away from the city, sitting farther north. The closest designated landing zone from either was easily three thousand kilometers away.

"Well, that's going to be challenging," he admitted. "Whatever we do, I think it's probably best to save the closest landing point until the very last. Once we've accomplished the mission, we become expendable."

"Imperial City is coming up," Evan Brodie said. "It looks like it took a direct hit. Perhaps more than one. The Imperial Palace area, on the other hand, seems to be mostly undisturbed. At least on the scale I can detect from orbit. It probably took collateral damage from the hits on Imperial City, but it wasn't destroyed outright."

That was good news. No matter how difficult it was going to be getting to the Imperial Palace, recovering the override was at least possible.

"Start loading the first crate aboard our remaining cutter," Jared said. "We'll start with the next landing zone past the Imperial Palace. Once we get down, we'll start getting an idea of how difficult this is going to be."

* * *

KELSEY GRIMACED as she stared at the representation of the flip point. It was as weak as the branch that led from the New Terran Empire to the Courageous system. The one that had trapped the original *Athena*. Using it would be a risk, even for *Persephone*.

She rubbed her face and sighed. They didn't have much of a choice. It was either use it or not get to Terra at all.

Carl had run the risk assessment, and the news was far from promising. The Marine Raider strike ship was small, so she would almost certainly make the flip successfully, but that might come at the same price *Audacious* had paid getting to Pandora. They might not be able to get back.

With that in mind, she'd pulled all the critical personnel she could onto *Persephone*. If they *were* stuck, she wanted to have everyone she needed to help Jared.

That meant the small ship was packed. Even though she'd been designed to carry a Marine Raider strike force, that wasn't a lot of people in the larger scheme of things. A single Marine Raider went a *long* way in a fight.

And then there was Fiona. She took up the largest previously open area on the ship, further reducing the available space. Well, she was an ace up their sleeves, so they'd have to make do.

Talbot had insisted they bring as many marines as possible, and Carl had needed his science team. That meant hot bunking, and all the people would stress the life support system if they were cooped up here too long.

Well, best to get this done. She left her quarters and made her way to the bridge.

Angela started to rise from the command seat, but Kelsey waved her back down.

"You're the commanding officer," she said as she planted herself next to the console. "I can stand. What's the status on loading supplies and people?"

"Just finished. The pilots are strapped into the fighters, and Raptor says they're ready to deploy. We haven't had time to rig up a way in from the fighters directly, so we'll have to extract them once we're ready to bring them back in."

Lieutenant Grappin and his people would be screwed if they got into a fight, simply because there were only six fighters and they had no way to quickly rearm them after a fight. If they got into a scrape, it would almost certainly end badly for them.

They'd still volunteered instantly for the mission. Like Marine Raiders, fighter pilots were a particular breed that ran toward danger. She was lucky to have them. They all were.

She'd considered bringing more pilots along, but that idea had made Raptor bristle. Apparently, one pilot to a fighter was the rule, and he wasn't pleased at the suggestion that he share his bird.

So be it.

"If we're loaded, then let's get over there and see what Jared has found for us," Kelsey said. "Flip the ship."

Even with her implants, the transition was a bit rough. No alarms started blaring, and a quick check of the ship's systems showed they'd made it without blowing their flip drive. She sighed in relief.

"What do we have?" she asked, even as she linked her implants to the scanners.

"We're in the Terra system," Angela said. "We're nowhere near detection range of any ship or station that we know of, but we knew that from the probes we'd already sent over. We're inside the asteroid belt between Jupiter and Mars, and almost on the opposite side of the sun from Terra, Mars, and Jupiter. Saturn is out system from us but is too distant for anything there to spot us."

"Then let's see if this was a one-way trip," Kelsey said. "We need to know if we're stuck."

Angela nodded to Jack Thompson at the helm, and he manipulated his controls. The flip drive engaged, but they stayed in the Terra system.

They were trapped.

36

Olivia worked with the others to unload the crate of reconnaissance drones. It was large, heavy, and bulky. She also wasn't sure if the AI could even see them doing the work. It might only be noting their landing from orbit.

The place it had dictated for the first landing spot that Jared had chosen was outside a devastated city that she didn't have a name for. It didn't look as if the city had been hit with a kinetic weapon but had rotted in place over the centuries.

Major Scala and some of his marines were keeping an eye on things just to be safe, but she hadn't seen any indication of human occupation. There had to be people out there, but they weren't showing themselves. If there wasn't anyone to worry about, the AIs wouldn't be deploying the Omega Plague here.

Once she and her helpers had the massive crate out on the ground, she sent the command to open it up. The drones inside were already prepared for deployment, but she took a moment to double-check the settings on each.

They'd programmed them to spread out in the pattern the AI had wanted, but for different reasons. The drones had no bioweapon to disperse, but they could and would take readings of the areas they patrolled. They'd forward that data back to the central control unit—a larger drone with significantly more capability—and it would sync that data to the other five control units via long range com.

In the end, if they were here long enough, that would give them a lot of information on the remaining human population, as well as an idea of what the planet still looked like so long after the occupation.

"The drones are ready," she said after a moment. "I'm sending them out."

Once everyone else had stepped clear, she activated the drones, and they began lifting off one by one and flying off in all directions. They'd spread far and wide, collecting data from many thousands of kilometers away.

That task done, she left the crate as it lay and headed back into the cutter. Even as she was strapping in, data began flowing in from the drones.

There *had* been people watching them. They were concealed in the ruins of several buildings and seemed concerned about the events they'd witnessed.

Olivia couldn't blame them. They had reason to be worried. If the drones were the ones that had started this mission, death would soon be spreading among them.

The lack of that death would eventually tell the System Lord that something had gone wrong. Probably before Jared and their crew were done here. That might make getting off Terra particularly challenging.

The marine officer brought the last of his people inside, and everyone strapped down. At her signal, the pilot lifted off and headed back for orbit.

"That took less than an hour from when we detached from *Athena*," Scala said. "Give us another twenty minutes to get back to the ship, and we can start loading the next crate. Call it two hours to deploy and recover from the mission for each crate. That gives us ten hours of work before the AI can get froggy with us."

"That's a little optimistic," Olivia said, turning to face him. "It might wait until we've deployed the last set and use the orbital bombardment weapon on us."

He shook his head. "Overkill. Besides, it would have to wait for the drones to clear the impact area. With that kind of time investment, it might as well allow us to return to orbit and deal with us there."

That thought made her rub her face. "How do we avoid that? It thinks it controls the ship and that we have bombs in our heads. When it makes its move, it'll expect results fast."

"The explosives are the first line of attack, I suspect," Scala said. "One signal and we all supposedly drop dead. No need to get fancy with that kind of option. The only question is what it does next. Does it want to recover the destroyer or eliminate any chance of contamination?"

"The latter," she said. "It's gone to a lot of trouble to make sure that we humans are the cutout. It doesn't risk contaminating itself or any other ships. Once it thinks we're dead, it won't risk verifying it. At that point, it'll get rid of the ship somehow.

"When it does, we need to be somewhere else, and the ship itself needs to respond to commands the way the AI expects. Sadly, I suspect that means *Athena* is going to be dropped into the sun to make sure there is no contamination risk."

The marine officer grimaced. "Or deorbited. We definitely don't want to be aboard for anything like that. We'll need to make sure everyone is off the ship by that point. If we're wrong, we can try to recover her later."

Olivia nodded. "And we need to get everyone down to the surface or to one of the stations. With the cruisers watching us like hawks, I think it has to be the surface. We'll have to rely on *Persephone* to get us out once we accomplish the mission."

"With the ships in orbit—and the AI for that matter—how will they get to us? Do we even know if they made it into the system?"

"They made it. Sean dropped a code word into the last communication from orbit. They wouldn't have risked a long signal, but they made it. Persephone and her pinnaces were designed to sneak up on the most advanced scanner suites without being spotted.

"The ship might not be able to get into orbit, though I'm not ruling that out, but the pinnaces can. They'll have to be much more careful in the atmosphere, but there's no reason they couldn't get some forces down to us and give us a ride out once we accomplish the mission."

By this point, they were back up in orbit and starting to maneuver toward *Athena*. They'd dock in ten minutes.

"The last drop is going to be key," Scala said. "We have to get everyone off the ship and still deliver the crate. Does the cutter have that kind of capacity? Worse, can it get back to the ship from the surface on automatics?"

Olivia didn't know about either of those things. "I hope so. If not, we're going to be in the position of leaving some of our people on *Athena* and hoping they can figure out another escape option."

And since the other options seemed pretty bleak, that might very well mean a suicide mission.

* * *

ANGELA WATCHED the scanner data flowing back from the stealthed probes grimly. It was building up an unpleasant picture. The AI had a lot of firepower out there. Trios of ships patrolled the system.

Since the damned AIs had no idea about multi-flip points or far flip points, that hardly made any sense. Why be so paranoid?

Kelsey was conferring with Talbot and Carl about the upcoming insertion onto Terra. As much as Angela hated the idea of sending the princess down to the surface, she was a significant asset and might make the difference between success and failure.

Yes, Talbot was also a full Marine Raider, even if he was still a little off on his use of his arms and hands, but that would fade in a day or so as he finally mastered his enhanced limbs.

The problem against arguing that Kelsey should stay in orbit resided in the other woman's implants. She had the codes that only the crown princess of the Empire could wield. A computer system down there from before the Fall would yield to her where it wouldn't do so for Talbot.

Inside the Imperial Vaults, there would almost certainly be security systems that only she could deal with. Admiral Mertz could use the key, but he wouldn't be able to handle any kind of computer lockouts.

So it looked as if Kelsey, Talbot, Carl, and a number of marines and scientists would be making the trip down. Only a half load for the pinnaces, because they needed to keep space open for the admiral and his people.

Once everything was done, the pinnaces would have one chance to slip out. Going back in was a risk they couldn't afford. Once and done.

She was still brooding about that when the ship's computer sent an alert to her. For a second, she was afraid the AI had found them, but it was only an anomaly detected by one of the probes. The one they'd sent toward the Alpha Centauri flip point.

Angela tapped into that specific feed and felt her eyes widen. The AI had invested the flip point with battle stations and ships. A lot of ships. Hundreds of them. Most were powered down, but not all.

That made absolutely no sense. Terra had three regular flip points. Two of them let out to the rest of the Rebel Empire, but the third was special. Alpha Centauri was a cul-de-sac. The system was only accessible from Terra and led nowhere else.

A guard force of this magnitude leading to a system that no one else could get to made no sense. And not just a regular guard force. A very powerful one. More so than what they'd detected at the other two regular flip points.

Taking a small risk, she sent a tight-beamed command to the probe to go a little closer.

While it did so, she contacted Princess Kelsey.

"What is it, Angela?" the princess asked.

"I think you need to tap into probe feed fifteen."

"What the hell?" Kelsey said after a moment. "A guard force on a dead-end flip point? That makes no sense."

"Exactly what I said. I've instructed the probe to get a little closer and take a look. Some of the ships are powered up, and all of the battle stations are, so we need to be careful."

"I'm on my way," the princess said a moment before killing the com connection.

Three minutes later, she walked onto the bridge with Talbot and Carl on her heels.

"How long until the probe is in position to give us more data about the ships and stations?" she asked.

"It was already close, so not too long," Angela said.

They all waited in silence as the probe inched its way closer. Finally, it was in position to see the closest ones clearly enough via passive scanners to tell them what they were looking at. Battlecruisers.

"Why are they here?" Kelsey asked. "What's in there? Is this force here to keep people out or something else in?"

"We're not going to be able to find out," Talbot said. "Just sneaking to Terra is going to be hard enough. No way we can get access to that while the System Lord is active. Maybe not even if we took it out."

Kelsey sighed and nodded. "Then we proceed with the mission as planned. We'll worry about this mystery at a later date. What's our status?"

"We'll be in position to launch the pinnaces in about three hours," Angela said. "You'll have a good bit of coasting to do at that point."

The princess's expression was grim. "Then we start the hard part. Talbot, Carl, get your people ready. We'll leave on schedule."

37

K elsey rubbed her eyes tiredly. She'd been helping load crates of drones and gathering everything they'd need on the surface between runs, and even she was feeling run down.

The argument she'd been engaged in for hours, off and on, with Jared Mertz, Sean Meyer, and Scott Roche hadn't helped her rest, though at least she'd gotten a few meals down in the process.

The cutter was on its way back up from dropping load five. This next one was the very last, and that was what had caused all of the disagreement. The matter was far from settled, and she just wanted it to be over.

She was in the mess hall, devouring what might be her last good meal for a while. Yes, they had plenty of field rations, but that wouldn't be the same. Scott Roche was sitting across from her, and Sean Meyer was to her left. Mertz had just sat on her right, and she was ready for the next wave of objections.

"Before you start this again, I know that I'm right and so do you," she said between bites. "How about we skip the argument part and just get to planning what I do next?"

Mertz sighed. "This is an extremely risky plan. The number of things that could go wrong are legion."

"And yet there's no reasonable alternative," she countered. "I'm the only one of us that has a chance of surviving, so unless you *want* to have a suicide mission for someone, why are we fighting? Didn't you tell me that I should trust more in my abilities and that I could do amazing things? Why the big turnaround?"

"Because this idea is crazy, Highness," Scott said in what he no doubt thought was a reasonable tone. "The chances of you pulling this off are damned poor, and I for one don't want to see you throw your life away."

She set her fork down beside her plate and gave him a level look. "If I don't do this, the AI will know we're pulling a fast one and drop a kinetic strike on site six, so I'll die anyway. If I give this my best, I might make it. And realistically, I have a better chance of making this work than anyone else we have."

Her friend rubbed his face. "I know you think that, but you're not a trained pilot. There are a lot of automatic systems on the cutter, so it will probably get you close, but then you have to dock with an unmanned ship. There'll be no one to assist or guide you.

"Let's say that goes off without a hitch. The AI might set off the supposed bombs in our heads and order the ship to drop into the sun. You'd have to verify that course, make sure the ship is following it, and then get off to the nearest station.

"That's the best case. The worst is that it has the ships following us open fire and destroys the ship with you on it."

"And what if it demands to speak to a human being?" she countered. "Then it'll know something is wrong. No, there has to be someone here to do the things that only a human can do, and I'm the best choice. I have a plan to get away, even under the worst-case scenario."

"Does it give you a realistic chance of survival?" Mertz asked in a steady tone. "I doubt that very seriously. There has to be another way."

"I'll do it," Sean said quietly.

"The hell you will," Mertz countered. "Olivia would have both our hides if she knew you even offered."

"Then let it be me," Scott said. "I commanded a destroyer and am more than capable of piloting this ship. Sorry, Highness, but I'm a Fleet officer. If the choice is between you living or dying, I'll do what I have to. I forbid you from this madness."

The rising testosterone level at the table made her roll her eyes. "You've forgotten who you work for, Commander Roche. I give the orders, and you obey them."

"I'll gladly sit for that board of inquiry when we get home, Highness. You can testify against, me and I'll accept whatever verdict they choose, so long as you're alive to be there."

She sighed. "That means so much to me, Scott. I know you mean every word of it, and it breaks my heart to ruin such a beautiful speech, but I will never let my friends throw their lives away for me again. I hope you'll forgive me some day."

With that, she fired the stunner she'd surreptitiously drawn from her belt holster and aimed at him under the table. The blue beam lit him up and caused him to spasm before falling out of his chair with a clatter, his convulsive grip on the tablecloth dragging everything off the table as he went down.

Everyone in the room lurched to their feet at the horrendous racket except her. She holstered the weapon and raised the taco she'd snatched off her plate to her mouth. It was the last one she'd have for a long time.

"Dammit, Kelsey," Mertz said as he checked Scott. "That was way over the line."

"Probably," she admitted. "He'll be *really* pissed when he wakes up, but I'll either be there to deal with it or I'll be dead. One way or the other, he lives. I've watched far too many of my friends die in the last few years to let that gallant idiot sacrifice himself for me.

"And make no mistake, if someone else tries to get froggy with me, I'll use my Marine Raider enhancements to put them down too. This is the way it has to be, and I will not accept any more arguing about this. Am I clear?"

With a bemused expression, Mertz nodded. "'Yes, Highness'

seems to be the only suitable response. If we can't stop you, then we need to work damned hard to make sure you have every chance of making this work. You need to finish that taco."

She nodded, finished the food, and stood. "Tell him I'm sorry if I don't make it. He was only doing what he thought was right, and I treasure his friendship. Don't let him blame himself. This was my decision."

"I can tell him that all you want, Kelsey, but it won't make a difference," Mertz said with a shake of his head. "He'll eventually forgive you if you live, but he'll never forgive himself if you die."

Honestly, death wouldn't be as bad as knowing that Scott had given his life for hers. Her life had been nothing but pain and failure anyway. It might just be a blessing.

"So long as he lives, that's a burden he'll have to bear," she said, her voice sounding hollow even to her own ears. "Let's do this."

"It isn't like I have much of a choice at this point," Mertz said with a sigh. "Let's get down to the cargo bay and make certain that everyone is ready. Still, I'm afraid your plan has one hole that still needs filling.

"The lack of a pilot for the cutter could ruin everything. Without one, the entire plan is ruined. Someone has to come with you, and I think it had best be me."

She stopped dead in her tracks and turned toward him. "Are you mad? Only you can open the damned vaults under the Imperial Palace. You have to be there."

"And I will be if you do your job. I'm going to risk a message to our Kelsey and have her pick us up from the nearest station."

She fought to keep her eyes from rolling but failed. "We've already been through this. My Raider armor will keep them from spotting me. Your suit won't be nearly as stealthy."

"Let me show you something," he said as he continued on into the cargo bay. Everyone seemed to already be there, waiting for the cutter to dock. They'd load the crate and then clear the ship. Everyone had whatever important things they could bring with them in bags at their feet.

Mertz led her over to the other side of the crate, and she stopped dead in her tracks. Spread out face down on the floor was a suit of Marine Raider armor. It looked just like hers, only it was a dark gray rather than black.

"What the hell?" she asked.

"Kelsey insisted I have this before we got separated. I'm not a Marine Raider, so I can't use it to fight like you, but I *can* use its basic functions such as stealth and the grav booster. After the last time someone tried to assassinate me, she wasn't going to allow me to be so vulnerable again.

"Carl hacked the interface and modified it to work with non-Raider implants. Mine, specifically. The armor is keyed to me, so I can't really let anyone else take my place."

"Why would you risk your life for me?" she asked slowly. "I'm not exactly your biggest fan."

He smiled and had the audacity to clap her on the shoulder. "Even if you don't feel about me the same way, you're my sister. I'm not letting you face this alone. We're family."

The idea caused an initial surge of anger, but she tamped it down. He wasn't the same man as in her universe. That was painfully obvious. It was time she really accepted that and worked at seeing him differently than the Bastard.

She forced herself to relax. "Okay. We do this together."

A loud clanging announced the arrival of the cutter. Mertz… Jared released her and started getting the rest of the people moving. It was time.

Talbot sat at the flight engineer's station in the pinnace's cramped control area. Kelsey was in the copilot's seat, though she wasn't doing any flying at the moment. Both of them wore Marine Raider powered armor, though his was locked down to normal human strength, just to be safe.

He knew Kelsey could act as a copilot in a pinch, but she was still getting experience with the small craft. Maybe she'd get her marine

small craft certification in a few months more, once she had the time
to devote to the in-atmosphere qualifications.

They'd left *Persephone* hours ago and were ghosting toward Terra.
The other pinnace, filled with marines and scientists, had separated
from them and would make their way to the landing zone separately.
No need for them to take risks on this rescue.

The pinnace he was on was empty except for the people in the
control area. If it went bad, only the three of them would die.

They were on their final approach to orbit. They were coming in
on the opposite side of the planet from the three ships watching over
Athena, as well as the moon so that they'd avoid being silhouetted
against it, but the AI would have line of sight on them. If things were
going to go wrong, this was the time they'd do it.

Kelsey had cussed a blue streak when word had come that her
brother was risking himself in the ruse that there were still people on
the destroyer, but it wasn't as if she could tear a strip off him for being
reckless when that might call lightning down on herself.

A less cautious individual than his wife was hard to imagine.

The final drone placement was in progress on the surface, and the
admiral would be on the way back to orbit in just a few minutes. This
pinnace needed to be near the station the others would be heading for
before then, or they wouldn't be in a position to adjust for
complications.

Kelsey stared at the viewport. Terra, her surface blue and green,
dotted by white clouds, hung huge in front of them.

"I never thought I'd see this," his wife muttered. "The homeworld
of humanity. I read everything I could about it as a kid, but I'm going
to see things no one on Avalon could even imagine now. If we can pull
off this insane stunt."

He laughed. "Pot, meet kettle."

"You aren't funny," she said with an annoyed glance at him.
"Jared is insane to take this kind of chance, even with a secret weapon
in his pocket."

"You keep dropping hints, but I'm not getting what you mean.
What secret weapon?"

She smiled smugly. "I didn't want to screw us up by revealing it too soon. You'll find out when we pick him up. You'll just have to trust me until then."

He shook his head. "I trust you with my life, but you can be so juvenile."

That made her laugh, probably in spite of her feelings. "I know, but I'm still worried. There are so many ways this can go wrong."

"Welcome to the universe in which we live. Jared is as resourceful as you are. Trust that he knows what he's doing."

"We're coming up to closest approach to the AI's station," Lieutenant Kada Erickson said, turning her head to look at Kelsey.

His wife focused her attention on the pilot. "Any sign it's seen us?"

"Not at the moment, but it'll have line of sight on *Athena* and the station we're going to use for cover in thirty minutes. We should be able to get into position before then, but the three enemy cruisers will be right there."

"And once trouble starts, they'll all have a chance to see us," Talbot added with a grumble. "In a perfect world, we'd pick the admiral up and wait for a clear moment to get down to Terra."

"But this is likely to get messy," Kelsey agreed. "If they start shooting and we have to get down to the surface in a hurry, what are our chances?"

"Slim to none," the pilot said. "With clear skies at that range, they'll spot anything dropping down into the atmosphere at once, even us. We'll be in visual range, so the scanner-dampening coating on the hull will do us exactly zero good."

Talbot knew they could get down to the surface safely when none of the hostiles were directly watching in about ten minutes, but Kelsey would never go that way. Neither would he.

They all watched the huge station holding the AI until it was over the horizon. Then Kelsey nodded. "Set course for the target station. Use its bulk as much as possible to keep the cruisers from seeing us. It's time to save my brother. And myself."

He wasn't sure exactly what that meant, but he couldn't agree more. Time to get this over with.

38

J ared took the controls as soon as they had everyone on the ground at the sixth landing area and had released the drones. Kelsey sat in the copilot's chair, watching him as he lifted the cutter away from the ground and set course back toward the ship. One of *Persephone*'s pinnaces—the one with almost all the people Kelsey One had sent to Terra—would arrive while they were going up.

"How soon after we get back aboard do you think the AI will act?" Kelsey Two asked.

"It won't delay long," he said grimly. "Whatever it has in mind, it has no reason to wait. I expect it'll jump as soon as it confirms it has complete control of the drones. Thankfully, the lockouts Austin installed will allow us to override that without the thing being aware of what we're doing."

"I had wondered about that," she admitted as the sky began growing darker as they climbed toward space. "So, we'll be in the drone system and able to use, what? All of them? Only those in range?"

"Each group has a central controller and backup that can communicate with all the others. We'll have access to all the drones, and none of them will report anything we don't want. Each has a fake set of instructions to report how much of the nonexistent bioweapon they're spreading to the AI, so it'll think everything is going along great.

"Right now, we're set up so that none of the ones in our general area will report anything not cleared by us. We don't want to give the AI any real intelligence about what's going on around us or that we're here at all. If need be, we can assume direct control of all the drones and lock the AI completely out, but that'll give the game away."

She nodded. "That's good. Do you think other me is in place?"

"Almost certainly," he said. "With the AI so close, she won't risk communicating with us at all, but she'd have gotten word to us if she'd been delayed. She'll be there."

The cutter exited the atmosphere a few minutes later, and Jared set course for *Athena*. The robotic destroyer had been a good ship. He was going to miss having her when the AI did something permanent to her, which he never doubted was coming for a moment.

He brought the cutter back to the dock and adroitly spun her along her axis to line up with the ship. With small nudges of the maneuvering thrusters, he mated the locks and sighed with relief when the automatic locking rings secured them together.

"There we go," he said. "Easy as pie."

"Why is pie easy? And don't you think it's rude to bring up food when I'm already hungry?"

He laughed. "Sorry. Let's get inside and up to the bridge."

"I might not have been able to do that," Kelsey admitted as she lay face down in her armor, which was lying on the floor of the hold. It sealed up, and she quickly levered herself to her feet, her blank faceplate coming to life with a view of her face.

"That's why they pay me the big bucks," he said. "Grab mine and come on."

She easily scooped his up and followed behind him as he traversed the empty corridors toward the bridge. "Shouldn't you armor up?"

"If the AI decides to call, I need to be presentable," he said as he held the lift doors open. "I personally doubt it will, but one never knows when it comes to homicidal AIs."

Less than a minute later, they exited onto the bridge. It felt wrong to see it with no one at the controls.

"What's your plan?" he asked Kelsey.

"That really depends on what the AI does," she admitted. "If it uses the head bombs, we can probably sneak out one of the personnel airlocks and slip over to the station. That's true even if it starts maneuvering the ship. We still have control of the ship's systems, so it won't know what we're doing. If it starts shooting, we'll have to go out the escape pod tube."

He shook his head. "It will see the escape pod and kill it before we even get to the atmosphere. Worse, we won't be able to get away from it in time to rendezvous with Kelsey One."

Even as they were speaking, he was linked into the destroyer's scanner network. The three cruisers were the most immediate threat, but he had his eye on the large station containing the AI, too.

At this range, he'd know the moment the enemy brought targeting scanners online and they could act. He just needed to decide what the best course was first. He hoped he'd have time to make a considered call.

The com system pinged with an incoming call, with video this time. So, the AI was going to talk after all. He wondered what it would say before it killed them, because he had no doubt as to the fate it intended for them.

He sat in the command seat and gestured for Kelsey to get off far enough to the side so she wasn't in the feed. Only when he was ready did he accept the call.

The video component was a sine wave that undulated across the screen. He'd barely had a chance to register it when the AI began speaking.

"You have done well," it said in a sonorous voice.

"Thank you, Lord," Jared said once he was sure that was all it was going to say as an opening. "We live to serve."

"I will see that your families are well rewarded for your loyalty, but no word of this mission must ever make way to your fellow humans. My personal reward to you is a quick death."

The scanners showed the cruisers bringing their targeting scanners online, so Jared killed the com and dove for where his armor lay on the deck. The end was upon them, and they had to act now.

Jared wasn't nearly as graceful getting into the armor as Kelsey had been, but it only took a few seconds. Hopefully, it would be enough.

He used his implants to give the ship one set of final orders as the cruisers prepared to fire. Not to fight but to shut down the fusion plants. If one of them went, it would incinerate Kelsey and himself in an instant.

The deck shuddered under his body. Not a weapons strike. Too subtle.

Jared levered himself to his feet and saw that Kelsey had ejected the bridge's escape pod. Not with her in it, but empty.

"What..." he started, and then cut off when he saw her slap a plasma breaching charge on the closed hatch.

"Back," she ordered, hurling herself away from the explosives.

He barely had time to emulate her when the charge went off. It felt like the end of the world. Even through the armor, his ears rang. Moments later, his implants registered a signal that he knew was meant to trigger the nonexistent bomb in his head. The AI was taking no chances.

The air venting through the hull breach picked him up like a toy and hurled him into space. Just in time to see the first missiles slam into his command. Even without the possibility of a fusion plant containment failure, that didn't mean the explosions were gentle for the two of them. The exploding missiles blew huge chunks of debris away from *Athena*, and something slammed into him, spinning him around and dazing him again.

Only as he tried to recover did he see a missile explode far below, no doubt killing the escape pod Kelsey had jettisoned. After a few seconds, he was able to bring his suit under control and arrow toward the station concealing his and Kelsey's pinnace. She'd be on the far side of the station, away from possible detection.

The plan was to hold up there until the cruisers left. Then, once the AI's attention was elsewhere, they could slip away. Chancy, but it was the best hope they had.

A small bit of debris hit his leg and spun him around just in time to see *Athena* come apart completely under the attack. It wasn't as violent an explosion as when a fusion plant went critical, but it was potentially deadly all the same. The attack was sending debris out in a terrible cloud, with several large chunks slamming into the station he and Kelsey were moving toward.

He felt another jerk as Kelsey grabbed his arm and leveled him out, just before she jetted forward and under the cover of the powered-down station.

Persephone's pinnace was right there, its ramp already down and an armored figure gesturing for them to hurry. The gray Marine Raider armor told him it was Kelsey. His Kelsey.

The two of them raced forward and past the ramp. It had only barely started to close when the hand of God crushed Jared against the wall, and everything went dark.

* * *

KELSEY HELD on for dear life as her pinnace violently rolled and jerked. Honed reflexes made her rotate so that her back slammed into the side of the craft rather than her head.

Jared wasn't moving, but his armor's telemetry said he was in decent shape, only knocked out. The other figure—the other her—was banged up but conscious. She was Kelsey, too, so she was tough.

"Kelsey," Talbot said, his voice strained. "Get up here right now."

"Get him strapped in," she ordered her other self. "Then get secure yourself."

With that, she made all haste back to the control area. She knew things were bad when she saw Talbot in the copilot's seat, struggling with the controls. The pilot was still in her seat, but limp.

"She went straight up and hit her head on the overhead controls," he said. "Bad luck, but she's out. We have worse problems, though."

Kelsey quickly pulled the woman from her seat and double-checked Talbot's assessment. The woman was breathing and had a strong pulse. Her marine implants indicated nothing more serious than a concussion. That was good. An impact like that could have broken the woman's neck.

She strapped the unconscious pilot into the flight engineer's seat and took the controls. "What happened?"

"The station blew up, I think. Not a fusion plant overload, obviously, but more than enough to knock us around. There's a lot of debris in the area around us and we're going to hit the atmosphere pretty fast on this course.

"I'm no pilot, but I'm worried we're on a really dangerous entry angle. We could burn up. Worse, one of the drives is out and some of the controls are amber."

Kelsey finished strapping in and checked the board. Yep, the port engine was offline, and some of the control surfaces seemed damaged. That was going to seriously complicate things.

"I really should've prioritized my atmospheric qualifications," she said as she projected their vector out. "I'll have to gradually adjust our course so as not to get the AI's attention. It can kill us just as dead as a bad entry, and everyone on the surface, too."

"Did you get the admiral on board? Who was with him? Are they okay?"

"Jared is out, but our other passenger has him strapped in. Who it is isn't important right now, so I'll explain when I have more time.

"Hey, one good thing is that we're going to end up on a decent course toward the area where everyone else is waiting down on Terra. It will only take a few tweaks in atmosphere to get us down to them."

"If we get down," her husband said.

She shot him a look. "Think positive. We'll make it."

In spite of her projected confidence, she was less than sure. Her atmospheric entry skills were rudimentary at best. With one dead engine and some damaged controls, this would've challenged someone like Annette Vitter.

She immediately regretted the thought. The fighter wing commander had been piloting an old-style marine pinnace when an asteroid impact on Erorsi had knocked them from the sky. The woman had somehow turned certain death into a crash that had scored a deep wound into the planet, but it had still cost the woman an arm and killed some of the people aboard.

Kelsey was nowhere in the other woman's league with small-craft handling. If things went badly, they'd almost certainly die.

She took a calming breath and focused on what she could do. Several adjustments to their course put them into a better entry angle, and she let that play out.

The initial wisps of air caused the pinnace to shake a little, but that was just a hint at what was coming. Within a minute, the shuddering of the small craft had her deeply scared. It was far rougher than she'd expected. Something on the hull must be catching air, and that could kill them fast.

Abruptly, the shaking ceased, but before she could react, an alarm blared. One of the control surfaces had just ripped off the hull.

"The good news is that we lost the thing dragging on the air," she said, trying to compensate for the new damage. "The bad news is that it's going to make a soft landing *really* challenging."

She was grateful when Talbot didn't say anything, leaving her to focus on the pinnace. The loss of the control surface was complicating the pinnace's stability, but only a little. The loss of the port engine was worse. It gave the pinnace a recurring tendency to slew to the side, and a spin under these conditions would kill them.

Kelsey lost track of time as she fought the crashing pinnace for every advantage she could wring out of it. Eventually, the buffeting eased, and the small craft was deep enough and slow enough that she was flying rather than falling.

A quick check of their location showed that the landing zone was coming up far more quickly than she'd planned on. She needed to bleed airspeed right now.

She put the pinnace into a series of S curves that dropped their speed, fighting for control when the pinnace bucked under her again and again. She only had the landing coordinates, as the people below didn't dare signal to them.

Kelsey imagined their entry looked catastrophic to the people on the ground. Hell, it felt catastrophic to her. Still, she reminded herself that this was far from the most violent planetary insertion that she'd ever experienced.

Using a drop capsule on Harrison's World had taken her from orbital speeds to a dead stop on the ground in about ten seconds. That bit of insanity had earned her the drop commando badge from Ned Quincy, and she was the only living person that could claim that level of crazy. Of course, she'd had no choice if she'd wanted to stop that madman with the nuke.

"I think I see them," Talbot said. "Off to starboard."

She looked over and spotted the strobe of a landing light. It wouldn't be visible from orbit, so they'd taken a chance.

Kelsey hit the general com. "I'm coming around for final approach. Hold on tight."

She killed the com. "We'll have one chance at this. If I don't nail it, we'll crash for real. The controls are getting worse by the second."

It was going to be a race to see if they could set down before the controls failed altogether. If they hadn't been on an approach vector, she'd never have been able to even get close.

"Altitude a thousand meters," Talbot said. "Start slowing us down."

"Can't," she said. "We're a damned flying brick. If I lose any more speed, we'll fall right out of the sky."

"We'll be a crater if we don't."

Dammit, he was right. She took a deep breath, let it out slowly, and activated the general com again. "Coming up on the LZ. This is going to suck. Thirty seconds to landing."

She somehow managed to balance losing speed with staying in the air for almost twenty-five seconds. Then the remaining engine failed catastrophically.

Kelsey forced the pinnace out of the skew the exploding engine had sent them into and saw the ground racing to meet them. "Brace for impact!"

The pinnace slammed into the ground, throwing Kelsey harshly against her restraints. They were on the ground but skidding wildly, and a new danger popped up right in front of them. They were headed directly for the other pinnace at an insane rate of speed.

The ground slowed them faster than she'd hoped but not nearly fast enough. They crashed into the other pinnace hard enough to shatter the console in front of her and crush her against the wreckage.

Thankfully, her armor protected her from what might otherwise have been a fatal impact, even for a Marine Raider. She sat there in her seat, blinking stupidly at the mess piled on her.

She used her enhanced strength to push herself back even as she was verifying the health of the three of them in the destroyed control area. Everyone was alive. Miraculously, no one was even seriously hurt.

"Allow me to be the first to congratulate you on a stellar landing," the pilot said weakly from behind her. "Just remember that all damage to the pinnace comes out of your pay."

Kelsey laughed in spite of herself. "I'm never going to be out from under the debt of destroyed and damaged equipment. You get used to it after a while. You okay?"

"My head hurts, but I'll damned well walk away from this landing. Seriously, good job, Highness."

Kelsey unstrapped herself with shaky hands as Talbot also dug himself out of the debris.

"I'll make sure she's okay," he said. "Go check on the others."

On unsteady feet, Kelsey got into the back of the pinnace. The floor sloped at least ten degrees to the side, but the body of the ship seemed intact, and one figure was standing. The other Kelsey.

"How is he?" she asked.

The other version of herself popped her helmet and shook her blonde hair out. "He has a concussion, but he'll live. I'm afraid I'm going to have to complain to the management about the landing. It did indeed suck."

Kelsey checked Jared's readouts and satisfied herself that he was going to make it. That relieved her no end. She popped her own helmet and stared at her twin.

She started to say something, but someone started banging on the outside of the pinnace by the ramp. That would be the ad hoc crash-and-rescue response team the others had put together. She'd better let them in before they had a stroke. If she could.

The ramp was crumpled and would never open again. There was an emergency exit on the side hull. It was visibly warped but might still be useable to two Marine Raiders in powered armor.

"Give me a hand here," she told her doppelgänger.

The other Kelsey stepped up beside her, and together they put all of their considerable strength against the jammed hatch. It groaned and finally popped open, letting in the sun and air of the homeworld.

Kelsey took a deep breath and turned toward the other her as the people outside looked for the best way up the gouged earth toward the opening. She clapped a hand on the woman from another universe's black-armored shoulder.

"Welcome to Terra, sister mine. Now the real work begins."

* * *

WANT to get updates from Terry about new books and other general nonsense going on in his life? He promises there will be cats. Go to TerryMixon.com/Mailing-List and sign up.

DID YOU ENJOY THIS BOOK? Please leave a review on Amazon. It only takes a minute to dash off a few words and that kind of thing helps Terry make a living as a writer and gets you new books faster.

WANT the next book in this series? Grab *Ruined Terra* today or buy any of Terry's other books, which are listed on the next page.

VISIT TERRY'S Patreon page to find out how to get cool rewards and an early look at what he's working on at Patreon.com/TerryMixon.

ALSO BY TERRY MIXON

You can always find the most up to date listing of Terry's titles on his Amazon Author Page.

The Empire of Bones Saga

Empire of Bones

Veil of Shadows

Command Decisions

Ghosts of Empire

Paying the Price

Recon in Force

Behind Enemy Lines

The Terra Gambit

Hidden Enemies

Race to Terra

Ruined Terra

Victory on Terra

The Humanity Unlimited Saga

Liberty Station

Freedom Express

Tree of Liberty

Blood of Patriots

The Imperial Marines Saga

Spoils of War

The Fractured Republic Saga

Storm Divers

The Scorched Earth Saga

Scorched Earth

Omnibus Volumes

The Empire of Bones Saga Volume 1

The Empire of Bones Saga Volume 2

The Empire of Bones Saga Volume 3

Humanity Unlimited Publisher's Pack 1

The Vigilante Series with Glynn Stewart

Heart of Vengeance

Oath of Vengeance

Bound By Law

Bound By Honor

Bound By Blood

ABOUT TERRY

#1 Bestselling Military Science Fiction author Terry Mixon served as a non-commissioned officer in the United States Army 101st Airborne Division. He later worked alongside the flight controllers in the Mission Control Center at the NASA Johnson Space Center supporting the Space Shuttle, the International Space Station, and other human spaceflight projects.

He now writes full time while living in Texas with his lovely wife and a pounce of cats.

www.TerryMixon.com
Terry@terrymixon.com

[a] amazon.com/author/terrymixon

[f] facebook.com/TerryLMixon

[p] patreon.com/TerryMixon

[BB] bookbub.com/authors/terry-mixon

[g] goodreads.com/TerryMixon

Made in the USA
Monee, IL
28 July 2021